DELAY OF GAME

MAGGIE RAWDON

DELAY OF GAME

She wants lessons to end her wallflower era, but the only thing I want to teach her is how to be mine.

Olivia is my best friend and the one person who was there for me when I wanted to quit football freshman year.

We're *just* friends. A fact I have to remind myself of every time I see another guy flirt with her.

She thinks I'm a nice guy. A good friend. Her grumpy protective "bestie". But what I really want? It would make her blush.

So when she tells me she's tired of blending into the background and asks me to tutor her, I can't say no. Even though I should, because my past means she's the last person on earth I should touch.

And with everything on the line right now—championships, the draft and our final year—I need her more than ever. So when it all catches up with me in the worst possible way, I have to face an impossible choice—or risk dragging her down with me.

And this game is one I can't afford to lose.

PROLOGUE

Liam

One Month Before

My hand connects with his jaw, and I can feel the reverberations through my bones. I feel the force of it up my forearm and even into my shoulder. It fucking hurts but no more or less than anything I feel on the field on any given weekend. If some pain is what it takes to get this guy off of Liv, I'm only too happy to be the one to deliver it.

Liv was my best friend, had been since freshman year of college. She'd gotten me through all kinds of shit, including wanting to quit the football team and she'd been by my side ever since. Entirely platonic because there were lines I wouldn't cross with her. Lines this fucker shouldn't be crossing either, because he didn't deserve to breathe the same air as her, let alone slide his hands up her skirt.

The blow lands hard, and he rubs his jaw, his eyes darkening as he tests to see whether or not I've broken anything. He eyes me again, sizing me up to decide whether or not it's going to be worth it to keep this going.

I can hear the shouts around us, mostly the football team either egging me on or shouting at me to stop. If I had perspective, I'd probably stop. If Waylon wasn't so distracted with Mackenzie at the moment, he would absolutely be stopping me from my current ill-advised foray into drunken brawling. But as it all stands, I have free reign to beat this hockey playing douchebag's ass into the ground for having his hands all over her. And I'm going to use the precious time I have to make it count.

He takes another swing at me and misses, and it gives me the opportunity to give him a smug little smile. One that he hates and reacts to by swinging again, a move that only makes him stumble and nearly trip.

"Liam, fucking knock it off!" I hear Liv's voice, but I don't heed it.

She hates scenes, especially anything public, and this is nothing but a giant prolonged dumpster fire. The whole party's gathering to watch their quarterback square off against one of their hockey team's D men. It's a fucking spectacle that will no doubt be the talk of campus by Monday, and I have no interest in either stopping or being the loser of this particular fight.

He takes another swipe and I dodge it, but the jab that follows catches the edge of my jaw. It stings, but it doesn't cause any major damage.

"Liam, I swear. Quit it now. This is stupid. He didn't mean anything by it. He was just playing around and it's fine!" Liv yells again over the crowd.

"He doesn't fucking touch you like that," I growl.

She comes closer, dangerously close given that this guy can't land a punch to save his life and she's as likely to be on the receiving end as I am.

"He can touch me however he wants if I say he can. You don't decide for me, Montgomery." I can tell from the tone of her voice that she's furious with me. I'm going to get a lecture when this is all over, on how I embarrassed her and she's not a child and doesn't need my protection.

And she's not a child, and she can stand up for herself. But I promised myself that I'd look out for her. I wouldn't let anything happen to her that I could prevent. And that includes not letting fuckboys like Mason Monroe feel her up at a party like she's a stripper.

"Get back, Liv." I nod for her to get out of the way.

"Liam!" I hear Ben's voice now, yelling for me in a tone that says I'm fucking up. I probably only have a few more seconds now before Waylon shows up and shuts this down.

The two of us circle each other once more, and he flails at me again. The benefit in this whole fight, probably the reason for it starting in the first place, is that he is very drunk. Much drunker than I am, and while I have no doubt this kid drinks his bodyweight in alcohol every week and has a high tolerance, it's clear he exceeded it tonight.

His brow furrows, frustrated with the number of times he's missed and that the baiting movements he's been making haven't made me rush him. So then he goes really fucking stupid and charges me, using his body weight—and I'd guess he has 20 or 30 pounds on me—to drive us both backward and straight into the glass coffee table behind me.

There's a massive roar from the crowd around us. A mixture of screams and gasps. The table shatters on impact, and I can feel the glass crunching beneath me as he rolls on top of me, trying to pin me to hit me again. A few shards scrape against my skin, but a quick mental survey tells me nothing's penetrated any vital organs.

I shove him off me and he rolls to the side, struggling to

stand again. His knees dig into a pile of the glass, the pieces biting into them, and he groans when he finally does rise to his feet. I jump up, ready to take an impact if he charges me again, but he's unsteady this time. Swaying like he can't get his balance and his eyes look muddy, like he can't quite see as straight as he'd like.

Nevertheless he takes another swing at me that I easily dodge, but it pisses me off. The broken table. The drunken sway of his body. Another vision of his hands creeping under Liv's skirt while she dances on the table. I see red.

So I take a step forward and plant my feet. Jabbing him twice in the ribs where I'm sure he's already feeling the urge to hurl up whatever liquor's swimming in his stomach and then I finish him with a right hook square to his nose. I feel his cartilage and his bones crunch under the force of my fist, crashing inward. The stream of blood from his nostrils comes half a second later, and he reaches for his face to try to stem the tide.

I doubted the broken nose was going to be a new experience for him either. I'd guess that the kind of attitude he has, out on the ice he probably averaged another broken nose every few games or so. Probably had a plastic surgeon on call to try to keep his pretty face straight.

He groans though, wiping the blood on the back of his hand and now he's well and truly pissed. Probably decently sobered from the pain and endorphins the break has brought on, and I can tell he wants to give me a matching injury.

"ENOUGH!" Waylon bellows as he steps between us.

I hadn't even noticed him walk up, but now he stands between us like a giant 6'5 mountain. I can barely see Mason's face over his shoulder, and the glare Waylon gives both of us is enough to make even my blood run cold.

Whatever problem he was having with Mackenzie was

putting him in a mood almost as foul as my own. I wondered if she was flirting with a jackass who didn't deserve her too.

He makes quick work of a lecture about how the two of us are too important to our teams to be fighting like this. That it could end up with us on the bench which no one needs. I don't give a fuck about ending up on the bench right now, but I do care about letting down my team.

"Seriously!" Liv yells. "What the hell is wrong with you, Liam?" Her hands are on Mason, rubbing his arm and no doubt cooing at him over his little injury.

I scrub a hand over my face and look to her with a pleading glance, begging her to understand that I didn't have a choice, but she gives me a look that ices me. A bone chilling look that makes me feel like I could shrink down and die, and now I know I went too far trying to prove my point.

"Liv, just listen-" I start but she's not hearing me. She's not even really looking at me, other than as the man who just delivered a broken nose to her new love interest.

"No," she answers me firmly. "Leave us alone!"

She coddles her bleeding hockey player, whispering something to him and glaring at me again, and I feel sick. I feel like I might vomit up everything in my stomach watching the two of them walk off together. My head swims with thoughts of her and Tristan. Imagining her with Mason like she was with him. Thoughts of the two of us and what it would mean for us to lose our friendship over something this stupid. That she might pick him over me if it came down to it. Lately the tension between us is more than I can handle. It almost feels like she's trying to get under my skin.

We'd already argued twice in the last couple weeks when she made jokes about dating one of the guys on the team. I'd told her I didn't need to hear my guys talking about fucking her in the locker room, that she was like a sister to me, and I wouldn't let any of those fuckers date my sister either. So apparently she was skirting the rules by trying to date a hockey player now. Which was going to make my life fucking wonderful.

Maybe I'd start dating one of her friends and see if she likes how that feels. I look to see where Wren and Mac have gone off to, and I spot Mac with Ben. I can tell he's giving her the brush off, yet again, and that it's cutting her. And Waylon's just standing there watching the whole thing unfold. Suddenly a ridiculously perfect idea forms.

I act before I can think better of it. Before I have a moment to reconsider, I've crossed the room and grabbed Mac.

"Play along," I whisper, right before I press my lips to hers.

Her hands tense and press hard against my chest, and I feel like I'm in serious danger of getting slapped. Mac is not someone I'd want to piss off either. I have a feeling she could probably hit better than the hockey player. But then, as if she's feeling as defeated and as don't-give-a-fuck-less as I am, she relaxes and kisses me back.

"Absolutely-fucking-not!" Waylon's voice bellows at the top of his lungs, and I step back before his arm wraps around her and snatches her up and off the ground.

Then he turns on me lightning fast, his face a mix of fury and disappointment. I know exactly what he feels like.

"Get some fucking ice for your hand and drink some fucking water. You need to sober the fuck up before you make any more bad decisions." The look he gives me is lethal, and I know the only reason I don't have a black eye right now is because he's my best friend.

I hear him mumble something to Ben, and I start to turn to move to the kitchen when I see Olivia standing there next to Mason. Her arms are pressed tight over her chest and her eyes are on me. Even from across the room I can tell I've crossed another line I shouldn't have. The tightness in her face and the disapproving shake of her head make me feel even smaller than I had before.

"Come on, man. Let's get you some ice." Ben looks down at my red knuckles with concern.

"Don't you want to lecture me first?"

"If I thought it would work, I would have."

I try to think of what I'm going to say to Olivia, how I'm going to apologize, but by the time I get to the kitchen she and her hockey player have disappeared. My gut turns, but I'm not going to think about the reasons why.

ONE

Olivia

Present

I'm pretty sure I have a crush on Liam Montgomery. A fact I'm coming to terms with because I just said Liam's name while I was pinned under my boyfriend Mason. My jaw droppingly handsome boyfriend who currently has his hand up my skirt and his lips hovering over my mouth. I have *the worst* possible timing.

Mason jerks back and blinks, looking at me through pale light that barely illuminates a room off in a corner of the sprawling hockey house. A room we'd stumbled in a few minutes before, hot and heavy after starting out on the couch in the middle of the party.

"What did you just say?" His breathing's still choppy. His brow furrows as he tries to make sense of what's happening. And I'm sure it's a really big puzzle for him because Mason Monroe is gorgeous. Like mind-numbingly so, to the point where I have no idea how I even caught his attention over so many other women who would gladly take him in heartbeat. I highly doubt he's ever been in this particular predicament, and he is genuinely perplexed.

"Nothing, don't stop," I whisper back, leaning forward to kiss him because I need to buy time to think of a more graceful exit from this situation.

"No..." He leans back on his knees and then stands. I can almost see the cogs whirling in his head as he confirms his suspicions. "You definitely just said *his* name."

He says *his* like it's poison. He doesn't need to say his actual name. I know exactly who he means. We both do. The man who broke his nose at the very beginning of our relationship, and the man who he always eyes with suspicion even though Liam and I are barely on speaking terms at this point.

"I didn't," I lie, because I don't know. What's the right thing to do here? Admit it, and crush his ego? That for a split second, despite having the looks, voice, and mouth that could rival Liam's in public opinion, I'd still been thinking of Liam.

He probably doesn't want to hear that.

"You fucking did. Jesus." He runs a hand through his dark hair, spinning around and then bending at the waist like he might be sick.

"I don't think so, but if I did it's just habit. It didn't mean anything."

"Habit? Why are the two of you fucking that much?" He glares at me from an ever-widening gap between us.

"No. We don't fuck at all. I've told you. I swear," I protest.

"Then how is it a habit?"

"He's my best friend, and I help out with football stuff. We're around each other a lot. I say his name multiple times on any given day."

"Yeah, well maybe when you're with your boyfriend, don't?" He gives me a hurt look.

"Mason..." I stand and move to touch him.

"Oh, you do know who I am. Good." He pulls back when my hand touches his forearm.

"I'm sorry. I didn't mean to. It's just been a long week and I'm tired. I've had a few beers and my head is all muddled. It didn't mean anything." Another lie because inside, my head and my heart are fucking rioting at exactly how much it meant, but again I'm standing in front of my perfectly sweet boyfriend. He's been nothing but a gentleman despite his reputation, and I really do like him. Just, apparently, not enough to overcome my feelings for Liam. *Shit.*

Mason stares at me for a moment, like he wants to believe me, but he shakes his head again.

"Olivia. Be serious for a minute. We're about to hook up and you say the name of the guy who broke my nose for touching you. Let's reverse that situation and you tell me if you'd believe you?"

I pause for a moment to consider, and yep. I'd be furious. I probably wouldn't be nearly as civil as Mason is being right now either.

"That's what I thought," he says quietly, his eyes on the floor. He makes a little sound at the back of his throat. "I really like you Olivia, but I'm not gonna try to compete with someone you have all that history with. I feel like I'm just a way to make him jealous."

"No. There's no competition, and I promise that there is nothing beyond friendship going on."

His hands tuck into his pockets and his mouth flattens into a line.

"That might be true, but only because you two haven't

worked it out yet. And I don't want to be in the middle when you do. It's been painful enough as it is."

I feel the tears clawing at the back of my throat and the stinging sensation at the corners of my eyes.

"I really like you a lot, Mason."

"Yeah. I like you a lot too. But it is what it is."

I stare down at the floor. "Is there anything I can say or do?"

"I just think you should go. I don't want to say anything I'll regret. You need a ride?"

"No. I can call a car. I *am* sorry, Mason."

He looks at me one last time, his gorgeous face marred by hurt I've inflicted on him both physical and emotional. He nods and I leave the room, the tears hitting the second I close the door behind me. Luckily I see a bathroom a few doors down and I duck inside.

I sit down on the edge of the tub and let the tears come, grabbing a few tissues out of my purse to blot them as much as I can off my makeup. I still have to get out of this house, and I don't want to look like I just melted.

My heart hurts like hell right now. For having feelings for someone who only sees me as a friend. For having hurt Mason. I *did* like him, and the guilt at having needlessly hurt him in all of this feels like a ton of bricks on my conscience. I'm not this woman, the one that leads another on when she really wants someone else. I'd been in denial about Liam for a long time, while my feelings for him only got stronger and stronger.

Mason had seemed like the real thing for me. He was hot, sexy, a hockey player which meant he wasn't off-limits per Liam's rules, and he was sweet. I really liked him, a lot. We had fun when we went on dates, and we had plenty in common. We texted and talked all the time, and there had been several days over the last month where I had very honestly forgotten all about Liam.

But it always came back. Especially now as our friendship is as strained as it has ever been, and I wondered what he was doing, who he was dating, and if he missed me as much as I missed him. And in my darkest moments, I thought about what it would be like if I said fuck it to our whole friendship and just went for what I really wanted—which was all of him. Despite the fact that Liam himself was off-limits to me. He had said so in very plain words—years ago, after one near kiss between us had ended in disaster.

I couldn't think about that right now. I needed to get out of this house and back home. Which was going to mean getting outside. I jump up and look at myself in the mirror, fixing my hair and makeup as much as possible. I look like hell—exactly like someone who was just getting ravished by her boyfriend and then broke up with him in the span of 15 minutes. I was the poster girl for that look, and it was not a great one to be honest. But I could walk fast, and then in the dark outside I'd be less noticeable.

I hurry through the house head down, feet moving like the place is on fire, but just as I'm about to cross the final threshold to the front door I bump into a hard chest. It stops me dead in my tracks and my eyes travel up the tall figure's body, meeting the face that's usually plastered with a self-satisfied smirk but is currently wearing a look that's positively murderous.

"Whose ass am I beating?" Easton sounds pissed, and he is the definition of "a lover not a fighter", so I must look rough.

"No one's."

"What happened to you?"

"Nothing. I just need to leave, okay?"

"Did he fucking hurt you? I will hurt him, and he'll consider it lucky that I got to him before Liam did." Easton's eyes start searching the room for my now ex-boyfriend. This is so far out of character for Easton that I'm worried about how bad I must look to prompt this reaction from him.

"He didn't do anything. I fucked up, okay?"

Easton's brow furrows. "You? How?"

"Can I explain this outside? I don't need everyone to see me looking like this."

Easton lets me get past him, and he trails me out to the porch. I pull out my phone.

"I just need to call a car and then I'll explain." I mumble.

"I can take you home."

"You just got here. Didn't you?"

"Yeah, but I'm not letting you go home like this until you tell me what's going on, so I might as well take you. I can come back after. And then I'll know whether or not to beat his ass for sure. And whether I should let Liam know."

"You cannot let Liam know I was upset like this," I snap.

"Whoa. Okay." He holds his hands up at my reaction. "My car's out this way. Let's get there and then you can explain."

I follow behind Easton on the sidewalk to the alleyway where he's parked his car. It's flashy as fuck, and I'm surprised he's willing to park it here.

"You're not worried about someone breaking in?"

He shrugs, "It's just a car. Besides it's my dad's old one."

He opens the door to the Maserati, and I slide in, wondering what it must be like to have that kind of money. He hops in next to me and starts the engine, turning off the stereo to bathe us in awkward silence.

"All right. Start explaining, because I fail to see how this turns out well for Mason."

"There's not a lot to explain. We were hooking up and then I said something that really upset him, and now we're not together anymore. Simple."

Easton makes a choking noise. "Okay. I might regret this, but I really have to know what you said."

"No you really don't."

Easton's face lights with a little smug smile. "Is it small? Oh god, the jokes that are gonna spread across campus."

"No it is *not* small. God you men are so childish."

"I figured that couldn't be it. It would have been wildfire across the sorority houses before now."

"It's not small. Again. It was my fault." I feel the need to defend Mason, because frankly he's the victim in all of this. My stupid shenanigans of trying to be someone different, less wall-flower, more badass.

"So what is it? He bad at it? You call his dick a name he didn't like?"

"Easton, oh my god." I roll my eyes.

"What? You can't say you were hooking up and then he broke up with you without explaining what happened in the middle."

"If I tell you... and that's a big *if*... Can you keep it to yourself?"

"Of course. Who am I gonna tell anyway?"

I give him a look. Like we both don't know exactly who he would tell first, or at worst second since he lives with Waylon and that might give Waylon an edge on Liam.

"I'm dead serious, East."

"Okay. I swear."

I raise a brow at him.

"I swear, Olivia. I can keep my mouth shut when I need to. I'm actually quite good at it. You'd be surprised at all the things you don't know."

"Don't say things like that. It makes me worry."

He laughs, and that makes me like it even less. "All right. Now tell me."

"I said the wrong name when he was getting ready to, you know..." I trail off and stare out the window.

Easton is a good friend of mine, but he isn't exactly Wren or Mac. They're who I really need right now, to tell me this is all going to be okay, somehow, someway.

"Oh fuck..." he curses under his breath.

"Yeah... That was his reaction too." I feel the tears sting again, and the guilt swell up a second time.

"Whose name did you call him?" Easton glances at me before looking back at the road.

"I'd rather not say." I play with the strap on my purse.

There's a beat of silence and then Easton bounces his palm off the steering wheel like he's just arrived at the right answer. *Crap.*

"Ohhh shit." Easton shakes his head. "Not... you didn't..."

I start to open my mouth to deny it, a little breath coming out and I can't. And it only damns me more.

"Fuuuuuck." Easton curses and shakes his head.

"So now you understand it's my fault, and why you don't need to beat his ass?"

"Uh... yeah. You handed it to him already tonight."

"Thanks. That's helpful," I say sarcastically.

"Sorry. I mean, did you... like him? Are you okay?" Easton does his best attempt at this, and I appreciate it. But again, not the best person for the problem.

"Did I like him? I was dating him. Of course I liked him. A lot. This is a huge mess. It was an accident, but I don't think he's going to forgive me."

"Yeah, that's the kind of accident a guy's ego usually doesn't come back from."

"You have personal experience?"

"Fuck no. But I can imagine it. And if I had a broken nose

from the same guy? God damn. I might need to go back and buy Mason a bottle of whiskey."

"Again, not helpful."

"Sorry. What would Mac or Wren say?"

"They'd tell me they're sorry and offer me ice cream."

"You wanna stop and get some ice cream?" He sounds amused.

"No. I just want to go home and cry."

"Fair enough." He glances over at me again when we reach a stop light. "And you're not going to tell him?"

"Are you insane? No, I'm not going to tell him. We're barely speaking and telling him that would really end our friendship."

"I think you two need to work through your shit. It's obviously causing a lot of collateral damage. And neither of you seems very happy."

"Liam's not happy?" I ask.

"He's been grumpy as fuck. Way more than usual. We don't exactly talk about it, you know. That's not my area. And he's not big on my preferred method of 'go fuck it out with a hot chick you found at the club', so I don't have any details to give you. But I assume your fighting is at least a part of it."

"Well, I don't even know where to start to fix things. I'm tired of him always bossing me around."

"Some part of you must like it." Easton laughs.

"Not funny. And I swear if you tell him, I will get the girls together and we will hide your body somewhere no one will ever find it."

"I'm not gonna tell him. The last place I want to be is in the middle of that drama."

I sigh. I don't even want to be in the center of this drama, and I'm the cause of it.

"Thank you. And thanks for the ride home," I say as we start to pull down the street to my house.

"Of course. I'm glad it wasn't anything else. I mean not that you all broke up but that you're okay otherwise."

"Yeah. I'm just a horrible person."

"As a fellow horrible person, I hear there's a recovery plan if you want it." He smirks as we pull into the drive.

"Yeah. Hopefully I figure it out before I make any more stupid mistakes."

"I'm sure you will."

I lean over and give him a half hug, as I see the light on the porch come on. One of the girls must be home, and since Mackenzie is likely at Waylon's it must mean Wren is off her shift from the bar.

"Oh good. Wren's home. At least I don't have to eat ice cream alone."

"Tell her I said hi."

"Uh huh." I look him over and narrow my eyes.

"Just being friendly."

"I bet. Goodnight, Easton."

"Night, Olivia."

TWO

Liam

EAST and I are parked in a booth at an upscale club downtown that we all like to attend when we can afford it. Usually that means when it's on Easton's dime. I'm not poor by any stretch of the imagination but I also don't have the money for bottle service on the weekend. East however, has plenty to spare and a black AMEX card that he's only too happy to wave around if it means we get special treatment. It's just the two of us tonight because Ben is busy working on some project for school, and Waylon has taken Mackenzie out on a date. I miss guys nights with all of us, mostly because Waylon and Ben temper East's behavior.

Going out with just East is always a dangerous bet, because if there's trouble or wild antics to get into, he *will* find them. As evidenced by the fact that he currently has a gorgeous redhead on one side of him and a gorgeous blonde on the other, both vying for his attention while he's busy surveying the first level of the club for a third.

As I nurse my drink trying to decide if I should just call a car and let him have his fun alone, the noise in the club rises, some hoots and hollers breaking out, and I watch as East's brows raise at whatever scene he's watching.

"Hang on sweetheart, can you sit back for just a minute?" he instructs the redhead whose hands had disappeared under the table several minutes ago and leans over her to get a better look.

"Oh shit," he mutters, a wide grin spreading on his face.

"What?" I ask, curious now even though I don't feel like leaving my reclined position on my side of the booth.

"You would not believe me if I told you. You should look for yourself." He looks up at me, eyes dancing with amusement as he grins even wider.

It's a look that makes me nervous, so I set my glass down and scoot forward, propelling myself out of seat and over to the edge of the balcony where I can look over. And he's right. I would not have believed him. I barely believe it when I'm looking at it.

It's Liv and Wren, dancing around one of the poles together. Liv's in a dress I've never seen her in. One that's short, strappy, with pieces of the material cut out in strategic places. She likes wearing the latest fashion, but this was beyond that. Wren was more conservatively dressed than her but was happily playing her wingwoman, dropping low and hyping up her friend's dance moves.

"I didn't think Wren had it in her." East smirks, standing next to me now, leaning his elbows on the railing as we watch them.

"What are the odds someone doesn't touch them?" I ask, annoyed that I'd been relaxing and now I was going to have to go break shit up because they decided to come here of all the bars in town.

"I'd say pretty slim. But you should let her have her fun. She looks like she's enjoying herself."

"It's not like her."

"Maybe she's trying on something new. Don't get me wrong, I love Liv. She's been great to us. But I've always thought it was a waste that she spends all her time being a football mom when she looks like that."

I shoot him a warning glance.

"Don't get your fucking shit twisted. I wouldn't touch her. No woman is worth drama. I'm just saying, objectively. I know she's practically a nun in your eyes, but you have to know that she's dream girl-next-door material for other guys."

I grunt in response. I did know. And I'd been reminded when I'd seen the way Mason had been with her. That had stirred up all kinds of shit I hadn't expected and didn't want to think about.

"Where the fuck is Mason anyway?"

Easton looks at me, puzzled. "They broke up. How do I know that, and you don't?"

"How *do* you know that?"

Easton makes a face and shrugs.

"Mackenzie's at my place all the time now, remember? She mentioned it."

"Liv didn't tell me."

"I thought you two shared all that kinda shit. Like two little girls who braid each other's hair and tell each ghost stories at sleepovers?"

"Fuck off man. That's not how it is." My stomach rolls at the idea she thinks of me like that. I had never cared before, but now the thought of her picturing me as some kind of girlfriend she gossips with makes me feel a little ill.

"Well fuck. Even I can't let that one go," East juts his chin, pointing to a guy that's currently grabbed Liv, picked her up and is practically dry humping her in the air. Wren is looking on aghast and that's our fucking cue.

We're down the steps in a matter of seconds, my hand on the guy's shoulder.

"Put her down," I say loudly, and he whips around to look at me.

Now that I'm up close I can tell both she and Wren are heavily intoxicated, and her eyes go to mine. A giggle popping out as she recognizes me.

"Liam? No way. *No way.* I must be seeing things." Another round of giggles.

Meanwhile, the asshole who is several inches shorter than me is surveying me. Deciding whether it's worth it or not, right when East comes up and stands next to me.

"Put her down, asshole." Easton repeats.

He drops her quickly, rolling his eyes at us and she stumbles as she hits the floor, and I reach out to steady her.

"What the hell?" She mumbles, grabbing my shoulder to steady herself as she watches the guy walk away. "Why did you do that?"

"Did you want to get fucked in the middle of a club with everyone watching?" I snap at her, irritated that she was this drunk and reckless.

"Maybe." She removes her arm from me, glaring at me through glassy eyes. She takes a step back toward Wren, and Wren wraps an arm around her, but Liv twists her heel and nearly sends them both careening to the floor except East manages to buttress Wren's backward motion.

Wren's eyes go to him, raking over him until she meets his

face and the wide smirk he has there, and she frowns, pulling herself away from him.

"Let's go upstairs and get you guys some water. East has a table," I say, trying not to worry about whatever the fuck was going on there. The last thing our friend group needed right now was more trouble in the water. Liv and I were already causing enough.

"And if I don't want to?" Liv smooths a stray strand of hair back, jutting her chin out in defiance.

"Too fucking bad," I grump, putting my hand at her waist and directing her toward the stairs. She follows my lead and I'm thankful for the small victory, because I don't have the energy after this week's practices to keep fighting.

"Do not touch me." I hear Wren complain behind me, and I glance backward to see East smiling at her.

"Why? Afraid you can't control yourself?"

"Oddly enough I don't have trouble staying out of the sewer."

"Maybe that's your problem, not enough time getting dirty."

"You wish, asshole."

When we reach the top of the stairs, I give East a look that tells him to knock his shit off, but he just gives me a little smirk and slides back in between the women who are still waiting for him.

"Of-fucking-course." I hear Wren mutter under her breath.

I motion for her to slide into the other side. There's not nearly as much room because there is a giant sculpture jutting out from the wall that the booth curves around, but there's still enough space that I can sit next to her.

I pull Liv down into my lap, wrapping an arm around her waist because I trust her exactly zero percent in her current state. I expect a protest, and steel myself for the fight but she just wiggles a bit.

"You have boney legs," she complains as she finally settles back against me.

"Maybe you just have a boney ass," I grump in reply. She didn't. Her ass was round, perfectly toned and if she kept wiggling like she was, was going to hit me in all the right spots. And *fuck*. This was half my problem right now. Thoughts like that from out of fucking nowhere. Ones I did not need. Ones I had done an excellent job of keeping buried up until now.

"How dare you," she gapes and narrows her eyes at me.

"What are you guys even doing here tonight?" I ask, wanting to move on from the subject of her ass.

"Dancing, obviously. What did it look like?"

"Was that what that was?" I raise a brow at her. "Looked more like a strip club audition."

"Don't listen to him Liv. From what I saw you looked good out there. Some raw talent," East pipes in.

Liv's face transforms into a self-satisfied little smirk. "Thanks East. You always know what to say."

I hear Wren grunt and look up to see her roll her eyes. She's trying not to be obvious, but I watch her look over the two women East has with him and then stare down at the table. And I'm praying East was not stupid enough.

"What do you ladies want to drink?" East offers.

"Oooh, where's a menu?" Liv stretches out her open palms, and he gives her one. I glare over her shoulder at East, but he just shrugs. Always the one to encourage bad habits and worse behavior.

"I just want to get a taste of you," one of East's companions purrs.

An incredulous little laugh bursts out of Wren before she

looks back at the menu Liv's just put in front of her for them to look over.

"You got a problem princess?" East's eyes jerk up and land hard on Wren.

She raises her eyes and levels him with a look. "Not at all. I find D-list porn highly amusing."

"Yeah? See if you can find something on there that'll untwist your panties and maybe we'll let you join in."

"Are you-" Wren starts.

"Ooh, can I join in?" Liv gives Easton a playful little smile, and I feel my stomach drop.

"Absolutely not," Easton answers without missing a beat. "I like all my body parts intact and in functioning order."

"See?" Liv twists around to look at me. "This is your fault. You ruin all of my fun."

"I didn't know you thought it was fun to have four-ways," I answer her bluntly.

"Well maybe I would. I don't know. I can't know because you're always there, lurking around the corner, scaring everyone off. I might be a completely different person if you weren't always around."

Her words land hard, and something like actual hurt flickers in her eyes. Our bickering is starting to feel more and more like fighting, and I hate it.

I can see out of the corner of my eye that Wren and Easton suddenly look painfully awkward, and the only people who look like they're still having fun are the two women who seem clueless to anything outside of the Easton bubble.

"How about we go talk for a minute?" I say softly.

"So you can lecture me?" she gripes.

"No, so you can get whatever this is off your chest in private."

"Fine." She hops off my lap, and I rise to follow her.

There's a little outdoor patio area off this level behind us, and even though there are heaters this time of year it's usually dead outside because of the cold. We walk that way, and I prop the door open behind us with a door stopper before I follow her out.

She's already out toward the railing and is pacing back and forth under one of the lamps, arms crossed over her chest looking heated as hell. I have no idea what I've done to rile her up this fucking much but the sooner we get it over with the better.

I put my hands in my pockets and approach her slowly, her pace picking up as I get closer.

"So?" I ask quietly.

"So? That's all you have to say? You come grab me from downstairs and take me up to sit in your lap like some scolded child. You scare Easton so badly he won't come near me, neither will any of the football players for that matter. You break Mason's nose, and while that wasn't a direct cause of our breakup, it played a part."

I take a deep breath before I answer her.

"Tonight, I just didn't want to see someone take advantage of you. You're obviously drunk. You know why I don't want you fucking my teammates. And I've apologized many times for breaking his nose. I don't know what else I can do to fix it."

"You can't fix it. And maybe I want someone to take advantage of me Liam! I'm so tired of being the perfect little football mom who makes sure everyone gets a snack after their games and helps them figure out how to do their laundry. I want to enjoy the last year of college. I want to get drunk. Get wild. Have hookups. Do stupid shit. Not be Betty-fucking-Crocker all the time."

"Then do it. Just don't do it where I am or with my teammates."

She whirls around, coming toe to toe with me and sticks her finger in my chest, her eyes meeting mine with a defiant look.

"If I want to fuck one of your teammates, I will. If I want to fuck East, I will."

And the threats hit just like she hoped they would, because I can feel the bubble of frustration rising in my chest.

"Yeah? Well you might want to pick a different night to fuck him because tonight he already has more pussy than he knows what to do with, and he's still flirting with your friend. Better luck next time."

"Fuck you, Liam!" She throws up her middle finger and takes off back to the door.

I am so fucking riled now myself; I think I might just stay out here for a while alone to cool down. Let the cool air take the edge off, and just listen to the sounds of the city until I can bring my temper down a notch.

"Fucking, fuck." I hear her mutter, and I turn around to see her pulling at the door handle to no avail. The door stopper that I left there is gone and the door is locked shut. Fuck.

"Hang on," I say, pulling my phone out. "I'll text East to come get it."

"You do that. Tell him he can absolutely come and get it." She gives me a wicked little smile, and instead of sending the text I tuck the phone back into my pocket.

I've had enough. I make a beeline straight for her. Ready for another round of arguing if we're going to be stuck out here.

"Oh no! Did I make daddy mad again?" she taunts me.

I draw up short and just stare at her. We'd had our fair share of arguments, especially in recent history when she decided she wanted to date some asshole D-man from the hockey team. Why she can't find a nice sensible classics or finance nerd in one of her classes, I don't know. But in all of those arguments, she was never like this. So blatant in trying to get a rise out of me.

"Why are you trying to bait me?" I ask and watch as something flickers in her eyes.

"I'm not baiting you. I'm just tired of this whole good-girl box you keep forcing me into."

"So do something different."

"I'm trying, and you keep fucking it up."

"Again, I was just trying to keep you safe."

"Maybe I don't want safe Montgomery! Maybe I just want to feel something!" she yells, but then her brow furrows and falls. "Although right now all I feel is freezing cold. East needs to hurry up!" She shivers and wraps her arms around herself. The dress she has on frames every perfect curve of her body but does about zero to keep her warm.

"Here," I offer, pulling my jacket off and holding it out for her.

"I don't want it." She bats it away.

"I thought you were cold." I hate the idea of her freezing out here because she's stubborn and angry with me.

"Yes, but I don't want you being Liam-y. All chivalrous and noble. Then I have to be nice to you, and I am fucking *mad* at you."

"Then why don't we go sit under patio heater? Unless you want to be mad at it too."

She glares at me, but she starts walking toward it before she mutters, "You're not funny, you know."

I follow behind her, and we sit down on the bench. After a minute she scoots closer to me but eyes me warily.

"Just for warmth. Don't get any ideas that I'm forgiving you."

"Okay." I shake my head and start to argue back before I

think better of it. "What's it going to take for you to forgive me?"

"I don't know. I'm sure when I'm sober in the morning I will. But right now, no."

"So you're just an angry drunk who likes to dry hump strangers on dance floors then?" My lips twist in amusement but I try to stifle it.

"How dare you!" She punches my arm. "I have justified female rage vis-à-vis your patriarchal ass, and I was badass out on that dance floor."

"Oh yeah?" I smirk.

"Yeah! Auditioning to be a stripper. Huh. You know what? Maybe I'll become a stripper for fun."

"Is that so?" I give her an amused look, and she does not like it.

"Now whose baiting who? I would make a fantastic stripper. Don't mock me."

"Like a Martha Stewart stripper? You're gonna wear a little frilly apron and then take it off and toss it into the crowd?" I laugh.

"No. Like a hot stripper, who wears dresses like this and gives lap dances and works the pole like a boss ass bitch," she sasses back and even though we're still fighting, it feels better, more like us again.

"Let me see then," I sit back and motion for her to get up and dance again. If she needs to get it out of her system, better she does it out here where no one can see than back inside where she's going to attract more attention from the creeps downstairs.

I expect her to deflect though, make another snarky comment about me bossing her around. Which is why when she gives me a devious grin and climbs into my lap a second later, I know I've fucked up.

THREE

Olivia

I'M NOT ENTIRELY THINKING straight and most of my ego and bluster right now are based on the fact that Liam Montgomery's grumpy bossy ass is on my last nerve. I love the man. He is my best friend, but he thinks he runs everything. The team. Me. All of our lives. He always knows best. And I am over it. And frankly over men in general right now because my first attempt at dating in so long went so craptacularly that his nose had barely healed before we broke up.

I'm in Liam's lap before I really have a chance to think better of it, straddling him while he looks up at me wide-eyed and confused like this was the last thing on earth he expected. It's enough to make me want to stop, but then he'll just see it as me backing down and I am not doing that tonight. He could back down for once in his life.

"What? Didn't think I'd take you up on the challenge?"

I raise an eyebrow at him when he doesn't answer, and I

place one hand on his shoulder to brace myself. I probably am too drunk to be doing this but it's not like I have to worry. He'll stop me before I do anything too stupid, because that's the one thing I can always rely on him for; ruining any stupid fun I might get into.

"I'm tired of always being the sexless good-girl spinster sister of Liam Montgomery. I'm going to end up like one of those women on the shows Mac and Wren are always watching. A sad little soul wandering the moors of England, and always looking melancholy in her giant drafty mansion of a home." I roll my hips around as I talk, circling them and swaying from side to side. I've never actually given a lap dance before, so it was my best approximation of one. More bluster than practice. I have to put my other hand on his shoulder when I nearly lose my balance, and his hands go to my hips to steady me.

"I have no idea what you're talking about," he mutters but doesn't look at me, his eyes stuck on my hips like he's worried I'll fall if he doesn't watch me carefully.

"Of course you don't," I roll my eyes and lower myself down, spreading my legs a little wider, so I can get a better look at his face. "Because I barely exist to you unless I'm doing something that irritates you. So long as I'm following the rules and doing everything according to plan, it's fine. I'm the invisible elf who makes everything happen behind the scenes for you and the guys."

"That's not true. I pay attention all the time. You're my best friend, Liv. And I've told you before how much I appreciate everything you do." He looks up at me now, something like actual remorse in his eyes.

"Really?" I slide down into his lap, my thighs resting against his. "Then why didn't I hear from you when Mason and I broke up?"

"I just found out about it tonight, when East told me, or I would have checked to make sure you were doing okay."

I stare at him, blinking as if that should be an obvious sign that he was not, in fact, paying attention all the time.

"Yeah, okay. I fucked up. I've been busy with extra practice time, and I've been trying to give you and him space."

The warmth of his body against mine feels so good, almost making up for the cold air threatening to freeze me into an icicle. I slide my hands under his shirt to warm them.

"Fuck! You're fucking freezing!" He lurches back.

"You're warm."

My fingers climb up his abs, and he has a really nice set. I've seen them before plenty of times, but I've never touched them. I think I might be enjoying the experience.

"Because I'm dressed." He grabs his jacket and drapes it over my shoulders and back without asking this time.

"That's too bad. I wish I could see your abs." My fingers trace them.

"What?" the breath rushes out of him.

"They feel nice. You have a nice body you know. You should show it off more. Like East does with the tailored and fitted stuff. You probably have a better body than him, but you'd never know it with all your baggy shirts and jeans," I babble on. It was true though, the man has very little fashion sense and no interest in being corrected.

"I dress fine," he says defensively.

"I know you think you do, but I'm telling you, you could pull more women if you listened to me. Maybe even three at a time to his two. You've already got the QB thing on your side. You'd have to work on that look on your face too though. That's intimidating. Scares a lot off."

"What look?"

"The resting bitch face you have. Like you're always pissed off."

"I do not."

"You absolutely do. You're literally getting a lap dance right now," I start rolling my hips against him again, remembering that was the original point of this exercise. "And you look grumpy as fuck." I touch my fingers to his cheek, running them along his jawbone where it's covered in two-day-old scruff trying to massage the gruff look off his face.

"Liv," he closes his eyes, tilting his head back and his jaw goes tight.

"See! That, right there. It has to go," I laugh, and I slide up and down over his lap, pressing my palms against his chest.

"Stop." His hands bite into the flesh of my hips, and he stills me.

"Why? Am I winning your little challenge? You want to admit my stripper skills are on point?" I grin at him.

His eyes open, something like fire in them and he uses his grip on me to slide me all the way forward, his hard cock pressing against his jeans where the seam of them meets the cotton of my panties.

I raise my eyebrows and bite my lower lip, hesitating for just a minute before I grin at him.

"So admit it!" I roll my hips again, meaning for it to be a taunt but it feels so fucking good, just the right amount of friction, a little gasp pops out of my mouth at the sensation.

"If I admit it will you stop?" he grits out.

"Why do you want to stop?"

"I can think of about a dozen reasons off the top of my head. The first being that you're drunk."

"So what?"

He tilts his head and narrows his eyes as if that answer is obvious.

"So keep your hands to yourself then. You can't be blamed for what I do. That's the whole point. Unless you want me to stop, then just say that."

"Liv..." my name is a warning on his lips, but it's all he says. I give him a little questioning smile, and he looks at me warily.

"Liam..." I mock in return and then roll my hips again, getting the friction that I need once more. He feels so good, the warmth of his body seeping into mine, his hands slowly creeping down my thighs and the feel of his breathing picking up under my palms. I want more. I want him, and right now, I desperately want him to want me back. I close my eyes.

"Please? I need it," I ask him softly, too scared to look at him.

I feel his fingers flex against my hips, and I'm sure if I opened my eyes there would be a war of emotions across his face. I'm sure he's got a lecture ready to go. But he moves underneath me, tilting his hips so that I have better access to him. The form of his cock in his jeans lining up against my center perfectly and I rock back and forth for a second to get the perfect angle against my clit.

"Fuck," I moan a little curse as I slide against him again.

"That feel better?" he asks in a raw tone I've never heard come from him before. "That where you need me?"

I open my eyes, and he's no longer looking at me like his irritating best friend. He's looking at me like a woman he wants to fuck. And holy hell am I screwed, because this version of him? I need more of it. So much more.

"Yes," I whisper, chewing on my lower lip because I want to kiss him, but I feel like that would be too far.

"Good."

I pick up the pace of my little lap dance, removing my hands from under his shirt and bracing them against his shoulders again, so I don't fall. I can only imagine what I look like right now, my dress bunched up against my hips, his coat draped over my shoulders as I dry hump him on a bench outside in the late October cold. But I honestly don't care. It feels that-fucking-good. He feels that good against me it's all I can think about.

"Christ I'm gonna come if you keep up like this." His hands are warm as they slide down my thighs.

"Good, maybe it'll improve your mood." I smirk, but I can feel my orgasm start to tighten, pulling low, and I lean into it, wrapping my hands around his neck. I feel hot, like I could break a sweat even though it's like 40 degrees outside right now. I pick up my pace, feeling like a few more touches might finally take me over the edge.

"Liv, fuck..." he curses, and runs his hands back up my thighs.

"Almost," I promise. I bend my head down and bite my tongue, trying to stifle any noise I make.

"Come for me," he whispers.

My body takes its orders from him just like I do, apparently, because a half second later the crest of my orgasm hits and I ride it out, slowing my pace as I come down until I finally collapse against him.

"Fucking hell, Liv." His breathing is almost as heavy as mine, and it's hard to tell from his tone if he's irritated or turned on.

"Well, I'm not cold anymore," I laugh softly.

There's a long pause. One that if my senses weren't dulled by the shots Wren and I had taken earlier, would have been eating away at me.

"Yeah... We should get you back inside though," his regular voice is back when he finally speaks, and I can feel the moment this is going to get awkward coming on even through my drunkenness.

"Yeah," I say, and stand slowly. I brush my dress down, trying to straighten myself out. I hand him his jacket back, but he refuses it.

As we walk toward the door, I start to ask if Liam ever got a reply from East when I see the door's open again with the door stop tucked into place. I cringe at the sight of it, because there's no way whoever fixed the door didn't see us. Liam stays silent though, so I stay quiet as we walk in.

As we get back to the table, I notice the two women who were with East are gone, and whatever discussion Wren and East had been having comes to a dead stop as we approach.

"Get everything all worked out?" East smirks over the edge of his glass as he locks eyes with Liam.

"Yeah," Liam answers, giving East a strange look in return.

I can't read whatever's going on between the two of them, so I scoot in next to Wren.

"What did you get to drink?" I see an array of shakers and mixers set out in front of us, along with a couple mixed drinks and shots sitting on a tray.

"I don't know. Whatever pretty boy here decided to order us. I gave up trying to find something on the menu. Apparently beer or vodka is too basic around here."

"Don't let her talk shit, Liv. Try it. It's good. I promise. We'll get you some water too. Need to stay hydrated if you're gonna work so hard tonight." East flags down the wait staff.

"That's enough," Wren barks, giving him a look that could kill from across the table.

"I'll be back," Liam mutters and then heads off down the hall.

I follow his progress with my eyes until he disappears, and I feel my heart drop. I had done a very fucking stupid thing outside, and I wasn't sure if he was going to forgive me for it.

And I have no idea if his participation in the whole scene was because he enjoyed it, or because he was just indulging me.

I grab one of the shots still sitting on the tray and down it. I don't care what it is. I need whatever will blot out what just happened before Liam gets back, so that I can act like everything is absolutely fine when it's not. Because my crush on him is threatening to become a real problem.

FOUR

Liam

THE NEXT DAY we're all sitting in the dining hall at dinner after practice; Waylon, Ben, East, and me. I can see East's eyes glittering with anticipation, dying to say something. I've been bracing for it all day, and I really would just like to get it over with.

"Whatever it is, stop looking at me like you want to fuck me and just say it." I glare at him.

"Am I allowed to talk about it?"

"Is there a chance it doesn't get back to Mac, and therefore back to Waylon and Ben?"

"Doubtful. Wren caught the same show I did when we went to find you."

"Show?" Waylon asks thoughtfully.

"Do tell." Ben eyes me curiously.

"Our guy here got one hell of a lap dance the other night," East smirks.

"Oh yeah? Which place did you go to? That hole in the wall down on Santa Fe or the classy one further north?" Waylon asks.

"Does Mackenzie know you know this much about the strip club selection around here?" I ask, because I'm sure the bookworm would rip out some of his long blond hair if she knew.

"It's former knowledge. No reason to go anymore. Trust me." Waylon grins.

"No strip clubs. It was a private show. Well semi-private since it was on a roof top where half the high rises in town could have watched if they wanted," East teases more information.

Ben and Waylon are both sitting up now, their rapt attention flitting between me and Easton.

"All right. The suspense is killing me. Who was it?" Ben stares at me.

"Liv," I mumble right before I take a sip of my energy drink.

A tight cough escapes Waylon's throat before the table erupts into cheers and a low whistle, attracting the attention of half the dining hall.

"Okay. Settle the fuck down," I gripe.

"So was it good? Did you, you know, get the *full* experience? I saw you run off to the bathroom when you came back in," East grins so wide I think his cheeks might break.

"It was what it was."

"Come the fuck on, man. You've been low over her since Mason came around. Speaking of—does Mason know you're letting his girl ride your lap? I need warning if I have to break up another fight this time." Waylon looks concerned.

"They broke up. So I doubt he gives a fuck."

"Huh," Waylon answers.

"Does this mean you're finally together?" Ben asks.

"No. It just means she was drunk, and I happened to be the guy who was there."

"Nah. Fuck that. She was riled up. Yelling at him and shit right before. She's got some serious repressed issues from wanting you to fuck her, and you consistently ignoring all the signs," Easton shakes his head.

"It's not like that." I shake my head staring at my plate. At least, I don't think it is.

"It might not be exactly like that, but you both have some serious 'we need to fuck this out' vibes rolling off you when you're together lately," Waylon scrunches his nose and tilts his head like it's hard for him to tell me but it's true.

I look to Ben.

"Yeah. Sorry man. They're not wrong. I don't know what's going on with you two, but you broke a guy's nose. You've been pouting. She's been yelling. The rest of us would really just like the two of you to get to the bottom of it."

"Hence why I locked them outside on the terrace," Easton grins.

"You fucking what?" My eyes snap up to his.

"This is the part where you thank me." A smug little look on his face has me wanting to wipe it off. But he's not entirely wrong. I want to strangle him, but I also do kind of want to thank him.

"Do you think we could just keep locking them out or in together somewhere? Like some sort of forced proximity therapy?" Waylon asks.

"Unethical. But maybe desperate times call for desperate measures," Ben shrugs.

"Fuck all of you. Very much."

"Nah. Just focus on fucking Liv," Easton smirks at me.

FIVE

Olivia

WHEN I WAKE up the next afternoon, my skull is pounding out of my head. I groan as I sit up, every nerve ending I have is protesting the movement.

"You up?" Mackenzie calls from the library in the hall.

"Yeah," I mumble.

"All right. Just give me a second, water, sports drink and Tylenol on the way. Anything else?"

"Maybe some crackers?" I ask, as I feel my stomach churn.

I lay back down, staring at the ceiling as I hear Kenz rummaging around downstairs. I'm trying to remember last night. I'd had a lot to drink. Pregaming. Two or three different bars. Hitting the club. Dancing our asses off. Liam stopping me from dancing. Liam and I arguing. Liam and I—Oh, *fuck*.

I sit up abruptly, and I feel nauseous.

"Okay, take it easy. Here's a trashcan." Kenz has magically appeared at my bedside, and she reassures me as she grabs the trashcan from the corner of the room and puts it at the side of my bed.

I dry heave a few times before my stomach feels like I might be able to have a few sips of water.

"I brought ice too, just in case. Wren told me you went a little too wild last night and would probably need some first aid when you woke up."

"Shit. Yeah. Thanks," I answer, taking the ice chips from her and putting a couple in my mouth.

"Anything else you need?"

"A time machine?"

"That bad?"

"Well, it's not good," I say, remembering the feel of his jeans between my thighs. "Fucking fuck."

"Care to share?"

"I uh... may have given Liam a lap dance?"

"What?" Kenz stares at me like I've just told her the moon has fallen out of the sky.

"Yeah, and not just any lap dance but one where I like... dry humped him to..." I trail off. I can't bring myself to say it. I just pinch my eyes shut.

"Arrival?" she offers helpfully.

"Mmm. Yes. That. Outside on like a terrace thing?" I bury my face in my hands.

"Um, wow. That is definitely a wild night for you," Kenz sits down on the edge of the bed eyeing me like she's even more worried than she was before. "What did he say?"

"Ugh."

"What?" She laughs nervously.

"No, uh I mean. *Ugh.* For me. Because I am pretty sure he tried to politely stop me from being an idiot a few times, and I was just like fuck it. Oh my god. I want the floor to swallow me whole and never be seen again!" I set the ice chips down on my nightstand and turn over, throwing a pillow over my head. I was never going to live this down or get out of it.

"Liiivvvvv. You do not want that. It sounds like a terrible way to go out. Also, it's going to be fine. I know Liam, if he wanted to stop you, he would have stopped you."

"It's not fine," I mumble through the pillow. "I'm an embarrassing train wreck, and now I've made our train wreck friendship catch on fire. He was probably just indulging me because my sad pathetic relationship fell apart a month in."

"You're being a tad dramatic, dearest." Mackenzie rubs my back. "Also, are we sure he hated it?"

"I don't know. He said some things that make me think he didn't but then he got really quiet, so I don't know."

"Can we revisit the idea that the rest of us all think you guys have had an unacknowledged thing for a while, or am I going to get into trouble for that?"

I pull my head out from under the pillow.

"You guys don't know the whole story."

"What's the whole story then?" Kenz pins me with a look and it's probably time I told her the whole truth.

"Liam was my boyfriend's best friend," I decide that dropping the weight like it's 100 pounds of lead is the best way to do this, because there's no easy way to explain how Liam and I ended up being so close.

"What?" She blinks at me.

"My boyfriend was Liam's best friend. That's how we know each other. How we met and got to be friends in the first place."

"Wait, was—does that mean they're not anymore? How come you've never told us about him?" Kenz gives me a shocked look.

"Because he died the summer before freshman year," I answer her quietly.

"Oh my god, Liv... What? How?" Kenz puts her hand on my arm and gives me the most pitiful look.

"And this is why I don't tell people. Even you, because it's depressing and then it ends up being this huge thing. I'm sorry I never told you though. I should have."

"Do not be sorry," Kenz pats my arm gently.

"It's okay. It'll help make everything make sense if I tell you, and then maybe Liam and I can have a breather without you all making wedding plans for us, you know?" I give her a little smile, trying to make the situation lighter.

"If you're sure." Kenz looks at me with concern.

"I'm sure. So... where to start. Um. Tristan. He was Liam's best friend and the guy I had a crush on through most of high school. Junior year he finally asked me out, and I fell in love pretty much immediately. Or whatever love is at that age. He was everything I could have dreamed of, you know? Outgoing, funny, a little bit wild, super carefree. That's probably why Liam and Waylon get along so well. I think that part of Waylon reminds him of Tristan. And you know, Mr. Serious needs a little levity sometimes," I smile and look up from my hands where I've been picking at my cuticle. Kenz is still watching me with rapt attention.

"We were inseparable. Just like now. Liam had a different girl or girlfriend all the time, so I never got my female bestie till I met you, but the three of us and whoever he was dating at the time did everything together. When Liam got the football scholarship there was no question where Tristan was going. Those two were a bromance for the ages. And then, where Tristan went I followed. He was the sun and all that stuff you feel when you're young and think it's the only love you'll ever know, you know?"

Kenz nods.

"Anyway, we all decided to come here to Highland. That

summer before freshman year Liam had to report for practice, and I had decided to come early to take a few summer classes. I wanted to get an early start, and I was anxious about the Classics program and being good enough. I'm not even sure how I got in to be honest. Tristan was a different story though. He probably would have put off college another year if it wasn't for us. He wanted to wander the world or take a job doing one of those chateaus or agritourism things in Europe. So instead of coming here early with us he went on a tour with some of his other friends, his cousin, and some guys from high school who didn't hang out with us as much."

I pause, rubbing my sternum as I remember the last time I saw Tristan standing in the airport. He kissed me so hard because I was crying and heartsick that we were going to be apart for so long. It was the first time since we'd started dating that we were going to go weeks without seeing each other. I was convinced he was gonna meet a girl in one of the hostels and break up with me before he got back. He was so damn pretty, and so wonderful. It hurts every time I think about it. Who he could have been.

"You okay?" Kenz asks. "We can stop."

"No. I'm good. Just remembering what he looked like that last time I saw him. So he uh, went overseas and they were traveling around for a few weeks. Then they went down to Croatia, you know for all the outdoor adventure stuff. And I guess one day they went cliff diving. One guy decided to go off this high cliff and jumped in and was fine. So Tristan went next. They'd been drinking though and when he jumped I guess he didn't clear it quite as well. He hit his head on the way down. So when he hit the water—"

Kenz gasps and then wraps her arms around me in a hug as the tears start to fall down my cheeks.

"Damn. I really thought I could do this without all the

blubbering. I'm sorry." I wipe at the tears, embarrassed that this many years later it still makes me cry. More for his lost life than love now, but still painful all the same.

"Do not be sorry, Liv!" Kenz shakes her head.

"It's okay. I mean, despite the tears. I'm really okay now. At peace with it. But it sucks. I just, I hate that he missed so much of life. You know?"

She nods, and I blot the rest of the tears on my cheek with the edge of my sleeve.

"When he hit the water... The one guy couldn't pull him out, and the others were too afraid to jump obviously, so they ran down the hill, but it was too late. By the time they got him out there was too much water on his lungs and between that and the injury..."

"Holy shit that's awful." Kenz hasn't let go of me, but she looks up at me with another pitiful glance.

"Yeah. I... when his mom called me to tell me, I threw up. It didn't seem possible. Couldn't be possible. Tristan had done so much stupid stuff over the years and had never gotten so much as a scratch. And then just one little fucking jump and it's all over, you know?"

"Right." Kenz rubs my back.

"I was so heartbroken, but Liam. Oh my god, he was devastated. They'd been best friends since kindergarten. They did everything together. Tristan's mom said she couldn't handle telling him. That it would break her heart a second time and she didn't have it in her. So I said I'd break the news to him. But then I had to tell Liam, and ugh. It was the worst thing I've ever had to do in my life. I told him when he got out of practice. It was stupid. I should have waited and found a better place to tell him. I was just still in shock myself. And Liam, he collapsed right there in the parking lot. The trainer happened to be walking to his car and ran over. Thought maybe it was heat stroke. It was so awful."

I choke back a few more tears at the memory of Liam like that. He's the impervious one now. The leader of the team. The guy who never gets rattled. The one who's always focused. But that day, he had just crumpled like paper inside a fist. And I couldn't blame him. It's how I felt when I heard the news. I'd just been lucky enough to be inside and alone when I'd broken down. I should have waited, but at the time I couldn't think straight. I just needed someone else who would understand.

"They gave him some time off, but then he didn't want to play football anymore. He wanted to quit. Stay in his room and drink. Wouldn't talk to anyone, even me. I practically had to drag him to the funeral. I begged him, because I told him I couldn't do it alone. But even after, he said he was going to quit football. Go home, find something else to do. But I told him there was no fucking way he was quitting. Tristan was so proud of him. He loved watching him play because he was fucking terrible at sports. Loved them, but fucking terrible"

I laugh at another memory of Tristan and Liam and a few of their friends playing a pick-up game of basketball where Tristan tried over and over again to make a basket, and then finally just started saying hitting the board counted.

"So I knew I couldn't let Liam quit. I told him I'd be there instead. I'd go to every practice. Every game. I'd literally hold his hand if he needed me to, but that Tristan would be furious if he quit. And he would have been. So I did it. The first practice he said he'd try, but he didn't think he could. And he made it through that one, and then another. And we just took it day by day. And we'd talk about Tristan and laugh about the way things used to be. The coach started having him see a counselor, and I started seeing someone too. We didn't tell anyone when classes started because it was just too hard a thing to explain to everyone, you know? 'Hey! Nice to meet you. My boyfriend died this summer, how was yours?'"

"Fuck, no kidding," Kenz shakes her head.

"So, it just brought Liam and I closer. Sometimes it felt like he was the only one who could understand in the world, and I guess he felt the same way to some extent. But in his mind I was Tristan's girl. Sometimes I think to him I still am Tristan's. I think that's half his problem with Mason. That, and now I'm like a sister to him you know? We're like family after all that trauma and that's why he didn't want the football players dating me."

"It does make a lot of sense now. They'd been friends since kindergarten? Can you imagine. And then you all being so close."

"Right. So I get why you all think we're secretly in love or something, but there's nothing there. Well at least for Liam. He's not jealous, he just worries about me getting hurt again. Worries that he won't do right by Tristan if he can't keep that from happening I think."

She nods and I appreciate how quiet she's being. I don't think I could answer a lot of questions right now. It all still hurts more than I remembered.

"Fuck. I get it. That's a lot between the two of you."

"Right."

"But also who better to understand it, you know?" Kenz says softly.

"True."

"Anyway, for now you better rest up and take some meds. You can make decisions about the grump when your head is straight again. What kind of greasy food do you want me to order?"

"Um... Chinese and wings?"

"Both?"

"Yes."

"I think I like this new Olivia. I can't wait to party with her," Kenz smiles at me as she gets up to leave the room. "I'll let you know when its here."

"Thank you, bestie."

"Love you!"

She shuts the door and I lay down, wondering how the fuck I'm going to deal with seeing Liam again.

THAT NIGHT WREN and Mackenzie appear in the living room where I'd been mindlessly scrolling on my phone. Mac holds out a bowl of ice cream.

"We have a plan." Wren smiles.

"A plan?" I look back and forth between them, confused.

"About your whole predicament. We caught each other up to the present on your situation with Liam and we have thoughts," Wren offers.

"You know, just like how you always solve problems for us. This time we're doing it for you." Kenz's grin borders on devious.

I eye them both warily.

"I don't think there's a solution to suddenly realizing that you have a thing for your best friend. I think you just hold your breath and hope that goes away before he notices," I grumble before I take a bite of the chocolate peanut butter ice cream.

"Or... and hear me out here..." Kenz looks to Wren nervously. "You fuck him out of your system."

I nearly spit the ice cream out of my mouth at the idea of me fucking Liam once, let alone enough that he would be out of my system.

"Are you both mad? I'm going to be lucky if the grumpy jerk speaks to me after the other night."

"False," Wren shakes her head. "I had glimpses of things the other evening, *unfortunately*. And I saw what he looked like when you came back in. That boy was fucking rattled to his core. Like he just had a wakeup call of his own."

"Yeah, but that wakeup call could have been 'Wow! My best friend is a freak!' It wasn't necessarily a good wake up call."

"Eh. I talked to Easton, and he thought similar things."

"You and Easton talk?" I ask, curious about this development.

"Focus on the subject at hand please, Olivia," Wren chides.

"Fine. So what? I try to drunkenly seduce him?" I ask sarcastically.

"Ask for his help," Kenz suggests.

"What?"

"Tell him your confidence is shaken up after everything with Mason, and you need his help. He's your best friend, right? And you've helped him out plenty over the years? So now he can help you. Give you some confidence coaching... you know, *lessons*," Mac gives Wren a conspiratorial look.

"That's devious."

"Which is why it just might work," Wren grins.

"I don't know," I shake my head, taking another bite of the ice cream.

"If he agrees, you get to try things with him without risking your friendship by telling him about your crush. And he skips the whole guilt-over-his-friend because he's not pursuing you, he's helping you. It's perfect, honestly. Then you'll either get him out of your system for good, or you'll figure out exactly what your feelings are," Kenz explains like it's the simplest thing in the world.

And it sounds crazy. Crazy enough that it just might work. I shovel another bite of ice cream into my mouth while I ponder it.

"I don't like lying to him though," I say at last.

"It's not really lying. Your confidence is shaken—he just doesn't need to know he's the reason," Wren offers.

I'm really considering it now, and I wonder what that means for my sanity.

SIX

Liam

A COUPLE of days after the night at the club, I head over to Liv's. It's at a time we used to hang out and study together before Mason so I'm pretty sure she'll be home. I really just want to have a conversation with her, so we can move past what happened last weekend at the club.

Wren lets me in as she heads out for work, letting me know she's upstairs in her room, and when I get there the door is open, but I don't see her. I drop my bag, assuming she's in the bathroom, and I sit down on the edge of her bed to wait for her. Hoping I don't give her a heart attack when she gets out.

Except when I look up, I'm the one who's about to have the fucking heart attack. The door to the bathroom is open and she's wearing a full set of lingerie, it's nude and black, with lace. Down to the garters and the fucking thigh highs. And I really, desperately, need to be cut a fucking break when it comes to this woman. Because I am doing my level best to put her back in the friend zone where I've managed to keep her for years, and nothing in this universe seems to want to make that easy on me.

She has zero idea I'm here either, watching her like she's my own personal cam girl, and fuck, is it hot. I've seen her in tank tops and short shorts that showed plenty of skin. I've slept next to her in those clothes and done my best not to notice. But this, right now, is more than I can handle. Especially since it's reminding me of the version of her I saw over the weekend. The one who sat in my lap and begged me to let her come. Flashbacks of that come flooding into my memory and it's the last thing I need.

I need it all to stop now. Need to stop thinking about it. Need to stop looking at her. I tear my eyes away, trying to find something, anything else to focus my attention on.

I glance over at the chair by the door and there are several more sets of lingerie laid out across it, and when my eyes drift back to her, like a magnet, she's holding another little lacy, see-through, barely-there top up to herself in the mirror. Which is about the moment when I wonder what the fuck is going on that she needs this many sets of lingerie. I never knew she owned one, let alone the half dozen scattered around the room.

She and Mason aren't together anymore, and I have no idea how she'd already be dating someone else and at whatever fucking stage requires lingerie of this magnitude so fast afterwards. Unless they were back together. Or she was serious about this whole stripper thing. Except, these didn't look like stripper outfits either.

I notice when I look at her again, she has earbuds in, and she does a little shimmy and a twist on her tip toes that makes it impossible not to smile. And that exact moment, when I'm staring at her, smiling like a fucking asshole is the exact moment she realizes I'm in her room.

"Jesus Christ!" Her hand goes to her heart, and she rips her earbuds out. "What are you doing here?!"

"What are *you* doing?" I look at her and then at the pile of lingerie, raising my brow. Because the best defense when you're caught out like this is a good offense.

"None of your business!" she says defensively, pulling the bustier in her hands tight to her chest, like it'll do any good at all in covering her up.

"You're not serious about the stripper thing?" I ask.

She gives me a look like I'm an idiot. "I don't have the coordination or talent."

"Trying to win Mason back?"

I get another *you're stupid* look from her.

"You going to make me keep guessing?"

"You going to mind your own business?"

"Not so long as I can't think of a good reason why this is happening."

And I can't think of a single one that doesn't light fire under every impulse I have to try to stop her. She gives me a little glare and sighs.

"It's part of my experiment."

"What experiment?"

"The one that's been an epic failure so far." Her shoulders slump, and I hate the defeated look on her face.

"You're going to have to elaborate."

"I was serious the other night. I know I was drunk, and you probably weren't listening, but I really am tired of this whole wallflower era thing that's been going on. I want to try something different senior year. I thought Mason would be the answer, but that went terribly. And then you had to bust up my fun over the weekend."

I bite my tongue to keep from commenting.

"But Kenz had an idea, so I'm trying it."

"What idea did Mackenzie have?" Jesus, Waylon is already wearing off on her if she was talking Liv into whatever wildness that ended in her buying out lingerie stores.

"I don't want to tell you."

"Why?"

"Because you won't approve. And I don't care whether you do or not, and I don't want to argue about it."

I don't point out the obvious, that we're already arguing about it, and while she's in lingerie no less.

"Is Mac doing whatever this is, too?"

"Yes. We're doing it together."

"Good. Then I'll just find out from Waylon."

"Liam!" she protests.

"Or you could just tell me."

"God. Getting those two together might have been a mistake if this is what I have to deal with now." She glares at me, but finally relents. "We're going to have boudoir shoots done tomorrow."

"You're going to have photos of you, taken, in that?" I point to her barely-there outfit.

"Yes."

"Oh, okay," I shrug.

"You're not going to lecture me about this?"

"Nope."

"Why not?"

"Because I'm the only one that's ever going to see them besides you and Mac, and whoever this photographer is. And I *hope* you vetted the photographer, otherwise I'm going with you."

I wonder if part of this experiment of hers was temporary insanity that she was going to have photos of her half naked and in compromising positions taken. For what? For *who*? Hell fucking no.

"Liam," she tosses the bustier on the bathroom counter, and storms out of the bathroom to confront me. "I'm serious. I'm tired of being in your shadow all the time. I'm tired of being your mousy little football mom sidekick. Okay? I want to be seen differently. Seen at all really. And you might as well know now that I'm going to ask for Easton's help."

Easton? There is nothing good that Easton could help her with, and I feel the weight of that hit my chest like a ton of bricks.

"Help you with what?"

"Lessons, tutoring, whatever you want to call it—in not being... whatever it is I've been the last few years. I thought Mason would help me with that, but since he found me disappointing too, I'm moving on to Plan B: getting expert advice."

I stare at her for a minute. Trying to put these puzzle pieces together in a way that makes any kind of sense at all.

"I know you're not telling me you're going to ask Easton for sex tutoring."

"That's exactly what I'm saying, and you will *not* interfere."

"Oh, I'm not gonna interfere. I'm going to put a swift fucking stop to it. Over my dead body are you having the king of campus manwhores give you lessons in sex."

"Then I'll start shopping for something in all black." She stares up at me, and her eyes are burning with intensity, like she's ready to throttle me, and that combined with what she's wearing is fucking with me so hard right now. Even trying to think straight is a struggle, and I need to not lose high ground on this argument.

Close eyes. Breathe. Think. Form words.

"He won't do it anyways." I give her a smug little look. Because Easton likes his life drama free, and he knows that an arrangement like that would bring far too many problems his way.

Her face shifts, a bright smile forming where the frown had just been, and I do not like it. I feel like I've just stepped into a trap.

"You're right. He probably wouldn't, because of *you*. And this whole situation is because of you in the first place—breaking faces, ordering me around, telling me what I can and cannot do."

I stay silent, because again, I'm not stupid. I can feel the walls of a trap closing in and while I know I've stepped into it, I'm still not sure what exactly it is or how to get out yet.

"So you got me into this, and you can help me get out of it."

"What?"

"You can be my tutor, or my coach in this case."

I stare at her, because she can't be serious.

"What?" I repeat.

"Unless you don't think you have enough experience. You're not exactly at Easton's level."

"I have plenty of fucking experience," I say defensively, realizing as soon as I say it that I'm stuck in quicksand, and I need to think fast if I'm going to pull out of this.

I could not tutor her. I could not touch her. That was going to lead down a road that will spiral out of control for me, and I cannot afford it. I needed my best friend back in the box and on the fucking shelf. In the touching-free friend zone where she belonged, and where she had been happily up until this weekend.

"Are we sure it's enough though? I want like, quality coaching. Expert level. You know?" she taunts.

"I have plenty. I promise. But that's not the problem," It's my turn to smile, because I've just realized how to get out of this.

And she does not like that I'm smiling, her little brow furrows and her hazel eyes light with irritation.

"What's the problem then?"

"Take that off," I smirk pointing to the corset she has on, because I know she won't. She will freeze. She'll stutter and then she'll back out of this whole idea. Then we can try to have a conversation like fucking adults again.

SEVEN

Olivia

"TAKE THAT OFF." He smirks, because he thinks I won't do it. That I'll be too shy, and it'll give him the perfect out. He'll say I need to chill out with the tutoring idea and everything else, and probably tell me I need to rethink my whole plan.

Because he would love for me to get back in my lane. The one where I stay quiet and make sure the guys have cake on their birthdays and ideas for places to take their girlfriends out for anniversaries. The one where I am his platonic other half, so that he never has to worry about girlfriends or plus ones to events. The one where I watch my friends hookup with hot football players and have fun one night stands, while I can't even keep the hot hockey player that finally noticed me.

Nope. I was not doing that anymore. I was not getting back in my lane, and if that meant stripping down in front of my best friend to prove my point? No problem.

My hands go to the tiny eye hooks on the front of the corset

I have on, and I start unhooking them one by one. They're small and it takes me a minute to get the hang of it, but before I know it I've got half of them undone.

"Liv..." Liam's voice is low, a questioning tone to it like he's not sure what the hell I'm doing. Like maybe I'm not in my right mind.

My fingers fumble a little as I pull the last of them apart, and I try to remind myself he's seen me topless before. It was a long time ago when we all went skinny dipping in high school when I had way less curves than I do now, but I lie to myself that this isn't new. It's not a big deal. Not really.

"Liv. Fuck!" I hear him curse, as I drop the bustier to the floor and then look up at him.

And his eyes are closed, his hands clasped and pressed to his lips as he takes a deep fucking breath.

"Yeah. See. This is the real problem. You won't even look at me."

"Because you're my best fucking friend, Liv," he growls.

"Plenty of people have friends with benefits relationships, Liam. And this isn't even that, you'd just be coaching me temporarily."

"Liv..."

"Fine." I fold my arms over my chest, because at this point I feel raw and rejected. A whole new kind of vulnerable I hadn't imagined possible; I was racking up fresh humiliation with him every few days at this rate. "But then stay out of the way of me asking Easton then, okay?"

I turn around and pick up the corset off the floor, ready to change back into sweats because the last thing on earth I feel right now is sexy. I briefly wonder if it's even worth going through with the photo session.

"Liv."

He's up off the bed and at my back, his hands on my shoulders stopping me from closing the bathroom door and putting a barrier between us while I sort my feelings out. I can guess what he's thinking, what he's about to say and I really don't want to have to sit through it.

"I know. I'm *your* best friend. I was *his* girlfriend. I *know*. But it's been years and I am tired of being that Liv. You can't help me, and that's fine. Like I said, just stay out of the way and let me figure out who I want to be, okay?" I cut all his objections off at the pass.

"I want to help you. I just don't want to cross lines that can't be uncrossed. We need ground rules, guard rails, something."

"Well I'm pretty sure this is gonna be hard to do if one of them is that you don't even want to look at me."

His forehead touches the crown of my head, and I can feel his breath in my hair.

"I want to look. If you were anyone else..." he says the words quietly.

"Who was I Saturday?"

"That's why I came here to talk to you."

"To scold me?"

"To get you to promise me we're going to be friends after all this. I missed you during all this Mason bullshit. I hate the arguing. I want my friend back. You promise me this doesn't fuck up our friendship, I'll help you however you want."

"I don't want to fuck up our friendship either. I promise. As long as you accept I might change sometimes. Because I need to. I want to."

"Okay," he agrees, and my shoulders sag a little with relief as he pulls me tight against him in a hug.

"Let me just get dressed and we can hang out for a bit, okay?" I relent, starting to pull away from him.

"Wait." He pulls his head back, his eyes meeting mine in the mirror. "You don't want to get started with lesson one?"

I raise a brow at him, and he gives me a little smile.

"Depends on what it is."

"Lesson one is that you don't need all this lingerie. If you like it, if it makes you feel confident... Go for it. But you don't need it. You've got that girl next door, approachable but hot as fuck thing down without it."

I give him a skeptical look. I didn't think I was ugly, but I also would never describe myself as "hot as fuck".

"I'm serious, Liv. You have a gorgeous face. And your body is a fucking wet dream." His hands slide down my sides. "You have soft curves, and perfect tits. And your hips and thighs are sexy as hell. But the best part... turn around." He presses against me, making me turn to face him with my back to the mirror. His hand slides down my back and over the panties I have on until he palms my ass, cupping one cheek in his wide hand. "Your ass is perfect, the way it curves here, the way it moves when you walk, and fuck your skin is so soft."

"Is Liam Montgomery an ass man?" I tease, laughing and turning back to look at him directly, without the mirror between us.

"When it comes to yours, yeah."

And my heart skips a little, because this is my Liam. The one who says kind things to make me feel better when I need it. The one who I could joke with easily.

"I thought mine was boney."

"That's what you remember from Saturday?" He raises his brows. "I said what I had to to get you to stop squirming in my lap."

"That didn't work out for you," I smirk even though I still feel awkward about it, shaking my head as I remember bits and pieces of the time out on the terrace.

"You were definitely in rare form." He looks down at me, studying my face for a moment.

"Thanks for not being a jerk about that. And I'm sorry I put you in that position."

"Uh, to be clear, I enjoyed that position."

"You went dead silent and then ran off."

"You nearly made me come in my pants like a fucking preteen. I had some adjustments to make. Cut me some slack, yeah?"

"Just talk to me next time, okay? If there is a next time I mean. Shit. I didn't think about that, is that going to be a problem?"

"What?"

"You getting hard? Not saying you have a problem, but with your whole Liv-is-just-a-friend thing."

"Liv." He grunts and squeezes my ass in a way I think I might like. "Lesson two is don't suggest a guy can't get hard and while we're at it, don't talk about how his friend is the superior expert in bed."

"I'm not saying that, I'm saying I might not be enough for you for these coaching sessions. We can do porn or whatever you need, if that's a thing. And Easton fucks a lot more women than you do, that's all."

"Easton fucks more women as a choice, and because his best friend isn't a living breathing cockblock."

"What?"

"You complain that I've kept you from dating because guys don't want to deal with me as part of the equation, and you never thought about the fact that that's a two-way street?"

"No."

"Well you should. It's definitely been a problem before."

"Shit. I'm sorry," I give him a pained expression.

He shrugs, "It is what it is."

"And the other thing?"

He takes my hand and puts his over mine, pushing my palm out and against the front of his pants where he is very hard under my touch.

"I think we're good there too."

My fingers twitch and I palm him lightly through his pants.

"Liv..." his eyes shutter.

EIGHT

Olivia

"LESSON THREE? Since you didn't finish the other night," I ask softly.

He doesn't say anything, but he palms my ass again, his fingers tightening around the curve of it like he was silently debating the idea.

"My blowjob skills are rusty, but..." I look up at him.

"*No.* No fucking way. One of the ground rules is we take this slow. Like pace-of-a-fucking-glacier slow," he answers me gruffly.

"So... just hands then, that's slow right? Very beginner level." I run my fingers over him again.

He gives me a doubtful look and scrubs a hand over his face. His eyes go up to the ceiling, and I know the look on him. It's when he wants to do something he thinks is a bad idea.

"I want to, and we have to start somewhere," I argue with his silent thoughts.

"Fuck... Like I can say no when you're standing there looking like that."

"So... yes, then?" I give him a little half smile.

"All right, just... fuck."

My fingers trace the edge of his jeans, and I don't know which of us is more nervous because I feel like I might need to coach him through this, given the way I can feel anxiety about it rolling off him.

"Tell me something you fantasize about," I say as I start undoing the button and zipper on his jeans.

"I don't know," his voice sounds hoarse, and he's quieter than usual.

"You don't know, or you don't want to share?" I tease him, as I run my fingers under the band of his boxer briefs. I'm thankful for Mason in that I at least shook off some of the cobwebs with him because I'd be terrified right now if Liam was the first guy I'd touched in so long. I start to push them down when he finally answers me.

"Kissing you."

My heart skips for a second, when he says it. My mind flashing back to our almost-kiss years ago and wondering if he's thought about it all this time like I have. But I only think that for a second before my mouth twists with amusement at such an innocent reply.

"Kissing someone is not a fantasy," I chastise him for cheating his way out of the question.

"Then you've never been kissed right." His hand goes under my chin and tilts my head up so my gaze meets his.

"How do you figure?" I raise an eyebrow, not entirely sure he's not just stalling for time because he's panicking about this being a bad idea. Which if he's changed his mind, I wish he'd just say so.

He leans forward, his lips brushing the shell of my ear. His hand ghosts down my side, resting on my hip, pulling me closer so that our bodies meet.

"Getting to feel that soft little puff of air across your lips, that little proof of want? Getting to taste you for the first time? Letting my tongue slide over yours, knowing it's the same one that's said my name a million times? Cheered for me from the stands? Threatened to kill someone 'cause they banged me up on the field? Making you imagine what my mouth would feel like on the rest of your body?"

Holy *fuck*.

"I'm sorry, who are you?" I ask when I finally stop assessing how far out of my depth I am with him.

"The guy who's gonna kiss you fucking right," he whispers right before he captures my mouth with his.

And he delivers on every promise he made. His mouth on mine makes me forget the world exists. Makes every thought I have absolutely consumed with how he tastes, how he sounds, how he feels. The way he slides his tongue in and out of my mouth, with rhythm and a dexterity I can't ever remember another guy having, it feels like he's fucking me. Feels like he's taking me and claiming every inch of me for his own. And I want it, more than I want the oxygen for my next breath.

He finally releases me, and my heart is rattling in my chest, threatening to come out through my rib cage. I take a little gulp of air and sway into him, his fingers biting into my hip to steady me, and I feel the brush of his erection coming through his unbuttoned fly. And now I'm desperate to bring him crashing down the same way the kiss has me.

My fingers slide underneath both layers and push, shoving them down his thighs. The outline of his hip and the perfect round ass—one I have admittedly appreciated before in his uniform—has me biting my lip. I wrap my hand around him, and he's thick and warm in my palm. He groans at the contact.

"Kiss me again," I whisper.

And he grants my request, but as his lips touch mine I start stroking him and it makes him messy. Not the deftly adept passes of his tongue that he'd given me before, but needy desperate little half measures that are broken each time my hand runs the length of him. I smile against his lips.

"You're fucking evil," he mutters, smiling back.

"You're supposed to be teaching me, not insulting me, remember Coach?" I tease.

"Yeah, well..." His hands wrap around my ass, and he hauls me onto the bathroom counter in one swift motion, his lips brushing over the side of my jaw. "You're doing good so far, Sunshine."

"Sunshine?" I ask, amused.

"If you're gonna call me Coach, it's only—" The words die on his tongue as I run my hand over him again.

"Fair?" I ask. Trying so hard not to grin at the effect I have on him.

"Fuck that's good. I forgot how good this could feel." He closes his eyes, his head tilting forward and some of his loose brown waves fall into his face. He rolls his lower lip between his teeth before he releases it. He's fucking pretty as hell, especially like this. It's a fact I normally try to forget for a long list of reasons, but I let myself appreciate it now.

"Any pointers?" I ask quietly, because I feel myself getting lost in thoughts about him, and I need to stay focused on why we're doing this.

"Lotion? Lube?" he asks absently.

"In the drawer to your right," I nod my head toward it when he opens his eyes.

He pulls it open and grabs the bottle out, raising his eyebrow. "Chocolate covered strawberry?"

"Don't hate it until you try it."

"I think I have questions," his brow raises.

"That you want to ask *right* now?" I hold out my hand, and he concedes by silently pouring some..

I warm it between my palms before I touch him again.

"Fuck," he groans and his eyes close again. "Like that, but a little tighter grip and faster."

I follow his directions, and my eyes drift back to his face again. Watching him, and the way his chest rises and falls in a heavier pattern.

"Good?"

"Yes, really fucking good," he mutters. "Just like that."

He sways forward, bracing himself against the counter on either side of my thighs, his head down and his breathing heavy. And for a brief second, I wonder if he'd fuck me now, because the way he looks and sounds like this, I want him to. But his earlier warning about pace echoes in my head and I keep the wish to myself.

"Fuck, fuck, fuck..." He curses and one of his hands slides up my thigh and hip, grabbing my ass again in a way that sends twinges of want straight to my clit. I want to say something, ask him, beg him, anything. But I know I can't, so I bite the side of my cheek and focus on making him come for me. And a few moments later, he does, pulsing in my hand as he comes on me, and I'm too distracted watching him to care where.

And it's only when his breathing slows and he opens his eyes to look at me, and I follow his gaze to see streams on my stomach and thighs that I realize the mess we've made.

"Fuck," is the grunted analysis on his part.

He surveys the state he's put me in, concern etched on his face, and he turns on the faucet next to me. He lets the hot water come on, always a slow process in our old creaky house, and reaches back to the little linen closet to grab a washcloth.

When he turns back, he kisses me one more time, languid

strokes of his tongue over mine before he releases my mouth. His eyes drift over my face and my body like he's assessing something new, or something he finally sees for the first time. But he doesn't speak.

His attention returns to the faucet like a spell is broken, and he tests the water temperature and then looks to me again.

"Give me your hand," he holds out his own.

I do as he asks, and he takes mine, turning it palm up under the water. He lathers his own with soap and then takes mine in it, rubbing the bubbles into my skin and washing it clean again. I had zero idea that an act this simple could feel like this.

"The other one," he motions, and I do as he asks. He repeats it again, and then hands me the towel off the rack.

I watch him, words on the tip of my tongue that I hold back because I don't want to say the wrong thing. The water finally puts off some steam and he runs the washcloth under it, squeezing it out and then he turns to me. He runs it over my skin, down my stomach and over my thighs, addressing every spot he left on my body. He studies me as he does it, his brow furrowed, and it feels more intimate than anything that's happened before this. My breath catches in my throat as I go to speak, and I have to swallow it to get my voice back.

"You don't have to do this," I whisper. "I can get it."

His eyes raise to meet mine. "It's the least I can do, and you shouldn't let any guy who wouldn't, touch you. You hear me?"

I nod. He looks intimidatingly serious, and I hold his gaze for only a second before I have to look away. This version of Liam is one I'm not ready for, even if I thought I was. This one is one I think I could fall for in an instant if I wasn't trying so hard to get him out of my system in the first place. Which means I need to get a grip, sign myself up for a self-help class that's designed to keep you from falling for the *wrong guy*.

Especially when that *wrong guy* has so many of the things on your checklist for the *right guy*.

He cleans the last little spot on my thigh and runs the washcloth under the water. He still looks distracted and lost in his thoughts as he finishes the task and puts himself back in order. I wish I knew what they were. If I did okay. If I suited his tastes enough.

"Thanks, Coach," I say, giving a bright smile that I don't entirely feel because I'm worried about his reaction right now.

His eyes flash up to mine, a storminess still there for a second before his lip twitches, and he gives me an answering smile in return.

"We'll have to work on pregame prep so it's not so..." He smirks.

"Messy?" I offer helpfully.

He grunts and squeezes out the washcloth, hanging it up on the rack to dry.

"Kind of fun this way though." I smirk, trying to get him to play even though I can tell he's lost in something in his thoughts.

He looks back at me, his eyes tracing over my body. "You should get dressed. Then we can go get dinner."

"At the diner?"

"If you want."

"All right," I hop up and kiss his cheek. "Just give me a couple minutes."

He nods, and I close the door behind him, my heart skipping a beat in my chest because he's agreed to try this with me, and the first lesson wasn't a total disaster. Only, he's not at all what I expected.

NINE

Liam

WHEN I GET BACK to my place after dinner, I feel fucking shell shocked. I'd gotten through the rest of the night just pretending like everything was normal. We sat together at the same place we always did, ordered the same things off the menu, but all I could think about was the way her mouth felt on mine, how hard I came in her hands, and worst of all how badly I wanted a repeat of everything.

And she was giving it to me. She wanted it from me. For me to help build her confidence back up in the wake of Mason and her general lack of dating through most of college. I was gonna coach my gorgeous best friend in confidence... and sex.

I need a fucking beer and time for my head to stop spinning. When I go to the kitchen, I notice the TV is lit up in the living room, and I wonder who's downstairs this late, just as I almost crash headfirst into Ben.

"Shit."

"Fuck."

"You look like you got rocked," Ben comments as he pulls a beer out and hands one to me.

"Something like that..."

"There you are," Waylon appears from the living room. "I came over thinking the three of us could have some guy time, but Ben said you went somewhere."

"To talk to Liv."

"Oh," Waylon smirks. "How did that talk go?"

"She wants me to fucking tutor her."

"What?" They both ask in unison.

I open the beer against the bottle opener on our fridge and take a chug.

"Not in fucking stats, in fucking sex."

"Holy fuck," Waylon sputters.

"Tutor her in sex how?" Ben asks.

"I don't fucking know. She wants a refresher course in the basics I guess. She just said Mason fucked up her confidence. It's my fault for getting in the way all these years."

"She's not wrong," Ben gives me a look, and Waylon makes a face like he agrees.

"Are you going to?" Waylon takes a sip of his beer.

"Yes? Or I already am? Fuck, I don't fucking know. I went over there, and she was wearing a whole set of lingerie and my brain just fucking short-circuited."

And my two asshole friends are very amused by this.

"Define 'already am' for me?" Waylon raises a brow.

"I'm not sharing fucking details."

"But there are details?"

I shrug and take another sip of my beer.

"I feel like this is a good thing. Why is this not a good thing?" Ben looks at me confused.

"Because you guys don't know the whole fucking story.

How she and I ended up close friends in the first place—she's my best friend's girlfriend."

"What?" Ben frowns.

Waylon just stares at me like I've said something impossible.

"You weren't here but Waylon will remember I took some time off during freshman training camp. I had to see a psych."

"Yeah I assumed you had the yips. You were doing great and then one day you just folded."

"Yeah, I found out my best friend died in an accident overseas. He was on a backpacking trip in Europe, and he died in a cliff diving accident."

"And he was Liv's boyfriend?"

"Yep. The three of us were close all through the end of high school. All planned to attend here at Highland."

"Fuck."

Yeah. *Fuck.* It's worse than that, considering the night before he died, we'd been at a party, and I'd almost kissed her. But I'm not that guy anymore and I'm not particularly proud or eager to share that part.

"Yep. She helped me through shit. I wanted to quit football. Quit college altogether. It didn't make sense to me that my life just went on and his didn't. So she started coming to every practice and game. She told me Tristan, that was his name, that he would have been disappointed if I quit and that she'd be there as long as I needed her to."

"I remember her showing up. I just thought she was obsessed with you or something until I realized you all were just friends," Waylon adds helpfully.

"No, she was just helping me try to get through it."

"Why did you never tell us?" Waylon frowns, and I figured he was gonna be a little pissed that something that big would never have come up before.

"I couldn't talk about it for the longest time, and then when I finally could talk about it, I didn't want to. For me, but also for Liv. I wanted to have the focus be on football. And she wanted to have a semi-normal freshman year where she wasn't just the 'girl whose boyfriend died'. And then it felt like it'd been too long to tell anyone. It's not the kind of thing you can just bring up in a random conversation."

"Fuck, that's a lot for you to have to go through. And it makes sense now why you were so close," Ben looks pained.

"And why you were so insistent nothing was going on," Waylon gives me a pitiful look that I hate.

"Yup." I shake my head. "Those two were... They'd probably be engaged if he were still alive."

"That's a lot to assume. I had high school girlfriends that there's no way I'd date now."

"Doesn't change the fact that he died her boyfriend though, does it?" I give a bitter smile.

"So you feel guilty?" Ben asks.

"Fuck yes, I feel guilty. I shouldn't be fucking touching her at all. And no way should I be tutoring her, but her alternative idea was to go to East for help."

"Oh fuck," Ben's eyes go wide.

"Yeah. And while I think he likes his dick too much to risk doing that, if not him it'll be someone else. And I don't want someone taking advantage of her."

"I mean also, you guys have a whole fucking vibe," Waylon interjects.

"We do not have a vibe."

"Jesus, don't make us have this conversation again," Ben mutters as he sets his beer down on the counter. "You might feel guilty wanting her, but you very clearly don't want anyone else to have her. She goes to *you* for tutoring. You're not that fucking dense."

I start to open my mouth to protest but Waylon cuts me off.

"Just admit you want to fuck her, even if it feels wrong. Yeah?"

I shut my mouth and glare at both of them.

"I'm doing this for her because she wants help and needs someone safe. I just have to figure out how the fuck to get out of it alive, because yeah, she's fucking gorgeous. And yeah, after this week I realize I have a fucking problem on my hands. Okay?"

"See. There you go," Ben grins.

"First step is admitting you have a problem," Waylon gives me a smug little smile.

"Fuck both of you. And don't repeat any of this. Not even to your girlfriend yeah? I'm sure she'll tell her, but I don't want it coming from this side."

"Your secret's safe with me," Waylon presses his hand to his chest.

TEN

Olivia

LATER THAT AFTERNOON after the girls and I finish the photo session and stop to get coffee, I meet Liam back at the house when he's out of practice. He follows me upstairs and he sets his bag down on the floor of my room and kicks back in my desk chair, spinning it once before his feet come to rest on the bench in front of my bed. He's in an oddly good mood, and I assume that means practice went well. Because how the team plays, how practice goes, and how well he does on the field absolutely defines this man's disposition most days of the week. Football is his life.

He'd come over to get dinner with us but we're discussing the rules of our agreement first, since we agreed that if we were going to keep doing this, we needed to come up with terms. There needed to be rules and boundaries before we took things any further.

"Good practice today?" I ask, as I sit down on the bed, trying to be casual.

"Hmm?" He looks up at me. "Oh. Yeah. It was pretty good."

"Well that's good. I'm glad to hear stuff's coming together on the field."

"Yeah," he says absently, and then his eyes bounce up to mine. "So, you still sure about this coaching deal?"

"Yes. If you're still up for it."

I know the elephant's in the room with us, and I'm just waiting for him to bring it up.

"Yeah, I said I would."

Or maybe I was going to have to bring it up.

"Is it still weird for you? I know it was years ago, but I also know you had strong opinions when things got weird between us then."

And I see a little flit of his eyes, a clench of his jaw. It's subtle but it's there.

"It is what it is. It was years ago. And like you said, it's your senior year and you want to experiment and need someone safe."

"True," I say quietly.

"But one of the ground rules should probably be that we don't talk about that."

"About the time we almost kissed or about him?" I ask, braving out the bluntness I feel like we need to have if this is going to have a chance of not crushing our friendship into dust.

"Both. It's just an experiment, so no need to rehash the past."

Just an experiment. Just friends. I needed to keep reminding myself of these facts if I was going to get through this and get over whatever this weird crush was that I had on Liam Montgomery.

"Right," I agree. "Rule number two, if it gets weird for any reason, we stop."

"Agreed." He nods.

"Rule three, let's not break anyone else's face during this?"

"I'll do my best." A little smirk forms.

I give him a skeptical look.

"I can't promise anything when I don't know specific scenarios that will come up, but I will try my hardest." He puts his hand to his heart.

"Well talk to me first, at least? Part of this experiment is me not being a wallflower, which will eventually lead to me having to flirt with and maybe date other guys. And I don't need you looming in the background."

"Maybe don't jump in the deep end with one of the biggest fuckin' players on campus then, yeah?" His eyes get a stormy look to them, and I really don't want to revisit that chapter, for a long list of reasons including this reaction he's having right now

"He was a gentleman to me." I try to move on.

"Until he dumped you for not being wild enough in bed, you mean?" he asks sarcastically.

Right. My cover story. I was really bad at lying, especially to Liam.

"Until that." I stare at the wall beyond him, hoping it's not possible for him to realize what a liar I am just by looking at my face.

It's his turn to give me a skeptical look, but after a beat he smiles.

"Okay. Are you wanting this to be a formal thing where I sit down with a play book and run you through it and we review game tape, or?" I can tell by the way something dances behind his eyes; he's teasing.

"Uh, no. I think it can be more casual than that. Just, I

guess rule four is we discuss anything beforehand so there's not weirdness or confusion?"

"Yep. Same page. Works for me."

"Okay. Anything else?"

"Rule five. We've got to end this before the make-or-break games in a month. I'm happy to help you with whatever until then, but then my focus needs to be on the field."

"Understandable and agreed."

"If we fuck... Hopefully it doesn't come to that, but if it does... I don't want things getting weird, or our friendship getting fucked up over this. That's the focus here. You repairing your confidence, and hopefully me doing enough penance that you're going to finally forgive me over the broken nose and the rest. But I need us to be okay when I'm out on the field, all right?"

"I know. I'm your lucky charm," I give him a playful smile, because the man was more than a little superstitious. His game day rituals were sacred to him, and me being in the stands for home games was a thing I'd promised long ago.

"You joke, but I'm serious. I need you, and I need our friends. The last month or so it's been fucked, and I want that to get better, not worse."

"I'm with you. I need you too, you know. Who's gonna yell at me and tell me to not dance on tables if not you?"

He shakes his head at me like I'm a pain in his ass, and I just smile.

"So that it then? Are those the rules?"

"Seems like it."

"Shake?" I hold out my hand, and he rolls his eyes, but he takes mine in his and gives one firm shake before he lets go, sealing our fate for the next month.

"So where are these boudoir shots anyway?" He smirks at me.

It was my turn to roll my eyes, but I pull out my phone to show him some of the previews the photographer gave us before we left.

ELEVEN

Liam

MINE. That was my first fucking thought after I jumped head fucking first into this experiment with Liv. The way she'd looked at me after I kissed her. The eager way she touched me after. It was like I'd finally gotten something I didn't even know I wanted; didn't even realize how long I'd gone without until I had it.

But then I remembered she wasn't mine. Never was, and never could be. Tristan might be gone, but it didn't change the fact that I couldn't cross that line. So the only way out of this was to wrap my head around it. Think about the whole thing clinically, logically. What I'd do if I hadn't felt my world come apart the second I tasted her. I could do this. It was like any other difficult game. Patience. Focus. Eyes on the end goal.

I could handle coaching Liv. Help her get her confidence back and hopefully smooth things over between us in the process. I could be an adult about all of this. And if I was going to do that, I needed to remember that she was off-limits except for this experiment, that she was absolutely not mine as much as I wanted her to be, and that started by watching her flirt with other guys without trying to break their jaws.

"You should try hitting on someone here tonight," I whisper in her ear as we sit next to each other at the bar. Our friends are busy debating whether East or Ben could pull more girls on any given night and trying to decide how they might make a fair competition of it. And they're so engrossed now in a discussion of how to make that competition ethical without skewing the results that they aren't paying attention at all to how close Liv and I are as we talk.

"Yeah? Any guys in mind, Coach?" She smirks at me as her eyes survey the bar.

"I'll leave that up to you. But the challenge is to walk out of here with at least three numbers."

"Three? That's a lot. There's only been a few nights when I've gotten one."

Yeah. And I could guess why. For one, most nights we all went out together and I made sure that any assholes got the memo that she was off-limits to them. A quick friendly kiss to her temple, an arm around the back of her seat, a fuck-off glare over her shoulder when she wasn't looking. I made sure the jackasses stayed away. On the nights I wasn't there? Liv is fucking gorgeous, and while she doesn't show a lot of skin, she's always perfectly put together. Most guys don't have the balls to handle a woman like her, one that's so far out of their league they don't even know where the stadium is. So yeah, it took a special sort of guy to be willing to overlook all of that and go after her anyway.

But if she put out the right vibes? If I locked down my

hands-off attitude for long enough for her to flirt? She could probably go home with a half dozen numbers in an evening.

"Yeah, well you don't usually flirt though, do you? You've gotta put the effort out there, and then you'll see."

"And how do you suggest I do that?" She looks at me skeptically.

"Guys are easy. Make eye contact, hold it for longer than three seconds. Then smile at him and look away. Accidentally bump into him and run your hand over his arm when you apologize. Make a dumb joke or say a cheesy pick-up line to any dude who's up at the bar. I guarantee you'll get interest."

A FEW MINUTES LATER LIV, Wren, and Mac are up at the bar getting drinks and shaking their butts to the music the DJ's playing tonight. It only takes a few more minutes for a couple of guys to approach them. I watch Waylon stiffen as a tall, tattooed guy leans over and says something by putting his mouth up to Mac's ear, but she laughs and then shakes her head. A second later the guy walks off looking shellshocked and Waylon relaxes again.

"Fuck, I love her." He flashes a grin.

"You don't mind when she verbally rips other guys' balls off like that? Thought that was a fetish you liked to keep between the two of you." I glance between them. I give Waylon a lot of shit, but I am happy the two of them figured things out.

"Yeah, but I don't mind if she uses her talents to get rid of those fuckers. Warms my heart," he grins even wider.

"You do realize this puppy-love phase you're going through is sickening to the rest of us," Easton shakes his head.

"Ask me if I give a fuck," Waylon raises his brow.

"Leave him alone. Let him have it after everything she put him through," Ben gives Easton a look.

"You mean including you?" Easton smirks.

Waylon stiffens at the comment, but his smile doesn't fade.

"Having a rough time with a chick or something? You're more than your usual dickish self tonight," Ben gives a nod to Waylon before he needles East himself.

"Me?" Easton laughs a little too loudly. "I've given a few of them a rough ride."

Ben shakes his head.

"Well fuck. And here I thought we'd have some peace tonight," Waylon cracks his knuckles across from me, and I follow his line of sight.

A guy is talking to Liv, his hand touching her hip and he's leaning in to tell her something that she's smiling about. I feel a tightness in my chest, but I take a sip of my beer and turn back to the table.

"You're not gonna go put a stop to that?" Easton looks at me skeptically.

"Nope," I shake my head.

"Why not?" Ben looks equally puzzled.

"Because I told her to do it." I shrug, playing with the label on the beer bottle to keep from looking at her again.

"You told Liv to go flirt with other guys?" Waylon looks at me like I've lost my mind.

"Yup."

"Is this a new kink you have or what?" Easton sits back against the booth, his eyebrow rising.

"Fuck, you all are fucking nosy. You know that? She wanted my help building her confidence after the whole Mason thing. So I'm helping."

"Helping?" East stares at me.

"Yeah."

"Helping how exactly?" East smirks.

"Like I'd fucking tell you."

I'd left Easton out of this conversation for a reason, mainly because I didn't want to tell him that he was her first pick.

"Just a clarifying question?" Easton sits forward again to grab his glass.

I look at him.

"Is she also *helping* you?"

"Fuck. Off." I tip my beer bottle back and take another long swig.

"Well she's helping herself tonight," Ben nods in Liv's direction and when I look over my stomach bottoms out because she is most definitely kissing the guy she had just been talking to. I look back at the table, suddenly very interested in the names and dents that have been carved into the worn-out, old wood.

I could fucking do this.

"Don't worry, Montgomery. You look like this isn't bothering you at all," Easton laughs to himself.

"Aren't you overdue to be getting your dick sucked in your car by some lovely young woman you met tonight?" I flash him a warning look.

"Probably, but watching you squirm like this is pretty fucking entertaining. I gotta say."

"Not fucking squirming," I mutter under my breath. I don't want to feed him anymore ammunition. Whatever has him in a fucking twist lately is making him extra dickish, and I could do without it.

I glance back over at Liv. I tell myself I'm not watching to see her reaction. Just watching to make sure the asshole can keep it PG. And when I look, she's smiling at him. Saying something and running her hand over his arm. But he's being decent. Laughing and keeping his distance. Nothing that would give me an excuse to go interrupt, even though I almost wish he would.

Mac and Wren return to our table, Mac plopping into Waylon's lap and Wren taking up the spot where Liv had been.

"You're being remarkably well-behaved Montgomery," Wren chirps, and fuck—do her and East have some sort of sixth sense?

I shoot her a glance, and she raises her eyebrows. "Forget I said anything." She smirks, and I decide I need a break from all this shit.

"Excuse me," I motion for her to let me up and she does.

I make like I'm headed for the bathroom, but instead I duck out onto the back patio. I need a dose of cold air to set me straight again. Because I could do this, if everyone would just fucking stop needling me about it. Her kissing someone else was fine. Perfectly fucking fine. I finish the rest of the beer and toss the empty bottle in one of the trashcans before I pull out my phone to text her.

> Might go home early. Can you get a ride with Mac or Wren if I do?

I'd driven Liv tonight since Wren had come straight from work and Mac and Waylon had been out to dinner ahead of time. But now I was thinking that watching her flirt tonight might not be as easy as I thought and making it an early night was a much better way to insure I didn't do or say anything stupid.

LIV:

> Are you okay?

> Fine just tired

> How are you going to know if I passed your first test?

> You can text me the numbers later.

> So you can text them all and tell them to fuck off? I think not

I hadn't actually thought of that but now that she'd mentioned it, it wasn't a half bad idea.

> Then I'll just take your word for it. And you should be focused on the task instead of texting me. Can you get a ride?

I BLOW a breath out into the night air, watching it curl toward the stars and tuck my hands in my pockets. I should probably find someone to flirt with myself. Someone who would distract me from thinking of her, except now that she's put her hands on me it's pretty much an impossible task.

"I can just leave with you." Her voice jolts me out of my thoughts when I realize she's actually standing out here behind me.

I turn around. "What are you doing?"

"Looking for you."

"You run off from a guy showing interest to look for another one, you're probably not gonna get a number"

"Already got one. And his friend's too," she holds up her phone

"Do I want to ask?"

"Probably not," She gives a little smirk.

"You still need a third, so you should probably stay. Wren's headed home, right?"

"If she doesn't leave with someone herself. There was a guy talking to her when I came out here."

"I'm sure Waylon would drop you off."

"It's fine. I'll just go with you," her brow furrows.

I give her a skeptical look. I don't want her going with me. If we get in my car, if I drop her off when no one else is home, I'm going to be way too tempted to touch her again.

"Oh. OH!" Her eyes widen like she's just had an epiphany. "I mean unless you're going home with someone."

"No, I'm not going home with anyone. Not with what we've got going on."

"What's going on?"

"As long as I'm helping you. Some women are already sensitive about me having a woman for a best friend and trying to see someone new when I'm physically involved with said friend for coaching purposes... sounds like a fucking disaster waiting to happen."

"I didn't think about that." She frowns.

"It's fine. With us on this championship run I don't need the distraction, and I don't have the time."

"Should you even be helping me then?"

No. My conscience answers her silently.

"You're low maintenance. You aren't asking me where we stand every five minutes or demanding I skip extra tape time to take you out somewhere."

"To be fair, you do spend way too much time watching tape and revisiting plays."

"Can't get better if I don't study where I fucked up."

"I guess. I feel like obsessing over the flaws that much can't be healthy."

"I guess we'll find out." I shrug.

"All right. Well let's go, so you can get some sleep."

She leads the way back inside, and I follow.

"Although I feel like I should still get credit even though I didn't get all three."

"Partial credit, maybe."

"Hey, the one guy kissed me. That should be extra credit."

"Was it good enough to be worth extra credit?"

"Honestly, it wasn't bad," she shrugs, and I'd been hoping that she would tell me it sucked. That he tasted like stale beer, that he was sloppy, anything that would give me some indication she wasn't going to text him when she got home tonight. "I have to close out my tab really quick!"

I follow behind her at the bar, glancing back at our friends' table to see them all lost in conversation. Suddenly I feel a hand on my arm, and I turn my head to see Mia standing in front of me smiling.

"Hey sexy, I wondered when I saw the guys if you were here or not." She leans forward and gives me a hug.

"Hey." I smile back at her.

Mia and I have been dancing around each other for a couple months. She transferred here at the beginning of the year, and we'd met at one of the parties the football team had thrown. It was during the Liv and Mason dating period, so I hadn't been as distracted as I usually was, and we'd talked out on the back porch for a couple of hours. We made out a little at the end, but I didn't ask her up, and she didn't press for more. Ever since, when we'd run into each other she'd given me vibes like she wanted me to ask her out, but I just hadn't brought myself to do it.

She was smart, funny, and had a sexy husky voice that was hard to ignore. But she seemed more like relationship material, and I didn't have time for a relationship. So I'd done my best to dodge anything with her, trying to keep things casual.

"Are you hanging out here tonight?" Her eyes light up with interest.

"Just getting ready to leave actually. Gonna make it an early one."

"Oh, that's too bad. We just keep missing each other."

"Yeah, seems that way."

"Listen, I can't figure you out so I'm just going to ask—do you want to grab coffee or food sometime? I had fun that one night. And I'd love to hang out again." She gives me a bright smile that makes it impossible not to smile back.

My mind races through possibilities, the first of which is that I go out with her because she's beautiful and I already know we get along. She's easy to talk to and I don't think she'd be the type to ask more of me than I could give right now. But most importantly I wonder if she might be able to keep my mind off Liv.

And like I'd summoned her, Liv appears at my side.

"Oh, hey Mia!" Liv reflects her sunshine demeanor with ease.

"Liv! Good to see you."

"You too." She smiles brightly like Mia is the exact person she hoped to see. It's unnerving how good she is at this.

"I was just chatting up your bestie here. Seeing if he wanted to grab food or coffee sometime because we keep missing each other."

Liv's lips curl up into a smile, and her eyes flash between me and Mia. And if I didn't know this was Liv, and know it was impossible, I would swear it was jealousy.

"Oh yeah? That's too bad. We were just heading out so he could get some rest. His schedule is insane lately with how the team's doing, you know? He was just telling me how he has zero free time and can barely sleep."

"Oh. Gosh. I didn't even think about that. I'm sorry. I'm an idiot." Her focus turns back to me. "I'm sorry—maybe a raincheck then for sometime after?"

I run my hand over the back of my neck trying to figure out what the fuck just happened. "Yeah that could work."

"Perfect. See you guys around," she flashes one last smile at me and then takes off.

Liv nods toward our friends, "Let's go say bye and then we can leave."

We give our explanations and then head for the doors after Liv gives a round of hugs.

"What was that?" I ask when we get out into the parking lot.

TWELVE

Olivia

"WHAT WAS WHAT?" I look back at him, even though I know exactly what he means.

"The giant cockblock you pulled back there."

"Oh, um you had just said that stuff on the patio about being busy. Not having time to date. I didn't realize she was an exception. You want me to go back in and explain?"

I can feel him staring at me, studying me as we get to his car. I don't know what he's searching for, but it makes me nervous.

"No, I have her number. She and I hooked up awhile back."

"When?" I ask, surprised because I had seen the way she looked at him when they first met months ago. She might as well have had a sign that said "Make me Mrs. Mia Montgomery". I hadn't liked her since that, no matter how nice she was. All that sugar she poured on every time she talked tasted more like the fake kind that eventually leaves a bitter taste in your mouth anyway.

"When you were hooking up with Mason."

"Well, I didn't know. You can text her and hookup with her again as soon as you take me home."

"Or you could get a ride with Mac, and I could go back in and talk to her now."

"Seriously?" I turn around and he's closer now.

"There."

"What?"

"The way your eyes just flared like that. What is that?"

"Irritation?"

"Jealousy?"

"Of her? Please," I bluster, hoping he'll drop this. "Do what you like Montgomery but its shitty of you to ditch me for her."

I straighten my purse on my shoulder and start to walk back toward the bar. It felt like a walk of shame since I'd just said bye to everyone and now I was going to have to explain what was happening. But I don't get far before his arms slide around my waist and he pulls me back toward him.

"I didn't like seeing you kiss him," he says quietly.

"You saw?" I had peeked in his direction when the kiss ended, but he looked engrossed in conversation with the guys.

"Yeah. Well, the guys saw and pointed it out and then I saw."

"You told me to flirt. That's kind of the end result of flirting, you know."

"Doesn't mean I want to watch."

"I don't really want you seeing other people while we're doing this. But I realize it's hypocritical, since me practicing kind of requires me seeing other people."

"I think I should be the only one you're practicing on. At least anything physical."

"You do?"

"It'll keep things simpler for both of us."

"Is that a new rule?"

"Yeah."

"And fine, I was a little jealous. But not of you two together. Just of her, a little bit." *Liar,* my conscience screams at me but I forge on. "She's just prettier than me. Smarter than me. Taller than me. And she just is so... I don't know... flirty. She gives off the kind of vibe I wish I could."

"A vibe?"

"You know the vibe. If you were hooking up with her, you fell for the vibe. It's the whole 'look at me, I'm gorgeous. I know I'm gorgeous. I know you know I'm gorgeous and you want to fuck me, so I'm going to act like I've got all the confidence *that* gives me.' *That* vibe."

His lip curls up at the corner like he's amused.

"Don't try to tell me she doesn't give off a vibe."

"I'd never thought of it that way, but yeah, I guess so. If that's how you want to describe it."

"That's what I need to figure out. That's the kryptonite guy magic you have to help me figure out how to put out there."

He laughs at me, honest to god, laughs at me.

"Don't laugh!"

"I mean it sounds like she needs to give you lessons."

"If I thought she would, I might ask! But given she obviously wants another ride on the Montgomery Express I doubt she'll be excited to share with me."

His whole body is shaking with laughter. "Please don't fucking call my dick the Montgomery Express. Jesus, Liv."

"Fine, whatever you want to call it."

"And also, we didn't fuck. We just fooled around and talked."

"Oh well, that explains why she's extra eager to make plans." I smile at him.

"She can wait until my coaching assignment is over."

His eyes drift over my face and land on my lips. Almost like he might be thinking of kissing me, except we're not in the middle of a lesson. We're not doing anything but talking about a woman who likes him.

"And she's not prettier than you or smarter. Taller though, yeah," he grins down at me.

"She is definitely prettier than me. Don't lie to me Montgomery. Do your coaches lie to you when the other team is observably better than you?"

"Sometimes, if the occasion calls for it. Morale is sometimes more important than honesty."

"Is that what this is? A morale boost?"

"I mean hopefully, but in this case I'm just being honest. You are gorgeous, Liv. You're right that you don't have the same vibe as she does. Yeah. You're quieter. More conservative. But I also don't think you realize how beautiful you are."

I feel a blush coming to my cheeks, and I look away from him. I was bad at taking compliments and this one in particular felt different, especially coming from him.

"I don't feel beautiful."

"We can fix that." He captures my lips with his and pulls me close to him. His tongue slides over my lower lip and dips into my mouth, brushing over my own before he pulls back again. His lips slant over mine in little crushing collisions that send sparks shimmering through every nerve ending in my body. And every additional kiss just makes me want him more.

He leans back, his eyes studying my face and he pulls my body flush with his, so I can feel him going hard against me.

"That's what you do to me. That's how sexy you are. Just

looking at you, kissing you... makes me fucking hard. Okay? So, don't doubt me when I say you're gorgeous."

"Okay," I nod, feeling dizzy from the flood of sensations this man administers to my body every time he touches me.

"All right. Let's get you home." He nods toward his SUV.

I follow, dumbfounded and quiet. Because if that's what I do to him, maybe there is a chance for him to see me as someone else after all.

THIRTEEN

Olivia

WHEN MAC and Wren insist upon another rewatch of *Wuthering Heights* after the first movie ends on movie night, I get up to start rounding up the dishes. Ben and Liam are both passed out on the couch, and I think Waylon would do literally anything Mac asked to make her happy. Including his third rewatch in as many movie nights.

Our dishwasher, much like the rest of the house, is old and cranky, so I always prewash before I load anything in hopes that things will actually come out as sparkling clean as the dishwasher soap promises. I roll up my sleeves and put on the apron we leave hanging in the kitchen, a frilly one with Christmas trim and the broken glass scene from *Die Hard* on it. One Mac and Wren had made for me after they found me trapped in the kitchen barefoot one morning after I knocked over several glasses and they'd shattered all over the floor.

I'm halfway through when a sleepy Liam wanders in.

"Have a good nap?" I ask, smiling at him. Thankful that in addition to our little experiment agreement, we'd managed to patch up our friendship in the process. Having him back in my life at weekly movie nights, talking regularly again made me feel like life was getting back to normal.

"Yes. It's been a long week. Been running extra drills with the guys and getting up early for it."

"That sucks. You can stay here if you want."

"Okay," he gives me a little lopsided grin as he rubs his eyes.

"Just a warning though that there's an added soundtrack these days," I smirk.

"What?"

"Mac and Waylon," I half-whisper half-silently-mouth their names. The kitchen is far enough from the living room that they probably wouldn't hear, but I'm not about to risk it.

"Oh fuck," his face sours.

"Yeah."

"We'll just have to be louder then," he shrugs and grabs some of the dishes I've pre-cleaned and puts them in the dishwasher.

"What?" I ask, my breath catching in my throat because it's not a joke I expect out of him.

"What?" He smirks. "Louder not your thing? You want to try quieter?"

I roll my eyes at him and go back to scrubbing the dish in my hands because now I'm imagining the sounds he makes when he comes, and I have no idea how to feel about the fact that that's something my memory can recall now. I scrub a little bit harder at a bit of marshmallow stuck to the plate, and I hear a low rumble of laughter come from him.

A second later and he's behind me, one arm wrapped around my waist as he leans down.

"That all it takes to make you blush?" he asks quietly, his tone reflecting how amused he is.

"Liam..."

"Liv."

He pulls my hair back and kisses the corner of my jaw, just below my earlobe. My heart jolts in my chest, half because he's touched me and half because he's so casual about it. Like it's just an old habit of his.

"You want to try an experimental lesson right now?" he whispers, his voice low with promise.

When I'd asked him to do this, I hadn't expected him to play along so well. I thought this would be more of me dragging him kicking and screaming. Me initiating any lessons and him reluctantly and grumpily agreeing. And as such, I hadn't exactly prepared myself for this or him.

"Like what?" I ask, feeling a little twist of anticipation in my stomach.

"Like seeing if you can keep quiet enough not to attract attention. And if you like sneaking around."

I look up at him out of the corner of my eye, and his eyes light with amusement. I narrow my eyes in return but nod my yes, and his lips turn up on one side before he places another kiss against my neck. It sends tiny shockwaves over my skin that light up my spine and make my pulse tick up a notch. He continues his adventure down my neck and his hands slide over my hips and up under my shirt, brushing over my skin as he pulls me closer.

One hand braces my hip and the other travels upwards, sliding under the cotton T-shirt bra I have on and cupping my breast before his thumb swipes over one of my nipples. And I'm trying hard to focus on the dishes in front of me, but I can barely think straight enough to remember how to use a sponge because Liam Montgomery has his hands all over me.

"One of these lessons is going to have to involve you stripping down for me again. Because I want to see you. All of you, without all the lingerie," he whispers as his hand travels to my other breast, softly brushing his fingertips over me before his hand travels south again.

"Liam," I whisper.

"Ah. Quiet remember? Unless you're telling me to stop. You want me to stop?" he whispers back.

I look toward the living room. I can see a sliver of it from where we're standing, hear the laughter of our friends as they debate something happening on the screen. It's not that many steps from there to here, and anyone could make a quick snack run and be on us in seconds. And while I'm not exactly trying to hide our experiment, I'm also not ready to explain the details to all of our friends either. But his fingers dip under the band of my jeans and the temptation to let him touch me outweighs the risk of being found.

I shake my head.

"Good," he whispers, and his hands go to the button on my jeans. There's an amused tone to his voice, "I've always liked this apron."

He undoes the button and the zipper, and I can feel him going hard against me through his jeans. I take a breath, the lemony scent of the dishwater washing over me, and I realize I've been squeezing the sponge under the water for dear life and release it. His fingers slide a half inch under the band of my underwear, and he hesitates, pressing a kiss to the side of my neck like a question.

"Yes," I whisper, giving the permission I know he wants. Because whoever this version is, underneath it all he's still Liam.

His hand slides south, his middle finger parting me and

brushing over my clit where he finds me soaking wet, and he stops dead in his tracks. His breath stutters.

"Fuck," the curse rips from his lips loudly. Way too loudly for the quiet in the room.

"You okay?" Mac calls from the living room and I freeze, my hands clenching the little sponge again.

"Yep. Just bumped into the cabinet." Liam yells back.

"You need help with the dishes?" Wren calls out.

"We've got it," he answers her so I don't have to, because I'm not sure I could find my words.

"Okay. Just let me know!" she yells again, and then I hear them talking like they were before.

A little breath of relief escapes me, but Liam is still tense at my back.

"I thought we were supposed to be quiet?" I whisper, before a little laugh pops out.

"Yeah but..."

"You can't follow your own rules?" I taunt.

It's a mistake though, because it's answered with direct pressure on my clit. Three rough strokes that have me doubling over and gasping.

"What were you saying?" A gruff whisper comes at my ear.

"Nothing," I shake my head slowly.

"That's what I thought." I feel him smile against my cheek and place another kiss at my jaw.

His fingers stroke me again, more tentatively, light steady pressure against my clit that's just enough to tease the sensation through my body but leave me wanting more. I lean back into him, and he presses his lips just behind my earlobe.

"You're gonna have to breathe quieter than that, or they're gonna figure it out," he says quietly, his breath dancing across my skin.

My cheeks heat. I hadn't even realized I was breathing loud

enough to make a sound, let alone loud enough to worry people 25 feet away.

"Sorry."

"You're good. We'll just have to work on it. But that's what the practice is for right?"

"Yes, Coach," I sass, and I feel a little laugh rumble through his chest.

"You think you can come like this?"

I nod, because I think I could come in about two seconds if this man asked me to.

"But stay quiet, yeah?"

I nod again, and he picks up the pace. The stroke of his fingers coming faster and harder, more deliberate with each brush over my clit until I can feel it start to hit. My body quaking under him as my release starts to roll over me.

"Shhh..." he whispers a gentle reminder against the shell of my ear, and I bite into my lower lip to try to stifle the sounds of my breathing and the little moan I can't completely stop.

The last of the little aftershocks hit me, and he releases the pressure he'd been maintaining. His hand sliding out of my underwear and slowly rebuttoning and rezipping my jeans up for me, as he kisses his way down my neck one final time.

"Was a good first try. We might have to consider game tape options, so we can review in the future," he smirks, and I shoot him a little look of bemused shock before I can't help but laugh.

"Rude," I whisper.

"What's rude is how hard that fucking made me. I'm gonna get a quick shower in before bed. Meet you upstairs?" His admission lights a little fire inside me, and when his eyes meet mine, I almost kiss him before I remember myself and the context.

"Okay," I agree and give him a little smile.

I want to follow him into the shower. Make up an excuse

for needing a lesson there because the prospect of him naked and hard upstairs in my bathroom is something I think I need a visual of in my life. But I remember that if this was a real experiment and not me just trying to get him out of my system, I'd be going slower. Taking baby steps.

"See you in a few." He brushes a kiss over my temple and hurries back up the steps like nothing happened.

"You sure you don't need help?" Wren asks, and I jump back a little at her sudden appearance.

"I'm good."

"You look... flushed," she eyes me carefully.

"Just the hot water from the dishes. Trying to get the marshmallow off from the s'mores we had," I cover quickly.

"Uh huh. Well... I'm going to bed. Here's hoping I don't need ear plugs tonight."

"I think we probably just need to invest."

"Yeah, it feels like it's headed that way." She gives me a strange look. "Goodnight!"

"Night!"

FOURTEEN

Liam

I AM FUCKED. Absolutely 100 percent fucked and agreeing to this experiment with her is going to be the death of me. I'd been so fucking good up until now with her. Keeping my thoughts, my hands, and all the things I want to myself. I'd put her in a box, one labeled "best friend's girlfriend: do not fucking touch", and I'd kept it on a shelf, tightly sealed for years. Most of the time I was able to keep her firmly in the friend zone even in my thoughts. And she'd played her part, being the dutiful platonic best friend who helped me with just about fucking everything and never said a word edgewise about the girls I fucked or dated.

But then she'd come apart in my lap and dangled the opportunity to watch it happen again and again in front of me. And now it's all I can think about when I see her. All the ways I can make her fall apart. All the ways I can make her mine. Now all under the guise of this experiment where I can pretend she's only out of the box because I'm helping her, like a good fucking guy. So far from what I actually am.

"Fuck..." I groan as I fist myself harder, hearing her breathing replay in my memory as I worked her clit downstairs, her perfect ass grinding against me. All while she did the dishes and cleaned up after everyone, because that's who she is. The sweet, good girl who takes care of everyone. She'd barely laid the rules down, given me the go before I could get my hands on her again. Before I could treat her like she was mine. And that was exactly what I wanted to do—touch her, teach her, fuck her like she was mine all the while pretending it was a coaching assignment.

I use my free hand to crank the shower hotter, and then brace myself against the tiles. It takes a minute before the searing heat bites into my skin, and I bring myself to the edge imagining her at my feet, sucking me off while I fist her hair and tell her how good she fucking takes me. While I tell her to take me harder and deeper.

And if she fucking knew that's what I wanted from her, that's how I fantasized about her? The kind of coaching I'd offer if I had free reign? She'd run so fucking fast. She'd never look at me the same. Our friendship would turn to ashes faster than I could watch the flames burn.

Which is exactly why I'm coming hard against my own hand right now. I need to take the edge off and walk the line with her on this assignment. Make sure there is zero chance of me crossing it because as much as I want her, I also can't afford to lose her.

A LITTLE BIT LATER, just as we're climbing into bed the moaning starts. It pours through the walls, getting louder by the second. I freeze as I'm pulling back the sheet to get into bed, staring at the spot where it seems to be coming from.

"No..." I say, looking at the wall that Liv shares with Mac.

"Oh, yes. Every single night they are here," she shakes her head as she gets into bed.

"You need thicker walls," I say, just staring at the wall and cursing Waylon for making Mac moan this damn loud. I'd almost thought I was going to be able to get through tonight without issue. That we were gonna get through this without anything awkward. Just go straight back into normal friendship territory in between our lessons, but no way is that happening while we have a live fucking porn show going on next door.

"I need earbuds, which are coming this week," she grumbles as she fluffs her pillow.

Another stifled moan comes from the room next door, and I climb into bed.

"Have you said something to them? Do they know how loud they are?"

"Yes, and this *is* them keeping it down. You should have heard them before," she looks at me with a frustrated look on her face.

"Fuck," I mutter. This is the last thing I need.

"Yep."

I lay down next to her, adjusting my pillows and wondering how I'm going manage to ignore this long enough to get to sleep. Liv settles in at my side a couple minutes later, closing her eyes, her breathing steadying after a moment or two, and I wonder if she just might be able to sleep through it.

A few minutes pass in silence, and I'm hopeful that maybe they're actually done for the night. Maybe we only got the tail end of this performance.

"Night," I say quietly.

"Night," she answers.

But a few more minutes later, and there's another moan. Softer but more insistent. And I can guess what Waylon is doing to her just by the sound.

"Christ..." I mutter, throwing my arm over my face, irritated and wishing I'd just gone home. There's no easy way to say *yeah hey I uh, am getting fucking hard listening to them and thinking about us, and I don't think I'm going to sleep at all tonight so maybe I'll just head out.*

"I suggest putting a pillow over your head. It helps a little bit," Liv offers helpfully, but I'm curious if this affects her at all.

"It's kind of hot though, right?" I hedge my bets and ask the question out loud.

She turns over on her side abruptly, looking at me and blinking through the moonlight.

"I'll be sure to tell Waylon in the morning that it turns you on to listen to Kenzie moaning. I'm sure all of *your* body parts will remain intact," she grins at me, and the echo of the statement Easton had made to her makes me laugh.

"I mean, not that it's her. Fuck. I just mean in general. It's... you know..." I shrug. It's a great fucking soundtrack to fucking. But I'm not gonna say that out loud to her.

"Like live action porn? Until you awkwardly realize it's your friends?" A little fit of laughter escapes her, and I love the sound of it.

"Oh my god. Fuck yes. Fuck, Waylon. Yes!!" Mac's little shouts of approval pierce through the wall. Yeah. Definitely not sleeping.

"Literally was silent as a grave when she was dating Ezra. I'm just half-curious what he's doing to her."

"I can guess," I offer.

"I mean I've heard enough to know that he is generously sized," Liv smirks, and I feel a little tightness in my chest at the fact she's thought about Waylon's dick. I do *not* love it.

"Yeah, that's not what it is," I counter the statement, and look at her with my eyebrow raised to see if she can put the pieces together.

"What?" She looks back at me almost indignant that I'm analyzing it.

"That's definitely the sound of a woman getting tongue fucked." A little rumble of laughter rolls through me.

She bursts out into louder laughter in response, loud enough that I'm worried they might have heard her. She hits me with one of the small decorative pillows she keeps on her bed. I pull it out of her hands and toss it against the wall, and her eyes go wide.

"You would know," she says quieter, looking amused.

"I would. I've heard it enough," I say smugly.

She snorts in response like she doesn't quite believe it.

"You don't think so?" I ask when I struggle to decipher her meaning.

"I wouldn't know," she shrugs.

"What?" My tone's sharper than I intend.

"What?" she repeats, sounding unsure.

"You wouldn't know about me, or you wouldn't know because you wouldn't know?" I stare at her through the dim light. Because I honestly can't accept the idea that the second part is true.

"Both."

"What?" I sit up, propping myself on my elbow. "Never? Not even with...?" I trail off because I don't want to bring his specter into the room with us, it's one of our rules, but I have a hard time believing as much as he worshipped her that he didn't.

"No," she answers softly, playing with the edge of the sheet she has over her like she feels awkward.

The silence between us stretches for a minute as I try to

process the information. Another moan comes from behind the wall, punctuating the awkwardness of it all.

"Do you want to?" I ask before I can think to tell myself to stop.

"What?" her voice sounds breathy and fuck if it doesn't make me a little hard again.

I turn on my side to get a better look at her through the dark, trying to gauge her reaction.

"If you want to try it, I could..."

FIFTEEN

Olivia

THE QUESTION LAYS heavy between us. A momentary image of Liam between my thighs flashes through my head, and I suddenly feel hot, the sheets oppressive against my body as I shift underneath them.

"Liv?"

"I thought you were tired," I deflect.

And as if on cue, the dull sound of the headboard thumping against the wall starts up.

"Yeah, definitely not gonna be able to sleep through that."

"It does make it hard, huh?" I ask, my heart vibrating in my chest. Because I want him to, but I don't think I'm prepared for it. I'd barely been able to handle the way he made me feel downstairs.

"You can just say no Liv. You're not gonna hurt my feelings."

"Okay."

"Your loss," he tucks his hands under his head and his lip quirks up on one side.

"I said, *okay*."

I feel him go taut beside me. Apparently he was happy with my deflection. Oops.

"Okay, what?"

"Never mind," I turn my back to him because now I feel weird about this entire moment.

I'm overheated, confused, and annoyed with the sounds of the headboard thumping and Kenz's moaning. I am going to have yet another discussion with her about it tomorrow.

"I just want clarity on what you're okaying. Clear communication, remember?" His hand drifts down my arm, under the sheet and then coasts over my waist, tugging gently to pull me back toward him.

I roll back and look up at him.

"'Cause I'm happy to give you that experience if you want it. I'm turned on as hell right now, honestly, so you'd be doing me a favor. But I need to know it's what *you* want."

His face is etched with sincerity, and I feel the tiniest little tug in my chest. It's so small I could almost write it off. I shouldn't, but I do because I'm too curious to make better decisions.

"Yes, it's what I want," I say softly.

"Okay," his eyebrows knit together momentarily like he's determining something before he pulls the sheet back slowly.

I take a deep steadying breath as he slides down my body. His fingers grip the hem of the T-shirt I have on and press it upwards as his eyes travel over me. And I feel a moment of apprehensive regret. Like I should have saved this moment for a guy who actually wants me and not just one who sees me as an assignment. But it's erased the second Liam's lips meet my heated skin, just above the waistband of my underwear. He presses a line of languid kisses across the top of the lace, kisses that feel like warning shots. Promises of what's to come and they're already making me warm with desire for more.

His hands tuck under the fabric and he slowly slides them down my hips, kissing a trail in the wake of their retreat. A shiver runs through me as the cold air meets my damp skin. He slides them the rest of the way off, slowly, carefully and tosses them to the side. His hands come back up my legs, starting at my ankles and his palms glide their way up the backs of my calves, knees and thighs, spreading me carefully as he does it.

I take another breath because even though I would trust this man with my life, it's something else entirely to be trusting him with this kind of vulnerability.

He settles between my thighs and places a tentative kiss on the inside of the right one, and I can feel the little waves of sparks spread out from where his lips touch.

"You're fucking beautiful, Liv," he whispers against my skin before he kisses me again.

My heart stops in my chest at the words. The way he says it. He's complimented me plenty over the years. Told me I'm smart, that I'm fantastic at planning, that I have good taste, that a particular item of clothing I was wearing looked nice. But until the other night he never commented on my physical appearance, and hearing it now in this context, makes my chest swarm with all kinds of feelings I don't know what to do with.

He must sense the tension in me because his hands go to my thighs, his fingers coasting over them in tender little strokes of reassurance that gradually escalate to rough little kneads of his hands. There were a lot of things about him to like but his hands might be his best asset.

Then he leans forward, resuming the line he'd been following before, straight down my center. His lips brush over my skin, and I can't stop myself from the little reflexive squirm

I make as he approaches my sex. His fingers grasp my thighs, stilling me and holding me tight as his mouth descends on me.

He kisses me first, and then his tongue delves down, stroking over my clit in one smooth motion and then sucking me into his mouth. His grip on me is tight, it's the only thing keeping me on the bed. I would have already come off because I see stars as he works me over.

A little moan pops out of my mouth before I can stop it and my eyes go to the wall, panicked that our friends could have heard it. But I can still hear the steady rapping of the headboard drumming against the wall and I lay my head back again, clasping a hand over my mouth.

There's a little chuckle of smugness from between my legs, and I'm tempted to swat him, except he takes another long languid stroke at my core with his tongue, and I'm silenced by all the sensations it drags out of me. One of his hands leaves my thigh and drifts between my legs, two fingers slowly sliding inside me as I concentrate hard on my breathing, so I don't make another noise.

He tests me, sliding them in and out, his tongue moving in sync with them until he hits a rhythm that has my entire body humming under his control. I have no one to compare him to, but I have to imagine at least some of his smugness is well deserved because this combination of his mouth and hands is something I would sign up for any day he offered the lesson.

There's several more loud bangs against the wall, and I can hear the grunts and the moans coming from beyond it. It melds with the sound of Liam's mouth against me, and I can feel everything in me pulling low and tight. He senses it and his pace picks up, his tongue ruthlessly stroking against my clit while his fingers work me from inside, and I feel like I might come straight out of my body.

I raise up on my elbows feeling like it's all too much and not enough at the same time, and I catch a glimpse of him between my legs and it takes my breath away. His strong shoulders hold me in place, his beautiful face concentrating so hard on the task at hand. My fingers thread through his hair before I can think about what I'm doing.

He glances up at me when he feels the touch, his eyes glittering with amusement for a half a second before he returns his focus to the apex of my thighs, and I gasp as his teeth graze my flesh.

"Fuck," I whisper.

He does it again, and my hips buck involuntarily against his face. I feel a swarm of embarrassment, but he continues on like it was nothing. His teeth graze me again and then he sucks my clit into his mouth, hard and rough. His tongue working it until I see fireworks.

I don't realize I'm moaning or how loud until I hear a loud deep cough from behind the wall, and a quick throat clearing. Waylon. It brings me crashing down to earth.

Fuck.

I collapse against the pillows behind me, releasing my grip on Liam's hair. I glance down at him, wondering if he's as panicked as I am but his body is shuddering.

"Liam?" I whisper his name.

He glances up at me and the bastard is fucking laughing. Hard. Like it's the funniest damn thing that's happened in a long time.

"It is not funny!" I gripe quietly, pulling my legs up and away from him.

He climbs up the bed beside me, wrapping an arm around my middle.

"Oh it is. They deserve it."

"It's going to ruin the lecture I was going to give Kenz."

"You're probably going to have to get used to that with this whole 'new Liv' thing you're trying out."

"Is that what we're calling this?" I ask softly, because we've crossed yet another line between us with this lesson.

"I think so," he answers but his voice sounds as unsure as I feel.

"And you don't mind being part of the experiment?" I ask the ceiling because I can't bear to look at him right now. It's a confidence I haven't mastered yet.

"It's a real fucking burden but someone has to do it." I feel his chest rumble with laughter next to me.

I punch him gently in the arm, and he pulls me tighter to him.

"Now maybe we can get some sleep."

"Maybe. Sometimes there's a third or fourth round."

"Dear god."

We both laugh until we fall into a contented silence. The kind we're used to sitting in, and I feel like maybe, somehow, it's going to be okay.

"Night Liam."

"Night Liv."

SIXTEEN

Liam

THE NEXT FRIDAY night we're hosting the weekly football party at the football house. Since Waylon and Mac are coming, Liv's handed off her usual duties to Mac who is currently in our kitchen setting up food and drinks. It's part of her plan to hand off some of her football mom stuff. Mac's honestly just as good at it as Liv is, the two of them have been tag teaming the whole thing all the time lately anyway, but I definitely feel Liv's absence as the party starts to get underway. But I guess it was something I'd have to get used to.

Mac told me that she'd decided to go out for drinks with some of her friends from her Classics program after they finished up a project together, and I wondered where she was and what she was doing. Who exactly she was with.

I hadn't been able to get her out of my head since the other night, the way she'd felt, the soft little cries and moans she'd made, the way her hips had bucked up to meet my lips was haunting me everywhere I went. And when I wasn't thinking about that, I was thinking about the way she'd fucking dry humped me on a terrace for half the city to see if they'd bothered to look.

I was still struggling to make sense of it all. Who she was; if this was really her or just some frantic attempt for her to find herself before we all had to face reality. Because let's face it, we all knew that this little microcosm that we existed in now was not it. The parties, the booze, the friends, the movie nights and the always having my best friends a short car ride away, was going to end, and we only had a few precious months to keep enjoying it until the lights got turned low and faded out.

I wasn't an idiot. I had a decent shot at the NFL. It would mean a whole new world of lights and parties and women. But it wouldn't be the same as I had it here. Wouldn't be the same without her at my side. And now this assignment is blurring so many lines with her, it feels more and more complicated by the second.

I've always cared for her, always put her on a pedestal and wanted to keep her safe like anyone would a sister or a really good friend. After the almost kiss, I'd never thought about crossing the line with her again until I watched the way she reacted to Mason that night at the party. When I saw her dancing on top of the table, looking carefree and sexy. Watched the way he looked at her, the way he touched her. I'd felt like I might rip his limbs off if I had the chance.

I had no right to feel it. She wasn't mine. Even now, she wasn't mine. She was trying new things. Experimenting. Seeing if she liked a different version of herself. One that doesn't always involve me, and I owe it to her to let her have that space. To support her getting whatever she needs for her confidence the same way she had stayed by my side and rebuilt mine when I'd lost my shit after Tristan died.

LATER THAT NIGHT, I come in from a round of bags outside to grab a beer when I notice that Liv has shown up sometime while I've been out back. She's curled up in Ben's lap on a chair while he shows her something on his phone, and she talks to him and Mac and Waylon on the couch next to them. She has on a dress that's short and makes her gorgeous legs look even longer than they are, and I hate seeing them draped over Ben even though I know there's nothing going on there.

I grab my beer and make my way over to them. Leaning against the door frame to see what they're up to. She doesn't notice me, too engrossed in whatever Ben's showing her to look up.

"You just swipe. This way if you're interested, that way if you're not. You can change your location. Then if you both match, you can chat and see about meeting up," he explains.

"And why exactly are you on a dating app? The women of Highland not enough for you now?"

"My sister mentioned that someone we knew was using it and it just sounded interesting." He shrugs, looking a tad sheepish.

"Someone, eh?" Waylon gives Ben a look, and Ben shoots a glare back at him.

"Just thought it was worth a shot." Ben narrows his eyes, and I'd have to figure out what that was about later.

"Can you set other preferences? Like age and height and stuff like that?" Liv asks him, staring at the app and swiping a few profiles.

"Hey!" Ben protests and pulls the phone back out of her hands.

"You need some variety in your life Benny."

"For real," Mac echoes.

"I like what I like," he defends his choices.

"All right. You've convinced me it's worth a shot. At least a better shot then what I can find here on campus now that everyone thinks a broken nose is the cost of dating me," she sighs, and I wince a little.

Waylon looks up at me, a pitying look in his eyes, and I just stare back at him blankly, like I don't know what his problem is. Inside though, I'm panicking a little. When we'd started this post-Mason experiment, in my mind I was more or less going to be her only subject. Any other potential subjects were going to be of the kind who I could likely intimidate or have one of my teammates lay groundwork against. Then we'd agreed that it would just be us after the night at the bar. But now she was going to have dozens of men at her fingertips, and they were all going to line up to do any sort of experimenting she wanted if she got tired of me.

Ben tucks his phone back in his pocket and as he does he looks up, finally noticing me and grins. I could choke him right here. It would devastate the women of Highland State and several of the surrounding counties, but it would be worth it. I'm fairly certain East would even help me hide the body because it would mean that he'd have less competition.

Except then I'd be short one half of my magic receiving duo and I want the championship this year more than I want almost anything else. So he'd have to live for now.

"Who won the game?" Ben asks, and I frown trying to figure out what he means when I realize he's talking about bags.

"JB and Cash. I decided to get a beer and warm up in here for a bit."

Liv's eyes jolt up to mine when she hears my voice, and I give her a little chin jerk to acknowledge her. She smiles at me, and then pulls her phone out, presumably to use the app that was going to have her buried in dicks by morning.

"Shit. My phone's almost dead. I'm gonna run and get my charger. Be right back," she pops up from Ben's lap and jogs by me toward the door.

Ben stands and stretches. "I need another beer."

"They're in the back behind the week-old seafood you all have yet to throw out," Mac directs helpfully.

"Thanks for that," I say, only loud enough for Ben to hear as he walks past me.

He pauses for a moment and smiles. "Someone has to light a fire under your ass. You're welcome."

"If anything happens to her, I will kill you. After we lift a trophy. But I will do it."

"You can try," he smirks at me and then makes off for the kitchen.

SEVENTEEN

Liam

A LITTLE LATER THAT night I'm playing a round of cards, trying to keep myself distracted and away from Liv, when Waylon and Mac come up to me.

"Can we crash in the spare room?" Waylon asks.

"Go for it," I nod and watch as the two of them disappear upstairs.

A second later I feel fingers massaging my shoulders, and it feels good but I'm not in the mood for dealing with any of the jersey chasers tonight. I glance up to say something and jolt a little when I see Liv's face. She smiles at me, something flickering behind her eyes, and I feel a flutter in my gut. One that makes me nervous.

"Hey," I say, smiling back at her.

"You winning?" She nods to the cards in my hand.

"Depends on how you define winning. Better to say I'm not losing, yet."

I was very nearly ready to fold and call it a night, but I wasn't ready for bed, and I didn't want to leave her down here alone. Not that she'd really be alone. There were plenty of people still milling around, but anyone who would keep her company had already left or was headed upstairs now.

"Need a good luck charm?" She gives me a little smile.

"Couldn't hurt," I pat my thigh, and she sits down, straddling it and I wrap an arm around her to help steady her.

We'd sat like this a million times before. Usually when one of us was being subjected to some overeager drunk advances by a person we weren't interested in, especially if we were at a bar. But it felt different now, to feel the heat between her thighs seeping into mine. To feel the curve of her spine lean back into my chest. A memory of the way her body had lifted off the mattress as she cried out when I was sucking her clit comes flashing back. I force myself to try to think of something unsexy, so I don't get hard right in the middle of this card game.

She chooses that moment to lean back against my shoulder and turn her head, her lips nearly brushing my ear.

"I saw Mac and Waylon go up, and I was gonna ask them for a ride since I've had a few shots. Is it okay if I stay?" she whispers, and I immediately imagine her spread out in my bed.

"Yeah, you can stay." I nod, trying again to keep my focus on the game.

"You sure? I don't want to bother you if you had other plans for the evening..."

Mia was here somewhere. I'd talked to her briefly earlier, and I assumed this was Liv's way of asking if I had changed my mind on that front. I still wonder if there's a hint of jealousy there, one she doesn't want to admit to any more than I do.

"Just not feeling it. Might need to try the dating app like you and Ben," I shrug, tossing a card out into the pile when it's my turn. I don't even know which one it is, because I'm too distracted.

She laughs, the little vibrations of her chest moving through my own. "Neither you, nor Ben need a dating app. You don't need to swipe on people's profiles and chat them up. You can just look at a girl and tell her to get in your bed and she will. The last thing the men on those apps need is the two of you competing with them."

"Yeah?" I ask, studying her face and she looks at me incredulously.

"Yeah, and you know this. Don't play stupid." She studies me back, trying to read the look on my face, although I can guarantee she has no idea what I'm thinking.

Because what I'm thinking involves pushing things right over another line with her, maybe a cliff. I lean in close to her, making sure she can hear me but keeping my voice low enough that no one else can.

"Then go upstairs and get in my bed. I'll be up in a minute."

She blinks, her mouth forms a little 'o', and she stares at me for a beat, before she smirks. "Very funny."

"Not being funny."

She bites her lower lip and stares at my mouth, and now I know what she's thinking about.

"You can have more of that or I have some other ideas."

"And if I just wanted to sleep?"

"Then I can take a cold shower or sleep down here if you'd rather."

"Liam!" JB shouts from across the table, and I snap my attention back, realizing it's my turn again I toss another random card in.

"Goddamn bro, you're not even paying attention, or you have the shittiest hand I've ever seen," he grunts.

"Lucky for you then," I answer back, and then turn my eyes back on Liv, looking at her expectantly for what she wants from me.

Her eyes rake over me, a flickering interest, "Hurry up and lose then."

She gets up and I watch her head up the stairs. I can feel the pace of my heart quickening with every step she takes.

"I fold," I say, tossing my cards down on the table.

JB glares at me, his eyes tracking to the steps and then back to me but whatever complaint he has dies on his lips.

"More money for me then." Another one of the guys grins.

I walk to the kitchen, downing a glass of water and pacing the floor for a minute because I've got to remember the rules, the assignment, the lessons. My heart isn't getting the memo though and I can practically hear it rattling against my ribcage.

When I get up to my room, the lights are off and the moonlight that's spilling in from the window is the only thing illuminating it. I see her shoes on the floor and her dress in a pool next to them, and I immediately look to see what she's wearing. Semi-relieved that she's got one of my shirts on because if she'd been waiting for me naked, I don't know if I could have controlled my reaction to it. I take a breath, trying to remind myself I'm the fucking adult in the room, the more experienced one who's supposed to be calm and composed.

It's not unusual for her. Sleeping in one of my shirts is old hat on nights she decided to stay the night and was dressed up. But it feels different now, in the wake of everything we've done.

"Hi," she says quietly. She's laying on her stomach, playing with her phone but her eyes meet mine the second she realizes I'm in the room.

"Hi," I answer her in equal measure.

I sit down on the bed next to her, looking at her phone, half expecting her to be trolling guys but instead she's just playing a game where she's clicking on blocks. Eliminating them one by one as she goes. My eyes run down the length of her body, the T-shirt doing a lot of work to conceal her form but conveniently bunched up in a way that has it ending just above her hips and giving me a good look at her ass and thighs. My hand goes to the back of her knee, following the little dip there upwards.

She flinches and I still my hand, looking to her to see if I've done something wrong.

"I didn't plan for anything to happen tonight or coaching sessions, so I didn't finish shaving or put on cute underwear or anything. Sorry," she mumbles, as she turns her phone over and lays it down.

"Like I give a fuck," I shake my head, continuing my path up her thigh.

"Are you sure you want me up here? You had a long day. I can get a car and go home."

"Yeah, I want you up here," my fingers trace up her back, and I push her shirt up, massaging the muscles along her spine and she lets out a faint sigh.

"I can't stop thinking about the other night," she confesses softly.

"Yeah?" It's the only word I can manage right now.

She hadn't said anything about that particular lesson since it'd happened. We'd gone to dinner with our friends and met to study on campus together for a couple of hours at the library and she hadn't mentioned it. I'd been dying to ask her, but I didn't want to make it awkward if she didn't like it.

"I want to do that for you. Like I said, I'm rusty. But you're a good coach, right?" She looks back at me, the hint of a smile breaking over her lips.

It's not at all what I was expecting her to say. It takes my breath and my thoughts away for a second that it's what she's asking for.

"I know you said glacial pace and all that, but we only have a week or so before your game."

Right. The games. The timeline. The rules.

She sits up next to me, studying my face, "If you don't want me to, it's okay. I know it's probably not very hot to have your awkward friend go down on you. I just thought if you walked me through it, if I did everything you told me to—it would be a good confidence lesson."

"Christ, Liv," I groan, running my hands over my face to try to make sure I'm actually having this conversation and I haven't drifted off into a fantasy fucking my hand in the shower.

"What?" she asks anxiously.

I run my hand over her thigh, "You talk like that, and I can't think straight."

"Is that good or bad?"

"I don't fucking know, but you're not awkward. You're hot as fuck. And if you want to try that, yeah. I think I can make that sacrifice," I flash her a grin, trying to break the anxious tension I feel rolling off her.

She punches my arm and leans forward, kissing me briefly before she nips my lower lip, "Don't be an ass, Montgomery."

I grab her and haul her into my lap, "That's Coach Montgomery to you, Sunshine."

She smiles, and her lips return to mine, kissing me softly with gentle strokes of her lips and tongue that have me thinking of them elsewhere. She stands then and pulls me up with her. Her fingers go to the hem of my shirt, grasping the material and pushing it up so slowly I think she might be trying to torture me. Her knuckles drag over the skin of my stomach and chest as she does it, and honestly it feels like the first time I've ever done this. The nervousness. The anticipation. Especially when she looks me over and makes a little sound of appreciation.

Her hands drift back down over my shoulders and chest,

pausing abruptly when she spots the bruise that's already splashed across my ribs.

"Holy hell, Liam." Her eyes snap up to mine, and while I always love the way she worries about me I hate how it distracts her.

"It's just a bruise," I shake my head.

"A massive one," her fingers ghost over it, tracing the size and shape. "What happened?"

"Hit during practice."

"Who? I will kill him myself if Waylon hasn't. Did he not remember you're *his* fucking quarterback?"

"It's one of the younger guys. He's just excited to prove himself. It's fine. Mistakes happen."

"He could have broken a rib," her brow furrows and her nose scrunches as she continues to study the injury.

"Liv?" I ask softly.

"What?" The grumpy edge to her voice evident.

I give her a meaningful look and her face relaxes and she draws her lower lip in between her teeth.

"Right. Sorry," she looks sheepish at first, but then her hands continue to drift down my body, following the path her eyes are taking until they rest at the top of my jeans.

Her thumb flicks over the valley between my hip and abdomen.

"These should be illegal," she mumbles, more to herself than to me.

"Yeah?" I ask in a hoarse whisper because the sight of her hands on me has me so hard, so fucking desperate to have her touch me more, I don't have anything else in me.

"Yeah," she whispers back, and I can tell she's thinking this through. Whether or not it's a good idea. And I wait patiently, just listening to our breathing and the dull hum of the game console on the other side of the room. It's a delicate game we're playing, and I don't want her to do anything she doesn't want to, no matter how much I might want it.

When it stretches out too long I take a step back, trying to put physical distance between us so I can attempt to bring my senses back to earth, stop my racing heart, and have something sensible to say. But the motion makes her frown, her fingers hooking into the material of my jeans.

"If you…" I trail off.

"It just feels like crossing the Rubicon," she stares down at the button on the top of my jeans.

A stuttered nervous laugh escapes me.

"I don't think it's quite that dramatic."

She gives me a doubtful look in return.

"If you're not feeling it, it's okay to stop. Any time."

"That's not it. It's how much I want it that feels wrong."

Her statement sucks out all the oxygen in the room, and nearly drags me to my knees.

"Fuck… Liv…" It's all I manage to say, as I stare at her.

A look of determination crosses her face though and her fingers start to work the first button.

"I know you're my friend, but sometimes, especially like this… It's hard to remember that," she whispers.

"I know," I admit. I run my fingers along her jaw and tilt her face up to mine, and she searches my eyes for a second before I kiss her again. She takes the opportunity to finish undoing my pants, pushing them and the boxer briefs I have on down to the floor. Her lips pull away from mine as she studies my body, her hands tracing over my chest and abs, her swollen lower lip rolling between her teeth as she does it. And the way she looks at me makes me feel like my skin is on fire.

She takes me in her hand, stroking me tentatively at first, using the first lesson I'd given her to her advantage.

"Fuck, you're good at that."

"I took notes," she smirks.

"A lot of them apparently."

"I did get called teacher's pet in school."

"Fuck me."

EIGHTEEN

Olivia

"THAT'S THE PLAN," I answer with a hell of a lot more confidence than I have.

I lower myself to my knees, taking the tip of him between my lips and his eyes go wide and then shutter at the contact. His hand goes to my cheek, brushing against it softly and then sliding back into my hair.

"Fuck Liv," he grunts my name, and it makes the heat pool low in my body.

I stroke him again, setting a rhythm as I take him slowly inch by inch into my mouth. I'm out of practice, and I desperately want this to be good for him. I want him to remember it every time he thinks of me. Because I'm tired of being seen as his sexless spinster best friend. So I'm hoping that my eagerness and my desire for him will make up for the lack of recent practical experience.

I take him deeper with each successive stroke of my hand

and use my tongue for counter pressure. His fingers turn in my hair, gripping it and pulling me closer and the sensation of it slides down my spine. The entire scene making me wet and desperate for more of him.

I pick up my pace, getting a little sloppy in the process, but sucking him harder and using my hand to build the friction.

"Fuck yes. Suck me harder," he mutters words of praise above me, and it spurs me on.

I feel his breathing start to change and stutter. The taste of him spills on to my tongue.

"God damn. Your mouth is so fucking good, Liv."

His grip on my hair tightens and he gently pulls me back with it.

I frown, my eyes going up to his in question

"Gonna come."

"Let me? Please?"

His eyes shutter and he curses but loosens his hold on me, so I can take him in my mouth again. No sooner I do, he's coming, his breathing coming hard and fast as he starts to double over, and I swallow as he pulls out of my mouth.

He curses under his breath, sliding his hands under my arms and hauling me up. He pulls me close, and he kisses me again. Not the same seductive measures he'd taken before but something softer, more familiar like he's done it a million times. Another kind of emotion spilling out from me, every time his lips cross mine. And if you'd asked me if this man had this kind of talent even a few weeks ago, I would have said no. Would never have guessed it. Every time he touches me it's like I discover something I didn't know.

"That was so fucking hot Liv. I can barely fucking breathe," he says when he finally lets my tender swollen lips have a break.

I tuck my head under his chin, enjoying the heat of him against me. I lean into him, and into the feel of him.

"You were right about the kissing by the way. I don't think anyone has ever done it right before," I smile against his chest, but I feel him tense underneath me.

And then I realize what I've said. What I've admitted, and the ghost of the past is standing in the room with us, chilling the air and my heated skin.

"Shit, I didn't mean-" I start to say but his hand slides down over my thigh and in between my legs as I say the words.

"Are you wet for me?" he asks, his lips brushing against my temple.

His fingers drag against my soaked underwear and the friction makes me whimper. I can feel him smile, satisfied with the condition making him come has put me in and he gives me several long strokes that have me wanting more.

"Did you like it enough last time? Will you let me do it again? I need to taste you, Liv."

I nod, because I can't form words. Not when he talks like that. I don't know who this man is next to me right now, but it's not my best friend.

He doesn't hesitate after I give him permission. He slides to the floor, sitting in front of me and leaning back against the bed. And I can't help it. I stare at him for a second longer than I probably should. His naked muscular body sprawled out in front of me like he's a work of art. He gives me a smug little look that on most guys would be a turn off, but on him just sends a flickering wave of want through my body.

He drags my underwear down over my thighs and calves, letting me step out of them before he tosses them aside. His fingers run over my skin, like they're discovering something fascinating he hasn't noticed before. He presses a kiss to one of my knees, and then looks up at me.

"Put your knee up here," he pats the spot on the mattress next to his head, while his other hand coasts up the back of my right leg.

I look at him doubtfully, but the stern nod of his chin I get in response has me complying. The position has me balancing tentatively and has me wide open to him. His breath ghosts over my bare skin, and I desperately wish I would have prepared for this, because I feel like cringing over the imperfections I know must be there. And it's like he can sense what I'm thinking.

"I like you like this. When you haven't had a chance to make everything perfect like you always do. I feel like I get something no one else does," he says the words so quietly that they're barely audible but make my stomach flip in a way I haven't felt in a very long time.

His mouth goes to my thigh, kissing and nibbling against the tender flesh and it makes me jerk involuntarily, nearly knocking me off balance. My hand braces on his shoulder, and his left arm wraps around my right leg, holding me tight and keeping my knee from buckling. Then without warning he kisses me, his mouth working my tender swollen sex the same way he worked my mouth and tongue, and I gasp at the contact, my hips bucking forward unintentionally. My hand sliding into his hair. He groans as he takes a long lick of me, parting me with his tongue.

"Fucking fuck, Liam. I can't. It's too much," I whisper, feeling like I'm going to collapse and trying to take a step back.

But his arms lock around my legs like steel, holding me in place, and he looks up at me.

"I want you like this, Liv. It's all I've been able to think about. I promise I'll make it feel good for you."

And my body 100 percent jerks to attention at his offer. My nipples go hard, and I can practically feel my clit pulsing, desperate for the attention of his mouth. But the position is so awkward. I don't know if I can do it, just let go and enjoy it. And like always he can read my every thought.

"Get out of your head and just take what feels good. Like you did out on the terrace that night. That's part of the experiment, remember?" he challenges me, looking at me like he believes in me, like he's coaching one of his freshman teammates, and I can't help but smile a little bit.

"Got it," I whisper, and he answers with a devious little smile before his mouth returns to me.

He's just as good as he was the first time, if not better with the angle and my desperation for him on his side. Deft strokes of his tongue have me feeling the first tingles in my nerves in moments, and I moan softly when he slides two fingers inside me. Mine thread through his shaggy strands of hair, but I let loose when I feel like I'm being too rough. Massaging his scalp where I worry I might have hurt him. I only have a second to think about it before his mouth and his fingers take on a punishing pace, doubling me over and I can't think about anything other than how good he feels.

His hands knead and massage my thighs and he grabs my ass, pulling me down on to his face. I roll my hips and he spurs me on, until we match each other's rhythm, and I feel the familiar tight pull in my abdomen. I see searing white nothingness when my orgasm finally hits, my body flooding with every perfect sensation he created. He runs his tongue over me until the little aftershocks subside and my legs buckle under me. I slide down until my knees hit the floor, and I'm straddling him, his hands around my waist, bent over with my forehead against the mattress. He's breathing into my stomach almost as hard as I am, his chest rising and falling and his hand slides under my shirt and over my ribs, and then back down over my stomach and cradles my hip.

"The way you sound... The way you taste. Fuck..." he curses under his breath.

I collapse next to him, my eyes drifting down before I realize what I'm doing and look up at him instead. This was never a problem I had before. Not with Tristan, not with Mason. Every time I thought we might do something that would finally get him out of my system, it only makes me want him more. Want the things I haven't had yet.

"What are you thinking?" he asks, the look in his eyes when they meet mine telling me he already knows.

"How fast I could get you hard again. What you'd feel like inside me," I confess.

"Fuck," he curses, and leans forward, capturing my lower lip with his mouth and biting it softly before he releases me again. "Don't say that, or I'll fuck you right here like this. And that *will* be crossing a Rubicon."

NINETEEN

Liam

"YOU DON'T WANT TO?" Her lids are heavy with want and her eyes flutter up to mine after being locked long and hard on my cock. And fuck me, I'd need a few minutes still, but I'm tempted.

She's like a fucking siren begging me to crash against the rocks, and I want so badly to give in to her. Claim her. Make her mine. But I promised that I'd support her in her experiment and as much as I don't want it to, it might mean other guys, and I can't have her like that and give her up. Or at least, I don't think I can. My cock is trying to tell me I absolutely can handle it if it means getting inside her now. She was so wet, and so fucking eager for it that I can almost feel her sliding over me now.

"I don't think I have a condom anyway," I lie, because I won't fuck her without one.

"Since when? You always have some shoved in your night-stand." Her eyes lift to it.

"When have you been going through my nightstand?" I raise an eyebrow at her.

"You never notice that sometimes your room is cleaner after I stay over than it was the night before?"

"Yes, but I didn't realize you were going through my things."

"Do you have secrets you're hiding?" She smirks. "A secret fetish I don't know about?"

I had a few, and she was definitely at the top of the list now. But she didn't need to know any of that.

"I might."

"Well see, now you have to tell me."

"Maybe someday." I shrug.

She leans forward then, straddling my lap again, kissing me, her mouth slanting over mine and her tongue tracing over my lower lip as her wet heat brushes over the tip of my dick. And I thank my lucky fucking stars that she made me come first because otherwise I'd have zero self-control.

"Now?"

"Someday," I protest.

Her knees widen, her legs spread, and she's so close now she's just barely hovering over me.

"Liv..." I groan, because I can tell she's taking pleasure in the torment, a little smile breaking out over her lips.

"I know. But you're so sexy when you look pained like that." She carefully climbs over me and kisses my cheek, settling next to me again.

"Uh huh. I need a cold shower."

"Go. You're fast. I'll take mine after you."

"You sure?"

She nods. I kiss her softly before I go, thankful because

some reasonable part of my brain knows I need some distance, some perspective from all of this.

I flip on the shower, let it barely heat up and jump in. I hiss when the cool water hits my skin, but a deep breath that I slowly release lets my body and my mind adjust to the temperature. I lean against the tiles on the wall, letting the water stream down my back.

I know I'm fucked, deep down I can feel it. The way my heart twists in my chest whenever she looks at me. The way I feel when she kisses me. It's not like it's been in the past. It's not the easy hookups, or even the content feeling I've felt with a couple of the girlfriends I've had.

With Liv it's pure unadulterated *want,* layered over years of needing her by my side. I fucking struggle to imagine life after college without her there even though I know it's going to be something I have to get my mind around. And when she's trying to be free, experiment, have fun—the last thing I should be doing is trying to make her mine.

And that's before we even get to the elephant in the room. The past that stands between us anytime I stop to think too long about it. I could feel the guilt slither up my spine again, when she'd said I was right that she'd never been kissed right. How the hell we could ever actually be together without a third party in the room is a mystery I have no idea how to solve. Even if we wanted to. Even if we tried.

But when it's just her and me. When she looks at me with those gorgeous hazel eyes, the sounds she makes when I touch her, and the way she listens so fucking well every time I encourage her? I can't resist her. I can't walk away. And this entire experiment is like slow torture that I'm in no hurry to stop.

When I'm done, she takes a quick shower, and comes back into the room wearing nothing but a towel. I pretend to be asleep as she drops it, standing naked as she goes through one of my drawers to grab another shirt that she pulls over herself before she comes back to bed and climbs in next to me. My heart swells at the fact she's wearing *my* shirt and smells like *my* soap, climbing into *my* bed. Little things like this that I never gave a fuck about before, are a giant fucking red flag I keep choosing to ignore.

I wrap an arm around her waist and drag her close to me. A little grunt escapes her when she registers I'm not asleep, but then she melts into me. She curls up onto her side, her bare ass snug against me. And I have to remind myself again that she is my *friend,* not my girlfriend. I have to let her have her freedom. Give her space. Even if it kills me.

TWENTY

Olivia

"THIS WHOLE THING IS AN EPIC FAILURE," I slump into the chair in Kenz's room wearing my Montgomery jersey, while she puts on her Prescott one and puts the finishing touches to her makeup. Today was a huge game for the team. One of two must-wins if they were going to get a bowl game and make it to the finals. And theoretically the last night for our agreement unless Liam decides he has room in his schedule for an extension.

"How do you figure?" Kenz looks up at me for a second before she leans into the mirror to put her eyeliner on.

"It's not helping me get him out of my system. I signed up for that dating app Ben suggested, and I just flick through profiles and none of them appeal to me."

"Yeah dearest, you can't be comparing guys on dating apps to your sexy as sin quarterback who spends half his time on the field and in the gym and the other half trying to please you. It's not exactly fair."

"He does not spend half his time trying to please me."

"Oh, is it more like 40 percent with all the extra practice time lately?" she asks sarcastically.

I make a face at her.

"I think this was a bad idea. Because now I know a whole lot more about him I didn't know before."

"And you like it?" Kenz grins and raises a brow at me.

"Like what?" Wren pops into the room and settles on Kenz's bed. She's already dressed for work, and I wish just once we could get her to go to a game with us. But alas, being the manager at a sports bar near campus means you work game days.

"Newly discovered aspects of Liam's... Personality? Anatomy?" Kenz smirks at me.

I shoot her a look but turn to Wren, "I'm just saying that I think this whole plan might have been a mistake. I think it might have made things worse and not better."

"Operation fuck-him-out-of-your-system not going so well, huh?" Wren gives me a pitiful look.

"I don't know. I'm more confused than ever and time is basically up. And I have no idea what's going on in his head. I don't want to ask either, he has enough on his plate with everything football-wise and school-wise. The last thing he needs is me asking him to break down his feelings for me. Can you imagine how grumpy that would make him?"

"I mean, whatever his feelings might be, or however complicated given your past, it's obvious that there's more than friendship going on," Kenz tries to comfort me.

"Did you have an agreed end date to this whole thing?"

"Yep. That's the thing, it's tonight."

"Tonight?" Kenz looks at me wide-eyed.

"Yes, when we discussed it... that was part of our agreement. Not letting it stretch out too long and then him needing to focus if they got this far in the season."

"Have you... gone to the end zone yet?" Wren raises a brow, a little smirk threatening to form on her lips.

"No."

"Are you going to?" Kenz points her makeup brush at me.

"I don't know. I can't decide if that's a good way to end things or the absolute worst idea in the history of ever," I sigh, picking off a little piece of nail polish where I'd overpainted my nail in the team's colors.

"I mean, did he really complete his coaching assignment if he didn't take you all the way to the Super Bowl though? That's the question." Wren laughs.

"Yeah, how will you properly assess his coaching abilities without it?" Kenz adds.

"You two are nefarious twins when you get like this."

"That would be a great band name." Kenz nods her head back and forth like she's considering it.

"Backup plan if our post-college career plans don't pan out?" Wren looks to her.

"Deal!" Kenz smiles back at her.

I can't help but smile at both of them. I dreaded talking about anything post-college, because I didn't like the idea of being without them or the three of us not living together. It would also mean the end of Liam being close and thinking about all of that in rapid order has my stomach in knots.

"What's wrong?" Wren frowns when she looks back at me.

"I don't know. Just thinking about things."

The two of them exchange looks but don't say anything else before we head out.

WATCHING Liam play is an activity I've always looked forward to, because the man is fucking phenomenal. The way he reads the field, the way he reacts to the defense's tactics, the way he encourages his teammates, and the way that man can launch a deep ball down the field and nail a wide receiver in motion on a long route is enough to make anyone who loves the game weep. It was also enough to bring half the women on campus to their knees, well that and the way he looked suited up, which is why I was far from the only woman here wearing a Montgomery jersey.

But watching him play in a situation like this, where we're down by three and in the last few minutes of the game, where we need a touchdown, and he needs to manage the clock is honestly turning me on. His focus and determination never waiver, even though twice they've been third and long during this drive. He's gotten them into the red zone and the crowd are all on their feet, holding their breath as he looks for Lawton or Westfield in the end zone. The pass rush their opponent has been showing is phenomenal and Waylon and the rest of the guys have had their work cut out for them today, but they've played almost perfectly. So far, they've only allowed one sack and we're lucky it hasn't been more.

He hands off the ball for another run play, and JB gets us another first down and running clock that has everyone biting their nails. I take a deep breath and look to Kenz as the other team calls a timeout.

"I hate this. It is so damn stressful, especially since I still don't know everything," she shakes her head.

"That's supposed to be the reason it's fun," I smile at her, even though I don't feel it. Waylon's taken an absolute beating today and if I was her, I'd be more than ready for this game to be over.

"Maybe if you're not dating the guy on the field." She

crosses her arms over her chest, her eyes searching for the 6'5 center and smiling a little when she does.

"Let's just hope they get this next touchdown." I reach over and link my arm around hers.

They line up for the next play, and they run it again, running down the clock some more. And they do it again but come short of the line. And now it's up to Liam to pull out the game winning throw. East, or as they call him on game days East/West for how he covers the field, is in and Ben is out wide. The play clock winds down, and Liam takes the snap, faking a throw and then searching the end zone, but no one's open.

Kenz tugs me tighter to her as he dances out of the pocket, tucks the ball and runs for the end zone, leaping over a huge defensive guard to land just on the right side of the line. The entire stadium roars to life, screaming and high fiving each other as the refs call the touchdown. The guys line up to do their dance and the band starts playing the touchdown song.

"Oh my god!!!" Kenz screams, jumping up and down. And if you'd told me a few months ago that my bestie would be in the stadium with me this thrilled over a touchdown I would have never believed it.

"Fuck yes!!!" I scream. "Montgomery you are a fucking beast!!"

"You're getting laid tonight Montgomery!!" Kenz yells at the top of her lungs, and several people around us turn to look and smile at her.

"Kenz!" I hip check her.

"It's true and you fucking know it. Especially after that. He earned it," she smirks.

I burst out into laughter, and we start chanting along with the touchdown song as the band gets louder.

WHEN I SEE Liam coming out of the stadium after the game, I take off running to him. There are a million people surrounding him, but I am so fucking happy for him I can't stand it. He spots me as I get close and opens his arms, catching me and spinning me around in the air.

"You are extra lucky for me today, Sunshine." He kisses my forehead and sets me back on my feet.

"That was fucking amazing. You were amazing. I am so fucking proud of you guys," I gush over him, too happy for them to act the least bit sensible right now.

"Yeah. Wasn't too fucking bad, huh?" He grins, always the one to deflect any exuberant praise in favor of stoic assessments.

"An understatement."

"Everyone was just clicking today. If we can do that for the rest of the season, fuck... I don't want to get ahead of ourselves."

I grin at him and give him another hug as an onslaught of people start to push in to give him their congratulations and a couple folks ask for his autograph. It's a real possibility he's the number one draft pick next year, not that anyone wants to jinx it, and the more certain that seems the more people want a piece of him. It's a blessing and a curse for him, because as much as he lives and breathes football, he hates the attention.

Waylon and the rest of the guys have come out as well and are talking to people and razzing each other as they file out for the evening. I slink back to talk to Kenz some more while we wait for them to finish chatting with folks, and then we all gather together by our cars to start heading back to the football house for the party tonight.

WHEN WE GET BACK to his house, it's already filling up with people who are ready to party hard to celebrate the win, dozens of them who are already drunk and rowdy from the stadium. He grabs my hand as we snake though the crowd to head upstairs so we can change and have a few minutes of breathing time before he has to be the center of attention. Several people high five him on the way, and a drunken cheer breaks out on one side of the living room. I smile and hold on for dear life as he tries to outrun it all.

"You're going to have to get used to all of that you know." I grin at him as we make it into his room, and he closes the door. "It's only going to get worse."

"And I'll just have to get better noise cancelling headphones."

I laugh and set my bag on his bed to dig out my clothes. I've picked out something a little flashier than normal tonight. I told myself it's because we'd be celebrating the win, but in reality, it's because I was nervous I'd get lost in the sea of people who were going to want his attention if I didn't. Now that it was the only thing I had to change into I was regretting my decision a little. I loved to dress Kenz and Wren up in stuff, but when it came to me wearing the same things, I was a bit of a hypocrite.

"You could just wear that the rest of the night," Liam comments on the jersey I'm wearing when he sees me hesitate over the clothes.

I look up and his shirt is off as he pulls some clothes out of his closet, his back to me now and I watch him move because he looks like the Roman sculptures in my textbooks. Like he could have been one of the specimens they used to inspire the artwork. He tosses the clothes on the small couch he has in his room before he ducks into the bathroom. He runs product through his hair to try to tame the haphazard waves that have air dried from his shower at the stadium, and I smile at the way he concentrates in the mirror. I grab my makeup bag and go to stand next to him to fix my own hair and makeup which looks crazy from all the wind at the stadium tonight.

"What?" he asks when he sees me looking at him.

"Nothing," I smile and shake my head, but my heart squeezes in my chest.

He eyes me in the mirror as he washes his hands and wipes them on the hand towel, his brow raising as I put on some dark eyeshadow to smoke my eyes out.

"What?" It's my turn to ask.

He grabs the material of my jersey and bunches it in his fist and pulls me toward him, his lips landing on mine. His kiss is slow and hot, like we could just spend the rest of the night in here like this. My hands go to his chest, drifting down over his abs as I kiss him back.

"Any lessons on seducing star quarterbacks after big wins?" I smirk at him when we finally come up for air.

"Yeah," his eyes rake over me. "I don't think you need any help there."

My fingers run along the band of his sweats, and I can feel his eyes on me. The weight of us both knowing it's supposed to be the last night we're together between us. I don't feel like bringing it up now either. I'd rather pretend the end doesn't exist. So instead I palm him through the material and kiss him again.

"We could just stay up here," he mumbles against my lips.

"Zero chance they let you get away with that. You know you have to go down."

"Oh, I know," he grins.

I roll my eyes and laugh at his little pun. "Get dressed."

I do the same thing myself. Putting on the lacy top and the short skirt I'd brought and slipping on heels that bring me closer to his height. Once he's dressed and turns to look at me, his jaw practically drops, and I grin.

"That's what you're wearing? Here? Tonight?" A little storm of grumpiness crosses his otherwise serene features— Liam immediately after a win is usually the least grumpy version of him.

"Yes."

"Fuck me, Liv. Do you want me in another fight?"

"No, but I have to play the part if I'm gonna compete with all the other women who are going to throw themselves at you. That's part of the confidence game, right? Rock the sexy outfit?"

His mouth screws up on one side as if I've made a point he can't quite argue with.

"You don't fucking have to compete with anyone." He grabs my arm and spins me around, looking at my outfit. "I might have to though."

"Hey. It's like my championship tonight, right? Have to prove I put those lessons to good use. Also, rule three. No breaking faces, remember?" I raise a brow at him, hedging my bets by hinting at the date.

"I said I couldn't promise depending on the circumstances."

"Well, let's make sure the circumstances are that you don't break rules," I kiss him lightly, knowing full well I already want to break rules. Namely the one that says this has to be over.

He pulls me close to him again, holding both my hands and tucking them behind my back as he bends to kiss me again.

"Then the circumstances better be that my bed is the one you end up in tonight."

"Hmm. I don't know, is there any incentive to that?" I tease him, smiling as he pulls me a little tighter.

"Yeah, Sunshine. You already know I make you come hard

—guaranteed. You really want to gamble the end result when you put all this effort in tonight?" He smiles back at me.

"Probably not," I whisper, staring at how gorgeous his smile is. Thinking how warm he feels. How much I want him.

"Then promise."

"I promise."

"Good girl." He smirks.

I let out a little puff of indignation, but it's quickly swallowed up as he kisses me one last time while he grabs my butt and squeezes.

"Now let's get this party out of the way."

TWENTY-ONE

Liam

THE PARTY TONIGHT is wilder than usual, and I've had more than my fair share of shots and toasts. It's one of those rare nights where I feel like the success we had on the field was truly deserved, and I can actually relax and enjoy it. The guys seem happier than ever, and Mac and Liv have been having their own wild dance party most of the night. In the last hour, I've been getting ambushed by group after group of people who want to discuss the game; I've lost track of Liv though and I go look for her. When I finally find her, she's on the back porch dancing with Mac and Wren whose shown up after her shift. They pause to do a round of shots before the next song starts.

It's freezing cold outside so I motion for them to come in, but they shake their heads.

"It's too hot in there! We're just taking a quick break," Mac points to the house. It's a fair point, because it's overflowing with bodies tonight as people try to pile in to celebrate the win.

Wren, the sensible one, is still bundled in her jacket and she just shakes her head at their antics. Shrugging when she looks to me like they can't be helped.

When Liv finally notices me though, her face lights up and her smile makes my chest ache. A new sensation that I really didn't want to analyze tonight. She motions for me to come over and immediately wraps her arms around me when I do.

"Oh see, this is like perfect. Nice cool night air to keep me from getting too hot, nice warm bestie to keep my hands warm." She looks up at me like I'm the best thing she's seen all night, and fuck if it doesn't make me want her right now.

I shudder as she creeps her cold hands up under my shirt, her fingers dancing up my stomach to the beat of the song she's swaying back and forth to.

"How many shots have you had?" I raise my eyebrow at her.

"Not that many. Just having fun. How many have you had?" She smirks and I wonder what she's up to.

"Enough."

"Boo."

"Why?"

"I had an idea I wanted to try but I don't want to take advantage of you if you're drunk. That wouldn't be very ethical, even under the agreement terms."

I laugh, "Is it like Plato week in your classes or something?"

"Maybe. But don't mock it. Ethics are important Montgomery."

"Apologies. What was the idea?"

She leans in close to me, "It's less of an idea and more of a fantasy thing, really, if I'm being honest."

"Well, now you have to tell me." I slide my hand under her shirt and trace my way up her ribs, shielding her body so no one can see me do it. I have no idea who she's told about our agreement or how much and now that it's coming to an end I don't know if she wants to keep it a secret for good.

"Fine. You have to be in there though," she motions to the inside of the house. "Bonus points if you're doing your thing. You know, flirting with someone, like, your sex eyes."

"My sex eyes?" A laugh sputters out of me.

"Yes. Don't act like you don't know. It's a thing you do when you flirt with a girl you like. You smolder."

A laugh racks my body, and she does not love it.

"See this is why I'm not telling you."

"Okay. Okay. I'm sorry. I'm smoldering and then what?"

"Then I'll come get you."

"And then what?"

She just shrugs and gives me a little devious grin, her fingers crawling further up my shirt. I want to kiss her, but I stop myself.

"All right. Well I'm going back inside. Don't stay out here too long, okay? It's cold as fuck out here," I pull away from her and wink, and get another smile in return.

TWENTY MINUTES later I'm in a conversation with people about our upcoming game, and I feel a hand slip around my upper arm. I look over and it's Liv.

"Can I borrow you for a minute? I need your help with something." Her lips draw up in a little smirk.

I nod and excuse myself, following after her as she leads me to the pantry.

"Can't reach the chips again?" I laugh because Ben shoves them in a cabinet so high half the people here couldn't reach them.

"Yep." She shuts the door behind us and the night light that's plugged in for late night snack runs comes on.

"You want to hit the light?"

"Nope."

I turn to look at her, puzzled and then I realize. "Dark pantries are your thing then?"

"No, but you when you talk about football is. It's kind of like your smoldering face but better. You get all serious, and your jaw does this little clench thing when you disagree with people's opinions."

Liv has always been the type who loosens a little when she's had a couple of drinks, but she's being more raw and honest tonight than I can remember. And I can't tell if it's the alcohol or something else that has her this way.

"How many shots did you have again?"

"Just enough to overshare." She laughs.

"I can tell." I raise a brow at her.

She shakes her head, leans forward and kisses me, softly, barely touching her lips to mine before she pulls away and her eyes drift up to mine. Her silhouette back lit by the small light illuminating us and I grab her hips and pull her close to me.

"So we're in the pantry, now what?"

"Now you pretend like I'm not me, but instead I'm some bad bitch you want to fuck, and you use me to get off. However you want."

I don't know what I thought she was going to say, but it was *not* that. My lungs go tight, my dick goes hard, and my brain throws a fucking flag out, all at the same time.

"I don't use women to get off, and the door in here does not lock. There are people literally four feet away from us."

"Yes, Coach. That's all part of the fun. Obviously." She rolls her eyes at me, like I'm the one who's being crazy right now.

"If you want me to follow rule three and not break faces, I

don't need anyone walking in here and seeing you in any state of undress."

"Boo. You are no fun," she rolls her lower lip.

"I mean if you want to risk it..."

"No. We'll just have to stick to things where only you get undressed then. Partially of course, 'cause I don't want them seeing you either." Her hands go to my pants where she starts to work the buttons.

"Liv, I don't think—"

Her hand clamps over my mouth.

"If I wasn't me, but another version who brought you in here and said I wanted these things, would you be lecturing me right now, or would I be on my knees already?"

I roll my eyes up to the ceiling and close them, wishing for some way out of this because holy fuck did I want her on her knees. I want this Liv. The one who takes charge and asks me for things I've wanted for longer than I've realized.

"That's what I thought. So... what was it you told me? Shut up and just take what you want? I think that was it," she smiles and kneels down in front of me.

I'm so hard already that a few strokes of her hand already has me on edge, so when she takes me in her mouth, I slam the palm of my hand on the counter behind me trying to feel something other than how fucking good her mouth is. She takes me deeper, and I can hardly stand it.

I cup her cheek as she looks up at me, and she's so fucking beautiful. I don't deserve her at all, and especially not like this. I feel the whisper of guilt climb up my spine.

And she must see it on my face because she pulls back.

"Don't do that."

"What?"

"You know what. And it hurts my feelings. I really was

looking forward to playing this out. Being down here, having you in my mouth, you pulling my hair. So please, Liam."

"Fuck. Okay." I don't want to let her down, and I hate that I am. We both know it's the end after this, and if I'm honest I want her like this. I want the memory of her like this. What it feels like to have her pretend she wants me this bad.

I run my fingers through her hair a few times, brushing it out of her face and then I gently tug her forward.

"Take me," a hoarse whisper comes out that doesn't even sound like me, but she follows the direction well.

"Deeper, and use your tongue," I decide to coach her through it, because at least if I have that as a crutch I don't feel like I'm an ass taking advantage of her, even though I am.

My fingers tighten in her hair as she hits a particularly sensitive spot and she moans, honest to god fucking moans when I do it. It makes everything in my body hotter and tighter. I want her like I've never wanted anyone, and my mind is already thinking about all the ways I wish I could have her.

I'd debated it over and over again, whether it was a good idea or a bad one to take things further. I'd told myself it was too much. That it was crossing a line, but now like this, I want her. Not having her, all of her, would leave me fucking haunted with what ifs I don't think I can handle.

Just as she picks up her pace, getting faster and sloppier in a way that has me fucking mesmerized with how damn good she is, the door starts to swing open, and I grab it before it can open all the way.

"Hey!" The voice on the other end yells. "What the fuck?"

JB's head swivels around the door.

"GET OUT." I grit out, giving him a look I hope he knows means he's gonna lose his eyes and his dick if he keeps looking.

"Fuccckk. Sorry. Didn't see shit!" he yells out as he walks away, and I hear him talking to someone just outside the door.

I turn to look at her, worried that she's going to be upset but her eyes just glitter with amusement, and she runs her tongue down me and takes me a little deeper than before. Like getting caught gave her a little surge of adrenaline she was hoping for, and it spurs her on.

It's one of the hottest fucking things I've ever seen in my life and sends me over the edge in rapid fucking order. I come hard, the way she looks at me feeling like I might never have it this good again. She swallows me down just like she did the other night, and I have no idea how I got this lucky. Watching her do that and the freight train of an orgasm she just gave me leaves me weak as fuck, and I lean back against the counter to keep myself together.

"That was so fucking hot," she brushes off her knees, which are red from kneeling on the hard floor, and I reach forward to rub her kneecap where the indentation mars her otherwise perfect skin.

"I don't know if he saw you or not. If he knows what's good for him, he won't say anything."

"Oh, I hope he does. It's too bad it wasn't one of the jersey chasers. They would have been telling everyone."

"What?" I stutter for breath.

"What?" she echoes. "It'd be kind of hot to have them whispering about it. Plus then they'd know to stop touching you like they have been all night."

"Come fucking here," I groan, wishing she could be a little less hot right now.

She wraps her arms around me, and I pull her tight before I run my fingers through her hair at the nape of her neck and tilt her head back. Her eyes are so fucking bright, her face lit up like she's a fucking ray of light.

"Hey, Sunshine," I whisper.

"Hey, Coach," she whispers back, and I kiss her for several

moments before she pulls away. "You should get back out there before you're missed."

"Fine. Not much longer though. I'm getting tired of people, and I just want you to myself, without interruptions preferably."

She smiles and kisses my cheek before she sneaks out the door and looks back at me over her shoulder before closing it again. I'm left to put myself back in order, except the way she keeps rearranging me every time she touches me, leaving me different from the last, it makes me wonder if my new order belongs exclusively to her.

TWENTY-TWO

Olivia

"WHATCHA DOIN?" Kenz walks up and bumps her hip into mine. Her eyes drift to the frat guy who's currently talking to his friend next to me. Prior to his sidebar he'd been flirting hard with me, caging me in against the wall, giving me his best lines and trying to talk me into leaving with him.

"Being petty," I take a sip of my water that I'm still pretending is beer. I'd already been pretty sobered by the sight of Mia flirting her heart out with Liam about 20 minutes ago, and she has not left his side.

Kenz must be able to figure it out, "I mean, you know she has a losing hand, so I don't know why you're worried."

"Does she though?"

"Liv, be serious. He hasn't touched her or given her any sign at all he's interested. He's just being polite, and in the last five minutes all he does is look over here every 30 seconds like he might murder someone."

"Aren't you worried about Waylon?" My eyes drift around the room, and I see a group of people talking to him, including one younger pretty woman I don't recognize. My guess is she's probably new around here either from a different college or maybe a sophomore, because the way she's looking at Waylon right now, it's like she thinks she has a chance.

"No, honestly, I've kinda grown to like it. It's good for his ego and therefore good for other things," she wiggles her eyebrows.

"You're a sick woman," I shake my head at her.

"Maybe, but a happy one," she grins, and I can't help but smile back.

"Shit. I'm sorry." Frat Boy turns around to talk to me again, realizing he's being rude and when he sees Kenz standing there his smile widens. Ugh. Why were they always like this? *Fat chance, asshole.* "Hey, are you her friend?"

"And on that note, I'm going to go talk to my boyfriend," Kenz gives me a look that says I should do the same. Except my "boyfriend" is occupied.

"Where were we? Oh yeah," he reaches out and brushes my hair back in a way I assume he intends to be sexy but really just come across as a sloppy drunk move. "Discussing where you wanted to go tonight. My place or yours?"

Ugh.

"Mine," the word sounds almost like a growl and a hand snakes around my waist, fingers sliding under my shirt and over my skin in a way that sends shivers down my spine.

Frat Boy looks up and blinks.

"Montgomery, sorry man. I didn't know!" He holds up his hands and takes a step back.

"Now you do," comes the grumpy reply from behind me.

"Sorry, for real. I wouldn't have even thought it," he takes off without a backward glance.

"What are you doing?" The grumpy tone is turned on me now.

"Flirting."

"You probably should stop drinking if you think he's a good option."

"It's water," I hold up the glass for him to see.

"That's worse."

"Just keeping my options open."

"Your options?" His tone is incredulous.

"I saw your number one fangirl working her magic," I roll my eyes.

He sighs and leans down closer to me.

"The only one that has magic that works on me is you," he places a discreet kiss to the side of my neck.

"And given that you promised already, the only options you have tonight are how you want me to fuck you and how many times," he whispers against my ear as his hand tightens around my waist. And just those two sentences have my knees weak and my thighs pressing together, desperate for him to touch me. That want is even starting to overrun my desire not to make our whole thing public right now, and I'm hoping he's done getting worshipped by the crowds for the evening. And like he reads my thoughts, "So be the good fucking girl you are, and go up to my room and decide those things."

And if there was any part of me that didn't want this man, it just left my body with the rest of the oxygen in my lungs.

WHEN I HEAR him come in the room, I'm in his bathroom getting a glass of water from the sink. I've stripped down to my lingerie with a few pieces I added while I waited for him to come up. His eyes go wide when he hits the doorframe and he rests one hand on the top of it, leaning in as he runs a hand over his mouth.

"You like?"

"I mean I thought I liked it in the photos, but in person... fuck."

I smile at him. The truth is, I'm nervous, not that I want to admit it. The lingerie felt a little like armor. It upped my confidence, made me feel like I had an alter ego. The version of me in the photos rather than the one he saw all the time.

He takes a few steps into the room, leaning over me and kissing my shoulder and following it up to my neck, the sensation leaving a ripple effect of goosebumps. The smell of his cologne wafts over me and I wish I could just live in this moment forever.

"So what do you want for your last lesson?" he asks absently against my skin.

"You."

"You already have me..." he mumbles as he kisses up my neck.

"No, I mean you. The non-coach version. The things you'd want to do if you wanted me for real. Because I want you. Watching you play today... Watching you tonight. It's all I can think about," I confess, closing my eyes because I'm terrified to see his reaction. His hands still and he stops kissing me.

"Liv..." he turns me toward him. "Look at me."

Shit. I open my eyes worried for what I'll see there, but the way he's looking at me makes me feel like I am going to melt.

"Everything we've done, I've wanted. I want to help you. But fuck... I want you. I want you so fucking much lately, I feel dirty for how much I think about it. How often I get off to the thought of you."

"What do you think about?" I whisper.

And it's his turn to close his eyes, his beautiful long brown lashes shuttering them for a moment before he opens them again and meets mine.

"The way you taste. The way you come on my tongue. The way you look at me when you suck me off. Fucking you hard. Tying you up, pinning you down and teasing your pussy so fucking good that you beg me to come—"

"That. I want that," I interrupt his string of confessions.

"What?" He tilts his head, his eyes darkening.

"Tying me up. Pinning me down. The way you boss me around. I hate it sometimes don't get me wrong, but also... You're really fucking hot when you get like that. Hence the accidental lap dance..."

He rolls his bottom lip between his teeth, and his eyes go heavy.

"Oh, fuck me, Sunshine..." He closes his eyes and hangs his head, shaking it slowly. "You can't fucking say things like that."

"I'm asking you, please."

"Fuck." The curse rips out of his throat, and he gives me a dark look, and I think I might finally get the version of him I've wanted for so long.

"Take this off." He nods to the bustier I have on, and I fumble my fingers over the hook and eye closures, in a hurry before he changes his mind

"Slowly, you don't have to rush," he adds.

I do as he asks, and I let it fall to the floor, and it reveals the see-thru lace bra I have on underneath, and his eyes drop to my nipples where they're already going hard. His thumb brushes over one through the lace, and I press toward him.

"Have you had this on all night?"

I nod.

"You should have told me that."

I smirk a little, but he's unamused.

"Take it off." Another gruff command echoes against the tiles, and I follow the order.

He leans forward, cupping one breast in his hand and then draws my nipple into his mouth, rolling his tongue over the tip in a way that has me gasping. He moves to the other one, flicking his thumb over the tip of the one he's just freed from his mouth, and I realize it might not take me long to beg him.

"You're so fucking perfect," he mutters, his eyes raking over my body like it's the first time he's really seeing me.

My fingers go to his shirt, and I look up at him. He pulls it off and I could die from how pretty this man is. He's the perfect kind of fit, where he has all the muscles but the soft skin over them that makes it look like he likes the gym but not too much. His abs are framed by the valleys of his hips, a soft vee that teases how good the rest of him must be. And it is good. I have to bite my lip to keep from smiling when I think exactly how good it was in my mouth earlier.

"You already had your turn," he says, like he can read my mind. "Go lay down on my bed for me."

I look up at him, and a smug little grin, one that promises me that I'm going to have all I want answers my questioning look. I do as he says, trying to act as casual and comfortable as possible despite the fact I'm anxious.

He follows me into the room and bends down to grab something out of his gym bag before he comes over to me. He holds out his hand, showing me a black resistance band he'd pulled out.

"You sure you want this?"

And just imagining it around my wrists makes me clench my thighs. I nod.

"I want to hear it."

"Yes. I want you to use it."

His jaw clenches, his lip curling up just a little bit.

"Stretch your hands up then, grab the bars."

I do as he asks, the metal cold against my fingers. I'd always liked the industrial look of his bed but now I wondered if this was the reason he had it. I was definitely never looking at it the same again.

He gently wraps one wrist, threads the band behind the bars and then wraps the other one. He's tied them loosely, and if I really wanted out of them, I could slip them off easily but the illusion they create is still hot as fuck.

"You want them off for any reason, you just say so, yeah?"

I nod. Too worried if I talk I'm going to sound as breathless and turned on as I am. He smiles at me again and then his eyes run over me, and they darken. He reaches down, his knuckles grazing over me from the small dip at the base of my neck, down between my breasts, over my stomach, and over my panties. He climbs on the bed and settles between my thighs, still looking at me.

"Honest to god Liv, you're so fucking beautiful. That you needed help with confidence is a fucking crime. And if I contributed to that, I'm sorry for it." He runs his hand over my thigh and draws my right leg up, bending over to kiss the inside of my knee.

"What's also crazy," he hooks his fingers into my panties and drags them down slowly over my thighs and calves until he pulls them off and tosses them to the side. "Is how fucking good you taste."

He leans over and presses a soft kiss between my thighs, the rough stubble of his jaw creating a counter sensation that has me rocking my hips forward. He parts me with his fingers and takes a long languid stroke of his tongue that has me wishing I could have him like this every single night of my life.

"You're so fucking good at that," I whisper.

"You like this?" he asks, sliding his tongue over my clit again.

"Yes. So much."

He slides his fingers inside me, gentle strokes that have me rocking against him for more.

"This is one of the things I think about when I get off. The sounds you make. How no one else knows how good you taste."

He gives me his tongue again, a soft gentle touch at first and then the rough stroke of the flat of his tongue as he picks up the pace of his fingers inside me. I spread my thighs wider, not caring how desperate I must look because I just want more of everything he's doing to me.

Then he slows down, an agonizingly slow pace before he pulls away again. I whimper.

"Fuck you've got me so hard, Sunshine. The way you look tied up like that, making those sounds while you roll your hips."

"I want more of you," I plead.

"More of me?" His brow furrows.

"I want you to fuck me."

I feel like I've said something wrong because his fingers that had been working me at a slow pace go still inside me.

"You said you wanted to," I whisper, trying to explain why I'd ask for it.

"I do."

"So do it. I'll beg if you want."

"Liv..." I hear the hesitation in his voice. The bossy confident tone disappearing under it.

"Liam... I've never wanted it as much as I do right now. As much as I want you. So if you're worried about me, don't."

"Fuck," he curses and stands, stripping out of the rest of his clothes and grabbing a condom out of the nightstand.

And I could fucking explode with the anticipation. The silhouette of him as he stands next to the bed is one of the sexiest things I've ever seen, and I watch as he rolls the condom on and climbs back in between my legs, kneeling there before he leans forward again.

One hand gingerly strokes over my clit, a finger sliding through my wetness dragging the edge of my orgasm back to life before he reaches up and undoes the ties.

He looks down at my face, "I don't want you tied up like this when I take you the first time, okay?"

I nod, and the way he looks at me is like nothing I've ever seen before, a reverence like... like a word I don't want to say. Hopes I don't want to entertain. Because I just want to enjoy this right now. I'm getting him the way I've wanted him since we started this. I pull my hands from above my head; there's a little bit of soreness in my shoulders that's going to remind me of this tomorrow.

"You're sure?" he asks, his eyes soft as he studies my face.

"Completely." The most sure of anything I've ever been in my life is that I want this man, and anything he'll give me tonight.

He brushes his knuckles over my jaw, looking at me like he's trying to remember something, just before he slides inside me, and I gasp a little as he fills me. He swallows it up by kissing me, softly at first and then more desperate as he grabs one of my thighs and digs his fingers in. He fucks me in slow steady strokes that hit almost perfectly every time, and I just want to thank every lucky star I have that he's this good.

"Fuck, Sunshine. If I'd known this is how good you feel..." he whispers when he lets my lips go.

"Holy fuck," I can't help the little smile that comes because everything about him is better than I thought it would be.

He leans his weight on one hand and uses the other to cradle my jaw, his thumb swiping over my lower lip as he looks at me with an intensity that I feel like I could melt under. Something shifts in eyes, and it worries me.

"What is it?" I ask.

"Would you have kissed me back?" The question is so quiet I almost think I imagined it, but the serious look on his face tells me I didn't.

And I know what he means. What he's asking.

"Yes. I wanted you to kiss me," I confess, the dirty truth that's lain silent and unspoken between us for years. Because yes, I would have kissed him. It might make me a terrible person, because while I would have felt sick with the guilt, I don't know that I would ever have felt sorry for it.

His lips crash on mine then, like I've given him something he needed, and I kiss him back, rolling my hips and urging him on. He fucks me harder then, and it doesn't take much before I feel the first wave of my orgasm. He follows me a few moments later, telling me how gorgeous I am and how good I feel, until we're both spent.

After he takes care of the condom and I sneak back into the bed from the bathroom, I stare at him for a minute, studying his face before I kiss his cheek. Bringing us back to our usual ritual, one that feels safe.

"Night Liam," I smile at him before I close my eyes to sleep.

"Night Liv."

TWENTY-THREE

Liam

YES SHE WOULD HAVE KISSED me. Yes she would have wanted me even if he was still there. Yes she could have been mine. That's all I can think about as I finally drift off to sleep. I was an asshole for asking the question, but I needed to know. Needed some way to believe that she might have picked me if there had been a choice to make. If the worst hadn't happened.

The ease with which she said it, combined with the way she felt and the soft moans she made every time I hit her just right makes me feel so fucking good, so fucking close to perfect for the first time that I can ever remember. And that combined with the win I had on the field today makes me feel like I've gotten far more than I deserved in way too short of a time. But I'm too greedy to care. Too fucking high on the way she'd asked me for what I wanted. It was going to hurt like hell to come down from, but right now I didn't fucking care.

. . .

SHE STIRS in the middle of the night and when I open my eyes I see her naked silhouette as she drinks a glass of water. All the curves and valleys of her body lit up by the light coming in through the partially shaded window. She looks gorgeous. And in my room looking like this in the middle of the night she looks like *mine*.

She climbs back into bed, the scent of her perfume and her shampoo washing over me, and I reach out an arm to pull her close to me. She lines her body up against mine, a soft sigh as she finally settles in. My arm splays across her stomach and her touch runs over my arm to my hand, her fingers lacing with mine as she drags them down between her thighs.

My fingers brush against her, and she's already warm and wet for me. My breath catches in my lungs when she finally speaks.

"I want *you*," she whispers, rolling her hips back so her ass is nestled right against me as I'm going hard.

"Say it again," I kiss her shoulder.

"I need you, Liam, please."

Her soft breathy voice is like a direct line to my dick; a few words and she controls me. And it's me she wanted tonight. Me she wants again when she wakes up in the middle of the night wet and needy, and I'm not about to deny her.

"There's a condom in the nightstand," I kiss my way down her spine as she reaches to pull the drawer open and retrieve one. She hands it off to me and rolls over to watch me put it on, a little smirk dancing across her face.

"Something amuse you, Sunshine?"

"How hot you are. That I get to sleep with you."

The sincerity with which she says it makes my chest ache, and I reach forward to cup her jaw and run my thumb over her lower lip before I kiss her. I draw back and her eyes look heavy with want.

"Yeah, well I'm the lucky one. That you want me at all." I smile.

"I'm yours any time you want me," she brushes her lips over mine and pulls close to me, hooking her leg over my hip. She rocks forward, teasing the tip of my dick and I pull her lip between my teeth as I rock myself into her.

"Fuck," she gasps. "You feel so good. So perfect."

This woman is going to kill me with the things she says. The way she makes me feel. The way I want her. The way I love her. How I need her. And that chill runs down my spine, just as her fingernails climb up it, pulling me closer as she rocks her hips up and down.

I let her control the pace, let her take what she wants while I try to reconcile what's happening. Her fingers run over my body, and she kisses me slowly, like she can't get enough. And it doesn't take her long before she's coming apart again, taking me with her a few minutes later. Bringing me back down to earth.

As I lay there next to her still breathing hard, I realize how badly I've fucked up here. How often I've colored outside the lines of the assignment with her. I fucked his girl. The one he loved. The one he would have broken my jaw over. The one I tried to steal from him when he wasn't looking.

Not because she needed my help tonight. Her confidence was fine. She was flirting with a frat boy just fine until I'd said she was mine. Because I wanted it. I wanted her. My friends are right. She's right. I'm the selfish prick that fucks things up for her just before she can escape my orbit.

Worst of all I've betrayed her in the process. This was supposed to be about her. Her freedom. Her confidence. Her getting out from under my shadow. And instead I've taken advantage of her. Taken things I don't fucking deserve.

But my stupid fucking heart thinks it can fix it. Still trying to think of a way that this all works out in the end. Except I'm no good at relationships. Every single one I've had has been a short-lived failure, where we end up arguing about how much time football takes up in my life. Then there's the fact that I'm headed for the NFL, and she's headed for grad school and the real world.

None of this is going to end well, unless our friendship can stand it. That much we had promised each other. That was one of the rules. The rules were the guard rails. The things that were supposed to keep all of this on track. And the last one was the most important. Because I could not afford to lose her, especially not now.

So after tonight, this experiment is over.

"That was really... really good," she whispers, a smile dancing across her face as she looks over at me. My stomach tightens as I try to figure out how to be the coach again. How to be the bigger person and pull us out of this mess even if I don't want to.

"Yeah, it was. But it has to be the last time," I say quietly.

TWENTY-FOUR

Olivia

"IT HAS to be the last time," he says it so quietly I almost want to ask him to repeat it. But I heard him. I just don't want it to be real.

"The last time?" I ask, as though I can't possibly imagine what he's talking about. Even though I know our agreement.

"The last time. The last night like we agreed before."

And just like that he's done. Done with us. At least like this.

"Right. So what happens now?"

"We go back to being friends. Like we said we would."

"I see," I look over at him, trying to figure out how the man who could be everything he was to me tonight and every other night before this, could be the same one talking right now.

"Don't look at me like that."

"Like what?"

"Like I'm an asshole. I did what you asked of me. I did this experiment with you. The coaching sessions. They were supposed to be my penance to get you to forgive me."

The last bit cuts like a knife. The rest is reasonable. I'd pushed for more than he was willing to give. He had a right to say no. But acting like fucking me was a chore was too much.

"I'm sorry I put you through that," I say sarcastically

"Olivia... I did it happily. But we have to stop now. With everything on the line, and tonight just reminded me why this is... of why it's complicated."

"Complicated... got it," I stand up and start putting my clothes on.

"Where are you going?"

"Home."

"It's the middle of the night."

I shrug, "So there won't be much traffic."

"You were drinking."

"Hours ago, and not that much."

Hell even if I was drunk, having the guy I'd just had mind-blowing sex with tell me that fucking me was penance was enough for me to call a car if I needed to. I've got my clothes on and now it's just a matter of making sure I've got both shoes.

"Liv. Fuck!" He stands up and rounds me, putting himself between me and the door.

"What?"

"Stop talking to me like that. Like you're a fucking robot."

"How would you like me to talk, Liam?"

"Like you're my fucking friend."

I take a deep breath. Like a friend. I could do that. Maybe.

"We just had sex. And yes, it is technically the end of our agreement, but it was still *us* having sex. So being told at the end of it that it has to be the last time, case closed. Like it was some sort of clinical assignment you've painfully managed to push through, is uh, less than ideal, *friend*."

"I didn't mean it like that. I just mean this feels like it's getting complicated, and I want things to go back to normal before it ruins our friendship. I need you, Liv—my best friend—right now. With all the pressure coming up. I need you there with me. I can't afford to lose you. I did what you asked, so please do what I'm asking. What we agreed to."

"You're not losing me. I'm just going home, Liam."

"It feels like more than that."

"Because I feel more than that. I have feelings for you more than that. Okay? And I know that wasn't the agreement, but if you want me to stuff them back away it's going to take time and distance."

I'm mentally begging him to say anything here. He doesn't even have to tell me he has feelings for me, he just has to say something, anything that will take the sting out of this burn. Something that will make me feel like I'm not a complete idiot who started this whole mess trying to fuck him out of my system and only managed to get dragged down under the riptide. But he just stares at me, like I've lost my mind. Like I've said the worst possible thing he could imagine.

"You *cannot* have feelings for me!" He practically shouts the words at me and given that it's late I'm now hoping he doesn't wake half the hungover people in this house.

"Don't yell!" I whisper shout back, trying to get past him out of the door, but he continues to stand in the way. He takes a breath and then levels me with another look, one that makes my heart pound and sink at the same time. This was going to be the lecture about how I fucked up. Lovely.

"You don't have feelings for me. There was attraction between us, sure. But that's not the same thing as feelings. You're confusing the line here and that's exactly why I said it's complicated. This was just a friends with benefits thing. We did it so you could build your confidence. So you could go date and fuck other guys. You know I have to focus on football. You know that he is always going to be there even if we don't talk about it. This wasn't an arrangement where you can catch feelings, Liv."

"Oh, well. Thank you for explaining that to me. I'll be sure to give my heart the mansplained memo, Liam."

Fucking fuck. How *did* I have feelings for him? He was an asshole.

I grab my purse off his desk and stuff my phone into it, thankful I managed to notice before I left the room because that return trip would have been humiliating. When I reach for the door this time he doesn't cut me off, doesn't try to make me stay. Apparently telling him I have feelings was the easiest way to get Liam Montgomery to back off. If only I'd thought of it sooner.

TWENTY-FIVE

Liam

EVERYONE GIVES me their drink orders as I stand to walk up to the bar except Liv, so I turn to her just before I leave, trying to catch her eyes while she seemingly does everything she can to ignore me.

"Do you want anything?"

She doesn't even look at me and it cuts like a knife. It's been almost a week. She'd promised we'd stay friends, but she never said how good of friends, and this felt more like the relationship between East and Wren than it did her and me. I feel like I'm being iced out ever since we ended things the other night. It hadn't been like it was with Mason. Not the same kind of fight. Not screaming and glass breaking. Just her leaving in the middle of the night. And now there's a canyon between us and I hate it.

"I'll get my own, thanks."

She stands up and heads to the bar, and I trail behind her,

wishing there was something I could do to fix this. My eyes drift down to watch her walk, the swing of her hips and the way the skirt she has on tonight fits her curves perfectly. To be fair, I didn't know how to be friends anymore either. I struggled to look at her, because instead of my cute friend laughing in a cardigan over some joke one of the linemen told at party, I see the woman dressed in lingerie demanding I undo the damage I caused by giving her lessons. I see the woman who drags me into a pantry at a party. The woman who looks at me like I'm the only thing she's ever wanted in the world. And I don't know how you hit the back button on that. I don't know how to delete that version of her from my memory, and I desperately need to.

I flag the bartender down and we both give our orders. I try to distract myself by glancing at the TV over the bar to see what the scores are on the games tonight, but suddenly a familiar person appears beside us, one with a freshly healed face giving Liv a lopsided grin.

"You two still haven't worked your shit out, huh?" He gives her a once over I do not like.

"Mason..." her voice is a warning.

"I'm just saying. You really should. Then you could put a stop to all the collateral damage you two cause, you know?" He grins, but it doesn't go to his eyes and the glassy look in them makes me worry I'll have to break another part of his face tonight. She visibly winces at his comment, her shoulders slouching, and I instinctively wrap my arm around her waist, pulling her close to me. But I don't say a word. I know she won't want a scene and I don't want one either if it can be avoided.

"Hey, Mason," Easton saddles up next to us, surveying the scene like he's nervous for all the same reasons I am.

I glance back to see where Waylon is, because we might need him, but I can't see him anywhere in the crowd right now.

"Hey Easton." Mason's eyes light up at the sight of them. "I heard you took her home that night. Brave of you, considering. Doesn't look like he broke your pretty boy face though. He okay with loaning her out to friends, then?"

I feel every muscle in my body tighten, and I take a step forward. I'm ready to take him by his fucking throat and slam him against a wall if he says another word about her. Liv leans back against me, her hand wrapping around my wrist where my fingers are already balling into a first.

"Liam, please," she whispers and looks back over her shoulder.

"Listen friend, you've had a lot to drink. Maybe you should ease up? Get some water or some fresh air. Let me get the bartender to bring you some water," Easton smiles at him, staying cool like he always does.

Another smarmy grin from Mason comes in response.

"Haven't had so much that I start calling people by the wrong name though. She get your name right, East? Or she call you someone else's too?" His eyes drift between Liv and East, and I feel my heart rate quicken.

I want to beat his ass, but I also want to know what the fuck he's talking about. The way Easton and Liv don't immediately correct him or ask what he's talking about makes me feel like there's a vein of truth here, and I don't like it. If East fucking touched her. If they've kept it a secret from me. My eyes search both of them, and they look fucking nervous. Liv more so than East and my gut churns. A sick thought that she's been using me as practice to try to get East makes me want to break shit.

"What is he talking about?" I keep my voice low, low enough that I hope only Liv can hear me.

Her head whips around and the worried look she gives me only doubles my anxiety. Easton must have heard me too, because he gives a surreptitious glance to Liv and then looks up at me before he wraps an arm around Mason's shoulders and waves over some of Mason's mutual friends.

"Did you fuck East?" I try to sound normal when I ask the question, but I sound possessed even to my own ears.

"Is there somewhere quiet we can go to talk?" Her eyes dance with worry, as she turns and looks up at me.

I pull my wrist out of her soft grip. She'd told me not to interfere when she said she was going to approach him for help. He had been her first choice. Her lack of denial makes me feel like I already have my answer, and I can't process the information. I can't face that kind of truth. The two of them together? It feels like my chest is caving in.

"Answer the question," I stare at her.

"No. Nothing happened with East. But can we have this discussion alone? You're attracting attention."

"Right, and God forbid we have a fucking scene."

"I don't want us all to get kicked out and for you guys to have to answer to your coaches, okay?"

"I'm much more interested in what he thinks happened between you and East," I take her wrist though and start walking out of the main part of the bar, down a hall that leads toward the billiards rooms that's usually empty. And thankfully it is tonight. I watch her, waiting for her to explain. But she doesn't.

She studies the wall and the memorabilia on it carefully, like it holds real interest for her, her face overwritten with worry. It only serves to make me feel that much more anxious.

"Just fucking spill it, Liv."

"I don't really owe you any explanations at this point, you know," her eyes meet mine with a look of defiance that kicks my heartbeat up another notch.

"You can tell me, or Mason can tell me. But one way or another, I'm getting answers."

She shakes her head, like I'm a disappointment to her and then crosses her arms over her chest.

"I wasn't totally honest about my breakup with Mason."

"Yeah. I caught that much. Because why? Because Easton was the reason? What the fuck is Mason talking about with you saying the wrong name? Didn't realize you were such a fucking heartbreaker."

"Please. We dated a month. Mason's heart didn't break. Maybe his ego." She glares at me through the dim light.

"Why?" I practically shout the word.

"I may have called him the wrong name."

I frown, "Meaning what exactly?"

"When we were um... hooking up, or about to. We were at a party and things were getting heated, so we went into another room. His hands were up my skirt and—" her eyes float to mine like she's worried.

"He was fingering you. I get the picture," I grit out, because it's an image I really don't want of the two of them.

"And I might have moaned the wrong name. I tried to pretend like I didn't, but he wasn't having it. He was understandably angry and asked me to leave. I tried to talk him out of breaking up with me but yeah... So I was crying when I left the room and I ran into East on my way out of the party. East was ready to beat his ass until I explained it was my fault and then East offered to take me home, so I left with him."

"Did anything happen between you and East? You need to tell me the fucking truth here."

"No. Absolutely not. Mason is making shit up. But I did tell East what happened because I was upset, and he thought maybe Mason had done something to me."

I frown again, because this whole thing still doesn't make sense. Why Mason was so bent out over it. Why he was talking shit to me and East.

"Whose name was it?" I look up at her, and she freezes like a deer in headlights.

"That's not really relevant, is it? I just fucked up and I made him mad. Apparently, he's still bitter about it."

I don't like that she's still concealing this. Like she's still worried I'm not going to like it, and I can feel my temper flare again.

"Whose fucking name, Liv?"

"Yours. Fuck! Yours, okay?"

"What?" I feel like the wind has been knocked out of my lungs. It wasn't the answer I was expecting.

I stare at her. They broke up before anything happened between us. Before she asked to try this whole friends-with-benefits experiment. Their breakup was supposedly the reason she needed help.

"I said your name. And given that you broke his nose, he made a lot of assumptions about us. That I was using him to make you jealous."

"What?" I repeat the word again because I don't have any others. I just keep trying to process this information, and no matter how many times I rewind, it doesn't make sense.

"So I guess he thinks maybe I used East too. I don't know. I don't understand drunk Mason logic. We weren't together long enough for me to get the hang of it," she shrugs, and continues to look over my shoulder instead of at me.

I lean on the wall next to her, watching her and trying to puzzle this out. The swell of nausea I'd had over Easton and her finally subsiding, but a new well of something replacing it. Little patches of tinder setting up as I put the pieces together in my head. Realizing that the only answer is that my sweet little best friend was a hell of a lot more devious than I'd given her credit for.

"So let me get this straight... You and Mason are hooking up, and in the middle of it you moan my name?"

"Freudian slip?" She looks at me sheepishly.

I eye her like I don't exactly believe that.

"Then Easton, who you confessed this to, locks us out on a fucking balcony together. Where you climb in my lap and ride me like a fucking pro."

"I did not have anything to do with being locked out there. I was as surprised as you were. And very drunk if you remember."

"Uh huh. And then, when I talk to you about it to try to ask for a way to not fuck up our friendship, you ask me for lessons because Mason didn't work out."

"That technically was the truth."

"Yeah, I mean if a woman called me another name while I was making her come I think I might not have the greatest review of that experience," I level her with a look that tells her she's being obtuse.

"I didn't think you'd want that much detail about the encounter, given that you'd broken his nose over less."

"You didn't think me knowing you called out my name while you were fucking around with him was an important piece of information for me to have? Especially prior to asking me for help?"

"I didn't really want to admit that; no."

"Why'd you say my name?"

TWENTY-SIX

Olivia

"WHY DO YOU THINK?" I retort because I don't want to deal with him pretending to be dense.

"I don't want to think, Liv. I want to *know*."

We stare at each other for a beat, a battle of wills before I finally give in.

"Because I was imagining it was you. Okay? You happy now?"

"Was it the first time?"

I give him a look that tells him to fuck off, and the asshole has the audacity to grin. It makes my stomach flutter and a swirl of want wind its way down my spine. And I hate it.

"So when you asked me for the lessons?"

"I thought it would help me get over it. I thought if I just fucked you out of my system that I could move on. We could go back to being friends. And look! Here we are, being friends."

"Yeah. Back to being friends," he scrubs a hand over his

face and looks up to the ceiling. An exasperated smile flitting across his face. "It's impressive honestly. I had no idea you could be so devious. I thought I was helping my sweet best friend with a problem and the whole time you were trying to seduce me," his eyes flash to mine, and I can't read them.

"I wasn't trying to seduce you, Liam. Don't make it sound so scandalous. I just wanted out of the friend zone temporarily."

"Out of the friend zone temporarily," he lets out a derisive laugh. "And what about what I wanted?"

"Don't act like I had to drag you kicking and screaming. As I recall you were pretty happy to help. In fact, I was surprised by how little you fought me on it," I give him an accusing glance because I'm fairly certain, the more I think about it, I wasn't always in the friend zone for him either.

"Because like I told you, you're gorgeous. I wanted you, but I knew it was a bad idea. I knew it would fuck up our friendship, and I didn't want to lose that. But then you made it seem like I'd be helping you, making up for some of the things you were upset with me about."

"Well, good news. It helped. And then you being an asshole right there at the end? That really cleared things up. Now I'm over it, and we can be back firmly in the friend zone," I give him a bright smile.

"Until you call the next guy my name at least, right?" He flashes a smug look back at me.

The fucking audacity.

"You wish!" I turn to walk away because I don't need any more of this. Liam always makes me feel way too damn much—whatever the emotion is, I get in spades with him, and I can't take it. I don't have the capacity for it tonight. I'm still too raw, too angry and now too embarrassed from this whole confrontation.

But his arm wraps around my waist before I can get far, and he hauls me against him.

"I don't fucking wish. I know, because even now when you're pissed at me you're still giving me those big hazel fuck-me eyes."

"You're imagining things," I argue, frustrated that I'm this transparent to him.

Half of an annoyed laugh leaves his throat, and he bends down to bring his lips closer to my ear, his tone is sharp, as he brushes his fingers under my jaw. "Liv, you forget. I fucking *know* you. And now thanks to your experiment I know every single part of you. So don't lie to me."

"I'm not dignifying that with a response."

"You won't?" His hand drifts down my side and then up my thigh, grabbing my skirt and pulling it up.

"Stop me," he whispers.

I stay silent, because I want him to touch me. And he knows I want him to touch me. So there's zero use in pretending otherwise. His fingers slide under my underwear, finding exactly what he wants.

"I fucking knew it," he growls against my ear, and then presses a kiss against my jaw.

"Good for you," I snap back.

"Yeah, you're always *good* for me," I can feel him smile against my skin.

He slides two fingers inside me, slowly working me as his thumb brushes over my clit. I can't stop the little stuttered breath that comes out of my mouth, and he makes an answering sound of self-satisfied approval.

"Is this how he was doing it? How it felt when you said my name?"

Holy fuck. Every time I think I know this man, he does something else that I have no idea how to react to. I want him and I hate him in equal measures right now, and I have no idea what we're doing. No idea what he's thinking given that he was the one who wanted to go back to being strictly friends. Something I don't know how to do.

"Friends don't act like this, remember?" I try for a half-hearted scold, but it just comes out breathless.

"I'm not your friend tonight."

"I don't know if we're friends at all anymore."

"You're probably right," he pulls his hand away from me. "And in that case, take the panties off."

"What?" There's no way I heard him right.

"You fucking heard me."

I hear the sound of his zipper, and I turn to look at him wide-eyed.

"What are you doing?"

"Fucking you, unless you wanna lie again and say you don't want me to."

He pulls a condom out of his pocket, and it pisses me off. A little slice across my heart reminding me that now that we're over there are going to be other women.

"You just happen to have a condom? Planning to go home with someone tonight?" I know I'm being petulant and unreasonable, but I can't help it.

"No, but I knew I was going to see you." He looks up at me, his eyes going soft around the edges, and it melts all the anger I thought I had for him. Anger I really need to resist him.

"Anyone could see us here," I look back down the dark hall as I take my panties off. Knowing this is probably the worst idea I've agreed to in my life. It's still empty and quiet down here, but it wouldn't take much to change that.

He shrugs as he puts the condom on, "Let them."

I turn and put my palms against the wall, anxiously biting the inside of my cheek. I want him too much to say no to this, but I can't help the little voice telling me I should run. That this is only going to compound the pain and the problems between us.

"No," he grunts, grabbing me by the hips and turning me around, right before he grips my ass and hauls me up, pinning me to the wall as he slides inside me. "I want to watch you when you say my name again."

Yeah, this was bad. Liam's pissed off possessive side is hot as hell. And when he talks to me like this it melts everything—my panties, my heart, all my defenses against him. Plus he's right. He knows me. He's not some guy I just started dating or a quick hookup. He's the one who can read every look on my face, every inflection in my voice. I can't hide from him. And all of that is what has me pinned up against a wall in a dark hallway at a bar despite the fact I should be wiser than this.

"Fuck..." I whimper as he thrusts into me again. I wrap my legs tighter around him and curl my fingers into his neck.

"I can't get the sounds you make out of my head. The way you look at me. You have me all fucked up," he confesses as he quickens his pace, and his fingers dig into my ass.

"I'm sorry I didn't tell you the truth," I whisper, feeling guiltier than ever about how we ended up here.

He studies my face through heavy lids, "Yeah well, we both fucked up—a lot."

Not exactly forgiveness, but it felt like progress. I'd take it. I shut my mouth and my eyes then, letting him take us both to the edge. I was pretty certain I was going to have bruises on my back and on my ass to show for this, but I didn't care.

"Fuck... Liam..." I don't have a lot of words; he's fucking me hard enough it's nearly taking my breath away and each down stroke is edging me closer. I'm a mess, my body and my heart competing for which was going to fall apart first.

"Please," the word leaves me, and his eyes snap to my face,

falling hard on my lips like he wants to kiss me but won't let himself.

"Please, who?" he taunts, a hint of irritation still in his voice.

"Please, Liam," I say softly, hoping he knows that I didn't mean to put us here. To make a stranger out of my best friend.

He swallows the next whimper he pulls out of me by kissing me, and I feel my orgasm hit me in waves a moment later, racking over my body until the only thing holding me together is him.

When I can finally almost catch my breath again, he gently lowers me to the floor. He takes care of the condom as I pull my panties back on and smooth out my skirt. I dread the moment he walks back because I have no idea how he's going to react or what he's going to say to me. Usually, I know him. But this was the problem with the fact that I unlocked other versions of this man. I never know which one I'll get now.

"You okay?" he asks softly when he finally reaches me, looking me over with a hint of worry, like he might have broken me in the process.

"I'm fine," I answer as I sweep my hand over my skirt again, feeling like what we've done might as well be branded on me. I feel thoroughly fucked, so I'm positive I look it. And our friends will definitely know.

He brushes a kiss to my temple. "Let's go get a drink before we have to go back to the table. Something strong before we have to deal with them."

I smile a little that he's thinking the same thing as me and follow him down the hall back toward the bar. I have no idea what we're doing or where we're headed, and I still feel a little pull of anxiety in my chest. We needed to talk after this, really talk without the threat of it getting out of hand, but right now I was just happy to have a few real moments with him again.

TWENTY-SEVEN

Liam

TODAY IS the big fucking game against our rivals. The one we have to win if we want to advance to a championship title run, and everyone's adrenaline in the locker room is at an all-time high.

"You got this." Waylon looks at me as he tosses a bag in his locker.

"*We* got this." I answer him.

"Don't let them get in your heads boys. This is our fucking field. Our fucking game to lose." Easton yells out to the locker room, to resounding cheers that echo against the floors and walls.

I take a breath, looking down at my phone in my bag. I normally text Liv on game days. Our check ins are part of my game day ritual. She asks me how I'm doing. She tells me I've got this. But after the last week, and after how I acted last night I don't know if she'll answer. We should have talked, should have discussed where the fuck this was going but I don't know. I don't even know what I want to ask her for.

That wasn't entirely true. I knew what I wanted—I wanted her to be mine. But I didn't think I deserved it. Didn't think it was fair to build her confidence up, help her in her goal of having a senior year that wasn't in my shadow and then immediately try to pull her back in. Wasn't sure I could ever fully escape Tristan's shadow, or that his death and my weakness had meant she'd spent far too much time holding my hand.

Even this ritual where I texted her was part of that, had started when I wanted to quit, and she promised she'd be there for me. When she came to every home game and every practice she could make to cheer me on.

"You all right?" Ben looks over at me.

"Yeah. I'm fine." I shake my head. "Just in my head a little this morning. Warmups will clear it."

"Need anything?"

Liv. But she'd be here in the stadium. That much she'd said last night before she went home despite the fact we talked very little after I'd railed her in the hallway after I found out that she's had feelings for me all along. That she'd wanted me all along. Fuck, I still didn't know what to make of it. How to deal with it. But we'd talk after the game. That would have to be enough for now because I needed to get my head focused.

"Nah. I'm good." I jerk my chin, "Let's just get out there and throw a few, yeah?"

"Sounds good." Ben nods, grabbing his gloves and leading the way out.

TWENTY-EIGHT

Olivia

I'M RUNNING INSANELY late to the game. After my run in at the bar with Liam I drank a little too much and a little bit more when the girls and I got home and started rehashing what the fuck happened and what I was going to do. Which meant I forgot to set my alarm and overslept and have been hustling ever since to try to catch up.

I fire off my text to Liam, hoping it's not too late to catch him. The team has a designated period before the game that's a media blackout so they can try to get zoned into play and I'm worried I missed it. Although it's also strange I haven't heard from him. I've run late in the past and he always texts to check in on me.

A sinking feeling in my stomach makes me worry that's a bad sign for how he's feeling after last night.

THE GAME HAS BEEN LESS than great. You couldn't tell by the score as both teams have struggled to convert any of their down field progress into points, but Highland isn't clicking like it was the last game. Liam isn't having his best game either. He seems off, like he doesn't quite trust his instincts, the ones that normally serve him so well. The offensive line is struggling to hold the line too, and he's been sacked twice already. The second time for a major loss of yards on an important third down.

I can tell he's frustrated, trying to force plays even when they're falling apart, and I can see even from up here in the stands the way the guys are trying to boost each other's flailing confidence as the second quarter starts to get low on time.

They line up for the next play, and it's one Liam has executed well a million times. What should be a fade route between him and Ben starts to fall apart as the offensive line collapses under a blitz. He tries to scramble out of the pocket, but he can't escape as one of the defensive tackles breaks the line faster than he can see it. Huge arms reach out for him, and I gasp as I watch them fall.

The moment I see the way he falls on his knee, I feel my heart bottom out through my stomach. Even from the stands I can tell it's bad, and the way he grabs at it, his whole body contorting in pain as he slams his hand against the ground. I feel tears coming, and I start running down the steps. I don't know where I'm going or how I'll get down on the field, but I have to get to him. I hear Kenz running behind me, her feet on the steps as she yells my name after me.

Security stops me before I can cross the railing to the field. I cry to him, telling him that Liam is my boyfriend, and I have to get a better look to see if he's okay. I know I'm not being reasonable. That they won't actually let me down there. But I can't think straight. Fuck, I'd lie and say we were married if it would get me on the sidelines. I look out across the field and both teams are down on a knee, the whole stadium in hushed silence as the medical staff look him over.

I can hear a group behind me quietly discussing what they think happened to him. I hear another person say the game is fucked. And another one say it's his whole career down the drain. My anxiety ratchets up with every additional comment I hear murmuring through the crowd, every second longer that the medical staff sits by his side. I want a miracle. I want them to say he just overextended it a bit. He can sit out a few plays and get back on the field, but I know it's just wishful thinking.

"Liv!" Kenz catches up to me. "Come here, hon. Come here." She's winded from running after me but she wraps her arms around me. I look for Waylon on the field, and he looks like shit. Like he's about to lose his mind. His helmet's off and he nervously runs his hand over it. It was his missed tackle that had led to the sack. But it could have been anyone's.

They start to stabilize Liam's leg in a brace, and they load him onto a cart. I grab Kenz's hand and squeeze as they drive him off the field. The players take a time out, heading for the sidelines while they clear the field. I start fast walking to where I might be able to get someone on the sidelines to hear me, Kenz matching my pace as she looks to give Waylon reassurance.

"Where are they taking him?" I shout, to any of the guys who will listen to me.

Ben's on the sidelines, looking thoroughly rattled, like he's just seen the apocalypse unfold but he hears me. He looks up and realizes what I'm asking. He motions to one of the coaches and points to me. A moment later the coach comes over.

"You his girlfriend?" he asks.

I nod. It wasn't entirely true, but I did not care. "What hospital?"

"Memorial."

"Thank you."

I watch Kenz blow Waylon a kiss, holding her hand to her heart and mouthing that it wasn't his fault. He looks at her, but he looks rattled and distant, and the coaches have him sit the bench as they send players back out after the timeout. I turn and start heading for the entrance.

"Okay girl, you need to slow down. You don't need to get there before him. Give me your keys. I'm driving you."

"You can stay and watch the game. Waylon and them, they'll want you. He'll need you."

"Waylon would want me to drive you. We don't need both of you getting hurt on the same day. And you are way too anxious to be behind a wheel." She reaches for my purse and slides it off my shoulder. I don't stop her.

She's probably right. I can't see straight. I just want to get to him. I want to tell him everything is going to be fine. I can only imagine what's going through his head right now. How frustrated and heartbroken he must be. But he has to know we'd get through this like we got through everything. Surgery. Rehab. Whatever it was going to take, if anyone could do it, he could.

THE RIDE to the hospital is a blur, and when we get there they won't let me back immediately to see him. They want to vet who I am, and then they start telling me the family-only policy. I get snippy, out of character for me, but I'm mad because he needs to see someone who isn't hospital or coaching staff. I start demanding that they change their rules because they're asinine before Kenz intervenes for me, asking them if they can ask the patient who he wants to see. Explaining that he has no family who lives in the area and I'm the closest thing.

Smooth talking them in a way only she can, in a way that makes me seem like a well-meaning friend instead of the unreasonable ball of anxiety I am right now. They agree to check once he's been seen and send us to wait.

An hour later I'm pacing the waiting room. I looked up at the game which was playing on the TV here. We were by some miracle still winning even with the backup quarterback. East and Ben were playing lights out, and our linemen seemed as determined as ever to make up for the earlier sack. A turnover by our defense for a pick six means we're up by two scores and it's the end of the fourth quarter.

I'm wondering if they're letting Liam watch the game, if he can even bear to look at it when one of the medical assistants comes out and asks if I'm Liv. I jump up and Kenz follows me. I'm desperate to get back and see him.

"You're Liv?"

"Yes. Can I see him?"

"He asked me to let you know he's doing fine. We're just running some tests to assess the damage. There's not a lot of room for visitors and he's trying to rest."

"Trying to rest? But I need to see him." I feel dazed and my tears are burning at the back of my throat.

"I think he's in a bit of shock right now. It would probably be better to wait. Don't worry, okay? I know it's hard, but he's in good hands."

"Of course. His whole career is probably flashing in front of his eyes. Are you sure you told him who it was? I thought he'd want to see me," I say quietly.

"He didn't want any visitors, and like I said, there's not much room for people in the room he's in right now. So if you want to wait here, or I can tell him you'd like him to text you when he's up to it."

"Text me?" I mumble, still confused that he wouldn't want

to see someone right away. It didn't sound like Liam but who knows what he was thinking right now.

"Liv," Kenz wraps her arms around me again. "Thank you so much for the update. We appreciate it. We'll stay for a while in case he changes his mind. Will you tell him that? That we'll stay for a bit?"

"Will do." The woman offers me a pitying smile and nods at Kenz before she disappears back behind the doors.

"What the fuck is going on?" I look at Kenz, the tears rolling down my eyes.

"Hon, his world just fucking imploded, okay? And you know how he can be sometimes. He probably needs a few minutes."

"I know that; which is why I want to be there. He needs someone there."

"And we're gonna stay here, so that when that initial surge of adrenaline and pain killers clears he'll know we're right here waiting for him. Okay? I'm sure the guys are gonna come as soon as the game is over. We can get some dinner in the cafeteria."

"I don't want to eat," I grouch at her. It's unfair. I know somewhere in the depths of the more reasonable part of my mind that I'm being rude and unreasonable, but I can't wrap my head around the idea that he doesn't want to see me. Even after everything, the idea that he wouldn't want me there is... unfathomable.

"Well maybe just something to drink then. Okay? Not yet. We can sit here for a while still."

Kenz walks me back to the chairs and we sit down again. I stare out the window, wondering how any of this can be real.

SOMETIME LATER I hear Kenz talking to Waylon. She thinks I'm asleep, curled up on the chairs with my coat as a blanket, but really I've just been laying here wondering when or if he's going to see me. If he blames me for distracting him. Or maybe he just hates me after everything and therefore I'm the last person he wants to see. The thoughts have been spiraling through my head over and over again until I can't make sense of them anymore.

"He won't see her."

"What the fuck?" Waylon sounds as shocked as I felt. "I can get him not wanting to see us. Not wanting to see me. But her?"

"He won't see anyone I guess; the med assistant has come out twice now to tell us he's having tests and stuff but that's it."

"I'm gonna ask to go back. I need to apologize to him. It's my fucking fault. I fucked up. Whiffed on that play, and fuck Mac... fuck. I fucked up so bad."

"Waylon, it was not your fault. It wasn't even really the linebacker's fault. It was a freak accident. They've shown the replay a million times now on social media and it was obviously just an accident."

"If I didn't miss, the accident wouldn't have happened," Waylon's voice is laced with frustration.

"You can't be perfect, Waylon," I say at last, sitting up because I feel like an asshole eavesdropping on their conversation. "You're going to miss sometimes. It's the game. Kenz is right."

I wipe my cheeks, trying to clear the mascara stains I can see beneath my blurry vision.

"Are you okay?" Waylon gives me a pained look, and it sends me over the edge again. The tears start flooding and Mac and Waylon both hurry over to my side, wrapping me in a hug.

"I'm fine. I don't need the comfort. He does. But he won't let anyone back."

"I'm gonna see if he'll talk to me. Maybe he wants someone who won't sugar coat it." East stands from the other side of the waiting room where he'd been sitting next to Ben.

"Yeah, you should try," Waylon nods.

He heads for the information desk, and I just cross my fingers that Liam will let someone back.

TWENTY-NINE

Liam

THERE'S a knock at the door, and I look up to see East standing there wearing his post-game sweats and not his usual expensive shit.

"I thought you might be willing to talk to me," he comes around the side of my bed and leans back against the windowsill, out of the way of all the equipment in the room.

"I don't want to hear a fucking pep talk right now, and out of all of them you're the least likely to give it."

"Fair enough. Still gonna ask how you're doing though. They doing enough for pain management?"

"Yeah. Just with all the adrenaline and stress it still hurts like a mother fucker."

He glances down at my knee, the slightest wince crossing his face before he looks back at me.

"They tell you how bad it is yet?"

"They think it's just the ACL. They were worried it was

both at first. They don't see any stress fractures, but they want to do another round of X-rays and an MRI."

"Well, something to look forward to at least."

"Yeah. Something like that."

"Waylon thinks it's his fault."

"Fuck. You tell him it's not, okay? I know he won't listen. But it happens. I took too long to throw. Their blitz was phenomenal. I should have thrown or left the pocket sooner. He can't hold them all day."

"Trust me, we've all fucking told him."

"I'll text him later. I just... you know how he is. He'll fucking tell me it's going to be fine, and we both know it's not."

"Why don't you at least wait till they finish telling you that before you plan your demise?"

"I don't want to sit around hoping for things right now. I just want to face shit and get through the hard stuff first."

"Mmm..." East crosses his legs at the ankles and folds his arms, and I don't fucking like the look of it.

"I'm gonna regret letting you back here, aren't I?"

"I just think you should know; she's been here for hours. She's not gonna go home until she sees you. She's been curled up in a ball crying. It's hard to watch."

I shake my head, staring down at the sheet in front of me. I could have guessed that without him telling me. But I can't see her now. Now that I know for sure it has to be over between us.

"I can't fucking see her."

"I assume she told you the truth last night?"

"Yeah, and you're a fucking asshole for keeping that from me."

"She made me promise, and it wasn't my truth to tell. Besides you're the one who made her the football mom. You can't be surprised when we're all just as loyal to her."

I grunt. He's not entirely wrong, but I'm not about to admit it.

"So you pissed at her for that or what? You seemed off even before the game, and I know you two went off last night."

"I'm not pissed at her. Last night we worked things out."

"Worked things out or fucked things out?"

"More of the latter."

East gives me a sly grin before he lapses back into serious mode, and for a second I think I might get out of this without having to have a fucking heart to heart.

"So now you know she's been hung up on you for a while, and you already knew she worships the ground you walk on. So why are you letting her cry her eyes out in the waiting room?"

"This is the shit I expect from Ben or Waylon, not from you."

"Well maybe I'm getting soft in my old fucking age. Or just curious, because it doesn't fucking make sense to me."

"I can't be with her. I felt guilty enough before with everything. But now? I'm a fucking liability. You know she'll fucking drop everything again to take care of me. And that's not how she should be spending this year. That was the whole fucking reason I agreed to help her, so she could get confidence and come out from being in my shadow. I'm not gonna let her give all of that up, so she can take care of my broken ass. And for what? A fucking has-been with no future? Fuck that. Let her have a real life." A derisive laugh rips out of my throat, one that threatens to turn into something else.

Because right now, I want her more than anything. I want to see her face. I want to hear her voice. I want to fucking kiss her and remember that I have some good things left. But I'm not gonna drag her down with me. Not again. Not when I can do better this time.

"Have you met her? And the rest of her bad bitch squad? You think that's gonna work?" Easton eyes me skeptically.

"Eventually she'll give up."

East rubs a hand over his mouth and raises his eyebrows, silencing whatever commentary he was about to make.

"What?"

"I think it's a mistake. I don't know a lot about relationships, but I know Olivia well enough to know you're gonna fuck that up royally doing what you're doing. And I know you well enough to know you're probably gonna live to regret it."

"I won't regret it when I see her fucking happy and not wasting her time on me."

"Yeah? You want to see Mason back with her?"

"Please, you'd fucking go back to a girl that called you another guy's name?"

"If not him, another guy like him. He's gonna see her hurting and be so fucking happy to try and fix it for her. And you're not gonna be there to stomp around her and break his face."

"It is what it is," I shake my head, even though my stomach feels sour, and I wonder if I might fucking lose what little food I still have in it.

"You're a bigger fucking idiot than I thought. But that's your fucking choice."

"I appreciate you respecting it," I grit out.

"All right." East looks up when a nurse walks in the room and checks my chart. "I'm gonna leave you alone, but you text me and let me know what you need. I can pick your parents up from the airport. Sneak you some decent food in. Give you a ride home. You just keep me posted, all right?"

"Thanks. I'll let you know," I nod. East nods back and heads out of the room.

My parents wouldn't be coming though. I wouldn't let

them even if they could, but I know they're both involved in a high-profile case right now and don't have time to fly out here to deal with a non-life-threatening injury. I'll get discharged tonight or tomorrow. I'll have to have surgery. They'll video chat to check in on me. Maybe send my sister out for a day if shit looked particularly dire. But they'll be no more interested in wallowing in all the problems this created than I am and would likely just leave me to my own devices unless I ask for help.

The nurse looks me over and lets me know they'll bring me some food soon and that the doctor will come and go over some of the test results with me within the hour.

When I look down, my phone lights up with another text. It's Liv again. Another desperate request to come back and see me, begging me to let her just come back for a minute, promising that she won't be a ball of fucking sunshine. Swearing she can be as much of a dick as East can.

And it breaks my fucking heart to ignore it. But it would break it more if I watched her give up shit to help me. If I dragged her back down the rabbit hole of my bullshit, and this injury is likely going to cause a whole host of it once I have time to process.

East was right. I'd probably live to regret it. Right about the time I had to watch her with another guy and pretend like I was happy for her. But I'd take that any day over fucking up her life again.

THIRTY

Olivia

"SO YOU'VE SEEN HIM?" I come down the stairs in a hurry when I hear Waylon and Kenz talking about Liam in the kitchen, and the context sounds an awful lot like the great King Liam has deigned to let other people visit him.

Waylon whips around grimacing at the fact that I've caught him, and Kenz gives me a pained look. They exchange glances before Kenz looks back up at me.

"Yes, he finally let Waylon go talk to him. But it took a lot of convincing. Ben and them say he barely comes out of his room right now."

"I want to go see him," I feel my heart cracking, the fact that he refuses to see me is making it hard for me to eat and sleep. He must be pissed at me. Blame me or the stupid experiment for being a distraction. Us fighting the night before was probably part of the reason he wasn't completely with it that day. I feel awful. I want the chance to apologize in person.

"I talked to him about it," Waylon glances at me before his eyes dart back to the floor.

"And?"

"He won't see you."

"Why?" The tears come immediately. That's how it is these days, like I'm broken and the slightest nudge causes waterworks. "Does he blame me?"

Kenz rushes over and wraps her arms around me.

"I want to tell him I'm sorry, if he does. I want the chance to fix it," I blubber on, ugly crying and Waylon makes a face like I've broken him.

"Don't cry, Olivia. I can't watch you cry. Okay? I am sorry. He's being a dick. He doesn't blame you. He's just going through all the stages of grief about this right now."

"But he will see everyone except me, why?"

Waylon's eyes flash to mine and then back across the room. There's a guilty look in them, and I can tell immediately there's something more Waylon knows and doesn't want to share. But I need to know.

"He told you why..." I say bitterly.

"He... he did. But he also swore me to not get involved."

"You're fucking involved Waylon. You're his best friend, and you're dating my best friend. There's no way you're not involved."

"Liv..." Kenz says softly. She doesn't have to elaborate because I know she's doing her best.

"I'm sorry. I'm sorry. I'm being shitty. I'm just a wreck. I'm begging you Waylon, at least tell me why so I can know why this is happening. I won't tell him you told me."

Waylon takes a deep breath and looks to Kenz.

"Tell her," she whispers.

"Fuck!" He scrubs a hand over his face. "If I tell you... You have to promise that you won't kill the messenger or go storming over there. I'm only telling you because I think he's being an ass about everything right now. But it still makes me feel like shit to break my promise to him."

"And you know, you owe me, I was instrumental in getting you two together. So you can tell him I guilted you." I try to offer Waylon an out because I feel sorry for him too. Liam was being cruel to everyone these days it seemed.

"That too. That's going to be my excuse when he inevitably finds out I talked to you and tries to murder me for it."

"Good. So talk," I say wiping my tears away and trying to steel my spine for whatever I was about to find out.

"He didn't expand much on his thoughts. So don't expect much. He just said that you spent way too much time helping him before, that you sacrificed too much for him over the years, that you would again and that he wasn't going to let you do it."

"Sacrifice what? I just want to help my friend when he's going through awful shit."

"He said you just got your confidence back and you had plans for what you wanted shit to look like this year and helping him was going to ruin that for you."

"I get to decide what ruins things for me. Not his bossy ass. What's ruining things for me is the fact I can't sleep because my best friend is going through hell, and he won't even fucking see me." The tears return, even though I don't want them. Even though they feel like a massive inconvenience to my anger rather than anything remotely cathartic.

"And why the fuck can't he say this stuff to my face? Why can't we talk like adults?"

"I suggested that, but he said the two of you will just argue and he'd rather leave things the way you left them."

"I see. Anything else?"

"There's something else he wanted me to tell you. But I

think it's a lie, and I think it's going to hurt you. You'd be better off not hearing it."

I feel my blood go cold at the same moment my stomach is set ablaze with a fire that feels like it's burning me from the inside out.

"Tell me."

"I don't think—"

"Just tell me, Waylon, or I'll probably imagine something even worse."

"He said to tell you," Waylon looks to Kenz and then at the floor. His expression is so pained I feel like him telling me is almost hurting him too. "He said that he doesn't love you. That you're a good friend, and he cares about you—which is why he doesn't want you wasting more time on him."

I open my mouth to speak, but nothing but a small croak comes out. It's like someone's given me a knockout punch to my lungs. All the air in them is gone with one swift delivery of words.

Doesn't love me.

I could take that he didn't want to be with me. That he wasn't attracted to me anymore. That he didn't see a future for us. All of those would have hurt, but they would have been things that I could get over in time. But doesn't love me? A slideshow of moments of the two us, not just in recent history but a million more stretching all the way back to high school winds through my mind and then twists around at the end, leading here, catching fire with three small words. Doesn't love me.

Kenz hugs me tighter, and I sit down on the steps.

"Liv, I'm serious when I say I think he's lying. It's just him trying to push you away while he deals with shit. This is why I didn't want to tell you."

I shake my head, and then pull out of Kenz's grip and run

back up the stairs. I regret ever having come down them. I feel my stomach roil, like I might be sick, too many emotions and tears that I needed to get rid of.

I hear the patter of Kenz's feet up the stairs, and she jumps on the bed next to me, wrapping her arms around me as I cry some more.

"You know it's not true. We all know that it's not true," she repeats over and over again like it's some kind of balm that will keep me from falling apart. But it's too late. I'm a fucking mess.

"Even if it's not true, the fact that he would say it. That he would tell Waylon, Waylon of all people, to say that to me, knowing how much it would hurt. What does that say?"

I lay there for hours while the light turns to dark, while Kenz comes and goes several times. While I drift in and out of sleep, each time I wake up another jolt to my entire system when I remember that the person I'd relied on for so much didn't love me. That the thing that felt like a nightmare was actually reality.

I'D FALLEN ASLEEP AGAIN when my door creaks open and footsteps approach my bed.

"Liv?" Wren whispers.

"Yeah," my voice sounds hoarse from all the crying.

"I brought you some food from the bar. You need to eat."

"I'm not hungry."

"That doesn't change the fact that you need to eat."

"I'm not hungry," I repeat.

"Too fucking bad," Wren flicks the light on, and sets a box of food on my nightstand alongside a can of pop and a bottle of beer she pulls out of her hoodie.

"Dealer's choice on the drink. I'll get you another too if you want, but you have to eat."

I sit up slowly, and she opens the box to reveal a whole assortment of junk food, and I smile a little because she was always good at this. This was her superpower—comforting people when they were upset. It's probably why she has so many regulars at the bar.

"Fine. I'll eat a little bit. Just so you'll leave me alone."

"Like I'm going to leave you alone. Kenz caught me up on the big picture. That your surly white knight has turned out to be a villain after all."

I shrug. I still had trouble agreeing Liam was a villain. He had his reasons even if I hated them.

"He probably just wants to be grumpy in peace, without me hovering around."

"You hovering around? Doing what—holding his hand through everything? Helping his team? Making sure morale stayed high all season every season with cakes and parties and girlfriend help? Staying single for literally years so he could have you to himself without actually admitting he wanted it?"

"Well apparently, he didn't."

"Liv, be serious."

"I tricked him into letting me out of the friend zone. I didn't text him the morning of the accident. I knew how he felt about the Tristan thing. I know how superstitious he is. I forced it all on him. It's no wonder he hates me now. I wouldn't love me either after all of that."

"He doesn't hate you. And it's a fucking lie that he doesn't love you. There is no one—no one—who has seen the two of you together who thinks it's possible he could do anything but love you. He's just being a prick who's all in his feelings right now and has somehow convinced himself that pushing you away is the right thing to do."

"Or just what he wants to do. I still can't help but feel like he blames me."

"He doesn't blame you. And he doesn't know what he wants. He's understandably a mess right now. You know, like those bulls. They stab them and get them all hyped up in the ring, so they just run around kicking and running at everything in sight. That's him. A cornered hurt animal going after everything."

I give her a strange look.

"The bull riding championships were on the TV today at the bar, just work with me, okay?" She gives me half a grin.

"Okay." I nod, glancing down at the food in the box.

"So you know what you're going to do, right?" She opens the beer for me with a bottle opener she just happens to have in her pocket. This woman is magic.

"What?" I look at her as I nibble on a fry and take a sip of the beer.

"Take the bull by the fucking horns."

"Waylon specifically told me not to go over there."

"Oh you're not going to go over there. Not tonight. First, you're going to talk to the team."

"The team?"

"Yeah, you're going to remind them it's you who's been saving their asses over and over again. Who's helped them with their girlfriend problems. Their laundry. Their fucking home-work. And they are going to bow down to the Queen Consort of Football and do her bidding."

"My bidding? Is this from those movies you and Kenz are always watching?"

"Again, just go with it... Anyway, your bidding is going to be that they do absolutely nothing for their quarterback. No rides. No food delivery. Nothing. They're going to stay out of the way, until you're the only choice he has for help."

"That's just going to make him angry."

"There's no way through this that doesn't make him angry. Unless you do what he says, and do you really want to do what he says?"

"No," I scowl, taking another sip of my beer.

"Good. So, do it."

"I suppose the only thing that could happen is that he dislikes me even more after this, and if it's true that he doesn't love me then that doesn't really matter, does it?"

"He loves you."

"I guess we'll find out."

THIRTY-ONE

Liam

MY DOOR BURSTS OPEN, no knock, no hello, no nothing. Just flings wide open like the person bursting through it gives zero consideration to whether or not I could be sleeping or jacking off or any other number of things that I wouldn't want interrupted. I wasn't, but that didn't change the fact that they were an asshole for doing it.

"Tell me that what I just heard from Waylon isn't fucking true," Ben storms across my room until he sees the state of it and halts dead in his tracks. It's a fucking mess because I'm too fucking depressed to give a shit, and I don't want anyone else's help either.

"I have no idea what the fuck you and Waylon gossip about, so I can't tell you if it's true or not."

"You fucking *know*. You fucking know that you had him tell Liv you didn't love her."

Right. *That.* I didn't want to think about that. It had to be done, and I was too much of a coward to do it myself. So that's what friends were for.

Outwardly though, I just shrug.

"You're an absolute fucking moron!"

"Excuse me?" I shift on my bed. I'm not supposed to be bearing weight on my knee when I can avoid it. I'm due to have surgery soon and the less stress and strain, the better. But I'm tempted to risk injury rather than sit here and be fucking yelled at by the resident would-be relationship expert.

"You heard me. You're a god damn moron. You had the girl. *The* girl. The one you've been obsessed with for years. The only one who can get something out of you besides stoic thoughts on the game or your usual grumpy ass bullshit. The only one who can get you to pull your head out of your ass when you need it, and you fucked it up. Do you know how many of us wish we had our own version of Liv? And you fucking had yours, and you threw her away? Like fucking garbage, after everything?"

I have no idea why he's this fucking hyped up about my personal life, but I don't need my nose rubbed in the fact that my whole life has gone to shit. I don't need reminders that I'm losing the one person I want on top of the game and my future. Fuck him for thinking he can lecture me right now.

I jump off the bed, trying to only land with weight on my good leg, but I stumble, and Ben reaches out to catch me. I yank my arm back from him, embarrassed that this is how pathetic I am right now.

"Don't fucking touch me!"

"I don't need you breaking your fucking leg on top of everything!" he snipes back at me.

"Then maybe don't come in here guns fucking blazing about things you know fuck all about."

"I know enough. I've been around you two for long enough

to know that you are going to regret that move for the rest of your fucking life."

"Sounds like you're projecting Benny."

"Fuck no. If I got my girl, I'd walk on glass before I gave her up. She'd be the one I'd want here helping me figure my shit out when I was too depressed to do it myself."

"Yeah, well you don't have a fucked-up knee. No career prospects. No plans for what you're going to do after college. No fucking future at all."

"Liv doesn't care about any of that. She would have sat here and held your hand and figured out what you were going to do next. She would have done anything for you."

I shake my head, a bitter smile crossing my lips. "Which is exactly why I don't want her doing it. It's a waste of her time and mine. Let her get on with her fucking life."

"You realize her getting on with her life is going to be her having a million fucking dicks landing at her feet the second they realize you've called your dogs off, right? Half the guys on campus are going to be praying for a shot with her."

I shrug, "East already tried this tactic on me. It won't work."

Ben gives me a bitter look.

"That East is trying to talk you out of this should tell you everything you need to know about how much of an idiot you're being. Did you fall for her before or after she dated your friend?"

"After," I grit out. It was mostly true. It'd only been right there at the end that I'd been a traitorous piece of shit to him.

"So then other than the brief stint with Mason you haven't seen her with anyone else, have you?" Ben let's out a derisive laugh and shakes his head. "You don't fucking know what you're in for. If you think you're miserable now, just fucking wait. There's a whole world of hurt you haven't experienced yet."

"Get *the fuck* out of my room," I grouch and sit back on the bed, because the pain is still there, and I can't stand long without feeling it. It's pathetic.

"Yeah. I'll do that. This place is a fucking mess. I'm having a maid service come up here if you won't do it. And stop being a dick to everyone. Don't ask Waylon to do your dirty work anymore. You get to wallow, Montgomery. But you don't get to drag everyone else down into the pit with you."

"Fuck off."

"Love you too, asshole."

Ben slams the door behind him, and I flip him the bird before I lay back on the bed. An image of Liv immediately comes to mind and for a second my heart skips a beat, questioning what I've done. How I made the decision that I knew would hurt her. I couldn't bear to ask Waylon if he'd told her. I didn't want to know what her reaction was.

But I thought maybe, just maybe he hadn't told her. Because I thought she might show up here when he did. That she might yell and scream and tell me what an asshole I am. Some part of me I don't want to acknowledge hoped she would, just so I could see her one last fucking time before she never spoke to me again.

Now though, I know he told her, and she just accepted it. Quietly. Without protest. No visit. No call. No text. I don't know whether to be grateful for that or pissed that I made it so easy for her to believe.

THIRTY-TWO

Olivia

I'D TAKEN Wren's advice. Taken the locker room by storm after practice one day, after recruiting East, Ben and Waylon's help and gotten the football team to agree not to help Liam. It was going to start the day of his surgery. Waylon was supposed to take him, but I was going to show up instead, without warning him.

And now that I'm here, waiting for him to come down the steps after Waylon texted him that he was here to pick him up on my behalf, I feel anxious as hell. I have no idea how he's going to react. I haven't seen him in almost two weeks. It's the longest we've ever gone without talking since we got to college. I hear the door to his room shut, and I brace myself against the counter.

He hobbles down the stairs on crutches, his eyes glued to each step to make sure he doesn't fall. He looks like a ghost of himself. His hair disheveled. His clothes wrinkled. A week's worth of beard covering his jaw. But he's still my Liam underneath it all.

"Were you able to get the printer to work on campus? I need the paperwork they sent over," he says without looking up.

I wait till he hits the last step before I talk, because I am sure this is going to piss him off, and I don't want him to fall down the steps when he loses his temper.

"I've got it," I say, holding up the paper in my hands. "And I filled most of it out for you. Since we have to be there early, I think we can finish the rest while we wait for them to take you back. You ready?"

He stops dead in his tracks, and just stares at me. He blinks like his eyes must be deceiving him for several long seconds before he finally speaks.

"No."

"What else do you need?" I act like he's answering my question.

"Get out." His voice is cold and hard. None of the warmth I remember.

"I mean, I will once you're ready. But you just said you're not, so what do we need to get?" I plaster a fake smile on my face.

"No you are not taking me. Get out of the house. Where's Waylon?"

"He's busy."

"Then I'll find Ben."

"Also busy."

"Then I'm sure East can be bothered to drag his ass out of whatever sorority bed he's in this one morning."

"Nope. Also busy."

"Fine. I'll find someone. But you're not taking me."

"You won't find anyone else. They're all busy."

"Says who?"

"Says the fact that they all owed me favors."

"Then I'll get a car."

"Says right here on the paperwork that you have to have a friend or family member take you, stay and bring you home."

"Then I'll reschedule."

"You will not reschedule. There's a chance your knee is better before The Combine if you have the surgery now."

"The Combine," he laughs bitterly, as if I'm being ridiculous.

"Don't start. I've already heard about how atrocious your behavior's been. I probably didn't even need to call in my chips. They're probably all tired of your grumpy ass right now anyway. So watch what you say. Now what else do you need?" I give him my firmest voice. It's a confidence I don't necessarily feel, but my mama always told me I could fake it till I make it. And I was betting on that hard right now.

"Nothing."

"Then let's go. I've got your keys because I think it'll be easier on your knee to ride in there, unless you're worried about getting up in it?"

"Mine's good." He moves slowly toward me, like he still wants to buy time out of this.

"Okay. Then let's roll."

He glances at me, like he still wants to fight, but then his eyes return to the ground, and he makes his way out the door.

HIS SURGERY GOES EXCEPTIONALLY WELL and even takes less time than they'd planned for it because the damage isn't as bad as they'd expected. They have me come back to see him as he's coming out of the anesthesia, and I don't have the heart to tell them he wouldn't want to see me.

He looks weak laying in the bed, his knee wrapped, and the sheets rumpled around his waist as he lays in the hospital gown. When I walk in though, he gives me a bright smile and it makes my heart ache.

"Livvvvv..." he mumbles. "Thank fuck you're here. I was just talking to them, and they were saying that we should elope you know?"

I can't help but laugh. I realize the anesthesia still hasn't worn off yet, and he's not making any sense.

"Who says?"

"The pink elephants. I know it sounds crazy, but they were kind of wise."

"I bet they were," I smirk as I stand next to his bed.

He reaches out and grabs my hand, his fingers running over mine, and it's the strangest sensation to have him touch me again.

"So will you?"

"Will I what?"

"Elope with me? You know our friends would eat it up. That's all they fucking do anyways is talk about us being together. Fucking helicoptering around telling me what to do."

A laugh bursts out of me and he frowns.

"It's not funny. I'm serious," his brow furrows.

"Well we're not even engaged so how are we going to elope?" I deflect, trying to bring us out of this conversation because if he remembers it later, it's going to make him wildly grumpy.

"I'm not allowed to get on my knee right now, Liv. So we're just gonna have to skip the engagement."

"Oh, okay," I nod, my lips twisting.

The nurse comes in and she smiles at the sight of him holding my hand.

"Mr. Montgomery, is this the fiancée you were telling me about?"

"Yeah. This is her. She's stubborn as fuck. But I'm lucky I guess. Well not *that* lucky given the knee, but I guess it's a tradeoff. The elephants think I should try playing poker," he mumbles, and his eyes start to close as he talks.

"I think the elephants should tell you to try to get some sleep," I clasp my other hand over his and rub the backs of his knuckles.

"I can't sleep. We've got to figure out the elopement. Or Ben's gonna yell at me again, and I'm gonna punch him next time. His fucking pretty face could use the rearranging."

I laugh, making a mental note to warn Ben about this.

"You can sleep. We'll plan it after."

"Oh. Okay..." he mumbles and a moment later he drifts off to sleep.

The nurse smiles at him again and turns to me, "Are you staying with him today?"

"Yep. Not his fiancée though. Just a friend," I correct for the record, because I'm sure Liam would want me to.

"Ah, yeah the anesthesia can give them quite the imagination," she gives me a look like she's sorry, but I just smile. "All right, here's the paperwork and the instructions for aftercare..."

She runs me through his medications, the routine he needs to keep up, how to change the bandages, and how he can take a shower while protecting his incisions. I take a few notes based on her advice and then we sit and wait for the anesthetic to finish wearing off before we leave.

By the time they get him out of the wheelchair and into the

car, surly and sullen Liam has returned, and he barely speaks to me on the ride home, other than when I ask specific questions about whether or not he wants food and if he wants to pick up his medications now. Otherwise, he barely even looks at me, and I wonder if Wren's idea is such a good one after all.

THIRTY-THREE

Olivia

LIAM'S especially grumpy this morning as we roll into his PT appointment. He doesn't want help out of the car, he doesn't want me to do anything for him and as usual, he barely speaks. It's lovely. Just like old times when I was dating Mason, except worse because we're forced to be together since I won't let anyone else around here help him. And dear lord, is he bitter about that.

Though, he moves swiftly on his crutches already, and it makes me hopeful that he'll heal as quickly as can be expected from this. Because the man is not good at being down.

The woman at the desk gets us checked in, and shortly after they call him back for PT.

"Do you want me to go back with you or stay out here?" I ask softly as he goes to stand.

"I mean you're here; you might as well come back. Then

we can leave as soon as it's over and I don't have to come find you," he mutters.

The assistant gets us back to the PT room, where a hot-as-sin physical trainer is waiting next to some equipment. He's ripped, tattooed, well dressed and his eyes are a bright sapphire blue that are hard not to stare at. He stands to greet us, holding out his hand, introducing himself to Liam and then turning to me.

"And you're the girlfriend?" He makes the assumption, and I feel the flip in my stomach at the disappointment.

"No, just the driver," I offer a small smile.

"Huh. Lucky for him," he smiles and then leads Liam back to the therapy area to get him started.

AS THE SESSION ENDS, and Liam goes over the information the PT guy has given him, I start gathering my things up and putting them back in my bag. Just as I turn the PT guy appears in front of me. He'd talked to me a bit, while his PT assistant helped Liam through some of the exercises. He'd explained some of the exercises Liam needed to do and how I might be able to help, but I couldn't shake the feeling that he was just trying to find an excuse to talk to me. So I'm not entirely surprised he approaches me as we're leaving.

"Hey. I don't normally do this, but I just... I don't know. Something about you. Do you want to get coffee sometime?" He gives me a little grin.

I don't know how to respond. He's attractive, but my stupid heart still won't beat for anyone but the jerk who's barely speaking to me. But it feels stupid to turn down this guy for someone who blatantly told me he doesn't want me. Plus, it's just coffee.

"Um... sure," I answer, giving him a small smile.

He grins wide at my response. No sooner do I say it, I don't know why I agree. But now I'm committed to at least pretending to go along with it.

"Awesome. Can I get your number? I can text you some times and places."

I give him my number absently as I finish putting my reader back in my purse and look up to find Liam standing just over his shoulder, looking wonderfully pissed. It's unfortunate it's such a sexy look on him.

My phone dings and the PT grins at me again. "Talk soon. It was great to meet you."

Then he turns and sees Liam. "That was a great first session man. I think you're gonna make fantastic progress."

Liam grunts in reply, sizing up the man who is several inches shorter than him before his eyes flash to mine. He remains wordless though and heads for the door, moving at a pace I struggle to keep up with.

When we get in the car, his voice returns.

"Why did the PT guy need your number, and why is he going to talk to you soon?"

"He asked me out for coffee," I answer, setting my purse down before I start the engine. It's a freezing cold day, and I'm desperate to get the heat on. I'm also desperate not to look at Liam, because I feel guilty for setting up a date with his physical therapist. Awkward as hell.

"And you agreed?" Liam's tone is low and lethal. A brief glance and I can see his jaw clenched as he stares at me.

"Yes."

"Jesus Christ." He tilts his head back and closes his eyes. "You guys gonna fuck while I'm on the machines then?"

"Wow..." I glance over at him, giving him a look that says he's being immature and petulant. "It's just coffee."

He levels me with a look, "I taught you better than that."

I blush and kick the car into gear in order to keep myself occupied.

"I'll tell him I can't go," I mutter as we turn back onto the road.

"Nah. Fuck it. You have to date someone sometime, right? Might as well be the guy trying to fix my knee. Get some benefits on the side while you're hauling my hobbled ass around town."

"I will just cancel it. I wasn't that into him anyway."

"Don't cancel on account of me. It's fine. I like this new Olivia. She's ruthless. Goes for what she wants."

I want to snap at him. Remind him that he is the only thing I want and he won't let us just be together. Or he doesn't want me anymore. At this point I don't honestly know which it is. How deep his obsession with this self-punishment goes. But he needs kindness right now, and I'm going to give it to him.

"I'll cancel it. Do you want to stop and get lunch?"

"Sure. Then we can chat and figure out what you're going to wear for your date. I've got thoughts."

"Don't do that."

"Do what? I'm helping."

"You know what you're doing."

"Do I? I don't know. I'm such a fucking loser these days, without your assistance I don't think I can do much of anything."

And I've had enough. I change lanes, sliding into the turn lane when space opens up.

"What are you doing?" he grumps.

I turn into the first available parking lot I can find and put the car in park under a tree in the far corner and turn to stare at him.

"Does this mean we're not going to lunch?" he asks sarcastically.

"I'm trying to hold this friendship together. The one you said was so important to you. Trying to get you to see that you're more than just your fucking knee and fucking football. I've accepted that you don't want me as anything more than a friend, and that you're not even sure you want that anymore. I'm helping you, because I love you despite everything. Even if you don't love me. But that does not mean you get to fucking say awful hurtful shit to me. You hear me? I understand you're mad at me, but I need you to respect that. Okay? That's my boundary, the one you don't get to cross."

"I'm trying not to let you get dragged down with me. You can't hold my hand out of this one, Liv. This isn't just me being sad. This is my career over before it even started. I don't have a fucking backup plan. Football was it for me. You're wasting your time trying to help me, and you claimed your goal with the experiment was to get out of my fucking shadow and have a senior year where you actually lived your life. That's not what you're doing taking me to class and PT. Just fucking back off and do what I'm asking. Then maybe someday we can be friends again, when we've both fixed our shit separately."

"The whole goal with the experiment was to get you to notice me as something else besides your best friend's girlfriend or the football mom. It failed, but our friendship doesn't have to. And what I did for you freshman year is the same thing I'm doing for you now—being your friend. That was also the thing you made me promise, above all else, remember? That we stay friends."

"I don't want a friendship where I can't give you anything in return."

"You give me plenty when you're not being an asshole like you are right now."

"Right."

"Liam, you're one of the smartest, hardest working, kindest guys I know. You have a lot of good qualities. I didn't stay by your side all these years because you were a quarterback. I would have been your friend even if you did quit freshman year. I just didn't want you to because you loved it. I still think you have a chance. People take a year off, and still get drafted."

"Not with a bum fucking knee they don't."

"They're not you. You're exceptional—the way you play. The way you read the field. The way you lead that team. You're a lot more than just a guy who can throw."

He shakes his head and stares out the window.

"You have time to figure something else out. You can pick a new dream when you're ready. In the meantime, the team still needs you. Your backup QB needs you. Your friends need you. I need you. And you need to find a way to move forward."

"Fat fucking chance."

"I see the sports psychologist is helping."

His jaw clicks again, "I don't even need to be going. It's useless."

"What would help then?"

"A bottle of Jack and a blow job," he mutters sarcastically.

"Are you off the pain killers yet?"

He gives me a *what the fuck* look.

"You can't have the whiskey with them," I explain.

"I'm off the pain killers."

"Okay, then we'll stop at the liquor store on the way home."

"Good," he smirks. "Then what, you gonna stick around while I have some friends come over?"

"Oh, yeah. No. The only blow jobs you're getting in the foreseeable future are from me."

"The fuck they are," His eyes go wide, and his jaw sets hard.

"Let's imagine for a second, that I was the one hurt, fresh out of surgery, in PT, seeing someone for help with my depression and claiming the only thing that would make me feel better was whiskey and head. You're telling me you'd let some random guy touch me while I was vulnerable?"

"Fuck no."

"Well, then you should understand."

"Be serious."

"Oh, I am. Just as serious as you'd be. Payback's a bitch, isn't it?" I grin at him.

"You're being fucking insane."

"You said you liked that. New ruthless version, right?"

"You're not blowing me while you date my PT."

"Cool, I'll text the PT to never mind," I grab my phone out of my purse and open it up to text, but Liam's hand covers mine.

"What are you doing?" he grouches.

"Whatever you need, *friend*," I snap back at him.

He stares at me for a long fucking minute.

"Put the phone away. I've got a bottle at home I can drink, and I just need that and a round of video games with the guys. So just take me home."

WHEN WE GET to his house I follow him inside, much to his displeasure.

"I can get to my own room without assistance."

"Of course you can." I smile. "But all the same I'm going with you."

As he takes his shoes and coat off I go into the kitchen and grab the good bottle of whiskey that I know Liam keeps hidden in one of the cabinets away from party goers and two glasses.

"What are you doing?" he calls after me.

"Getting the whiskey you ordered."

He grunts in return.

"I could have gotten it myself," he says when he appears around the corner.

"And carried it upstairs while navigating them with your crutches?"

"I'm not fucking helpless. And why do you have two glasses?"

"Because your attitude drives me to drink. Now go," I usher him up the stairs ahead of me, and he reluctantly moves.

Once we get to his room he collapses on the loveseat in front of his TV. I set the glasses on the nightstand between the TV and bed and open the whiskey to pour us each a shot as he turns the TV on and grabs his controller. I hand him one and drink half of the other glass myself, the burn coating my throat on the way down.

I was about to do something stupid. *Very* fucking stupid. But this is what this man drives me to.

THIRTY-FOUR

Liam

I WATCH her out of the corner of my eye as she drinks the whiskey she poured for us. I both hate and love that she came up here with me. Hate it because it just leads to more competing impulses for me. I need her to stay away from me, to not think about her so much, to put time and distance between us, so I can try to move on from her. But she won't give it to me. She's everywhere all the time, helping me, being kind even when I'm an asshole. Telling me I'm doing great. Little thoughtful shit like getting the bottle of whiskey so I don't have to, and it starts thawing the icy exterior that I'm desperately trying to grow around my heart to resist her.

I turn the game on that I've spent way too much time playing lately. I need something, anything to keep my mind off real life right now. Thinking about football. Thinking about her.

Then the PT guy fucking hitting on her. At least he asked

if she was my girlfriend first, but that had fucking rattled me to my core. I knew she'd be moving on. Knew she'd date someone else, especially since she'd said she wasn't going to go back to being my mousy sidekick one day when I'd been needling her last week. I'd encouraged her to do it. I want her happy. But I don't want to have to watch it. Don't want to have to think about her with someone else.

"Shit." I hear a little gasp from her and look up to see she's spilled a decent amount of whiskey down the front of her T-shirt and jeans. She sets the glass down and her hands go to the hem of her shirt, grabbing it and hiking it up over her head. The move reveals way more skin on her body than I can handle and a lacy black bra that makes her tits look fucking fantastic. I immediately move my eyes back to the screen. Begging her silently to put something else on quickly.

"Do you know where my extra shirt and jeans are?" she asks, scrubbing her finger over the stain on the shirt.

She saunters across my field of vision to the closet. I know exactly where they are. In the bottom drawer on the left of my dresser where she keeps them. I'd washed it with my stuff the other week when I'd found it at the bottom of my laundry basket and smelled her perfume on it. But I just grunt a noncommittal sound in her direction.

"Is it in here?" Her back is to me as she opens the closet and peeks inside to look for her clothes.

I watch as her hands go to her jeans, and she unbuttons them and slides them down her thighs. And holy mother of fuck, she has on a barely-there thong and she bends over to pull her jeans off, revealing way more of her than my body can handle right now. I feel the air leave my chest, my dick stirs to life, and the dull thud of my heartbeat in my ears as she kneels down to look in the drawers at the bottom of the closet. I grab the glass of whiskey and throw the rest of it back.

"Liam?" she asks again.

"Check the dresser," I answer, my eyes back on the TV again.

"Oh right," she smiles. But it's not her usual smile. It's the wicked little one she uses when she's up to something. That's when I get the distinct feeling I'm being fucking played.

I confirm that feeling when she puts her hand on my thigh to balance herself as she kneels down to open the dresser, and it lingers too long and creeps higher as she reaches into the drawer for her clothes. The one she knew they were in the entire time.

"I know what you're doing," I mutter, refilling the whiskey glass and trying to ignore how hard I'm getting for her.

Her eyes drift back to mine, a flash of guilt before it's replaced with a smug little smile.

"Is it working?"

No. Say no. That's all I have to do. One little word. Only two letters. So simple. Her clothes are already in her hand. She can get dressed, and I can send her on her way.

My mouth doesn't get the memo, and my dick wants what it shouldn't have.

"You're already on your knees, you tell me." I take another gulp of the whiskey because I can't believe I just fucking talked to her that way. I just pray it's enough of a dick move to send her scrambling out of the room.

But she doesn't. She tosses the clothes to the side of me and slides between my legs, her hands running up my thighs and over the front of the sweats I'd worn for PT. She pulls the elastic band down and fists me as she pulls me out.

"Olivia..." I do my best to give her a fucking warning, but as her hand slides down the length of me I close my eyes and my mouth. I'm silently begging for her to put her mouth on me one last time. One last fucking time getting to feel her before I have to give her up for good wouldn't hurt anything, would it? People talk about closure all the fucking time. I needed it with her. Like I needed my next breath.

"You need to relax, right? The doctor said the less stress you have the faster you heal. So..." she trails off, giving me the perfect excuse to let her do what she wants with me. But we both know it's not the real reason she's doing it. Not the real reason I want her to.

"Yeah," I choke out the word as she fists me a little tighter.

She doesn't say another word, just puts her mouth on me and fucking works me over. She wastes zero time and the way she uses her tongue, the way she sucks me it's like she's trying to punish me. Trying to remind me of exactly how good she is and how much she wants me. I take down even more whiskey and bite my tongue to keep from saying anything that will spur her on. I want this to last for as long as it can, for forever if that's possible.

But it's only another minute or so before she stops abruptly and pulls away. I worry she's finally had an attack of conscience, a realization that I don't deserve this or her. Especially not given how shitty I've been. Shitty doesn't even encompass it. I've been absolute garbage. But she leans over, opening my nightstand and tosses a condom at me.

"You're awfully quiet," she chastises.

"What do you want me to do with this?"

"Put it on. I wanna ride you."

Fuck me. Whoever this is in front of me, it isn't my Liv. Some pissed off reincarnated version I had created by being a complete and utter asshole to her. But not her. I open my mouth to protest, holding the condom out for her to take back. She ignores it, unhooking her bra and letting it fall to the floor.

"I've happily put up with all of your bullshit these last few weeks. The least you can do is let me come. And you want to fuck me. You just don't want to feel guilty for it. So don't."

The words kick me in the chest. They must, because it feels like it's just caved in. I stare at her for half a moment before I comply with her order.

"So you do listen to me," she smiles, one that travels to her eyes and the way it twists everything inside my chest takes my breath away. She pulls the thong off, tossing it to the ground. I let out an unsteady breath. Reminding myself not to say anything that's going to fuck this up. Not to bring feelings or regret into this. Just fucking closure.

"Get over here and fuck me then."

"Take your shirt off," she crosses her arms and raises a brow at me.

I grumble, but I do as she asks. And then she comes back to me, straddling my lap, my hands on her hips as she guides me inside. She makes an audible gasp as I fill her. One that will be seared into my fucking brain every time I imagine this moment to make myself come in the future. She runs her hands over my chest before she rests them on my shoulders, her fingers running over them in little circles. My hands go to her ass, gripping it tight as she rocks back and then slides forward against my hips. She's so close to me her nipples graze my chest, and I can feel her soft breath over my skin.

"I shouldn't tell you this, but you really do have the perfect fucking dick," she murmurs. "Like hits every single spot."

And fuck if that isn't enough to make my dead ego flare to life. Another little gasp and a moan pop out of her mouth as she rides me, and I can't stop watching her, just mesmerized by the way she moves and the way she breathes. The girl owns me, and the confidence that she's riding my dick with right now is like nothing I've ever seen her have before. Not like the first time on the terrace, or any other time we've fucked. Like she's just doing it to please herself and she could care less if I like it or not. But I do, so fucking damn much. Even inside her I still want more. More of her body, more of her fucking heart.

"Fuck it's so good," she murmurs, one of her hands slips around the back of my neck, her fingers teasing along the nape.

"You like it that much?" I say it before I can stop myself. I've been trying to keep my mouth shut but it's hard when my girl looks like this.

Her eyes pop open and she narrows them, watching me from under her lashes without missing a beat. They drift down to my lips, like she's studying the problem and wishing there was a way she could permanently silence me. I don't blame her given the things I've said to her lately. Shit she doesn't deserve but the only path I can see to driving her away. A path she refuses to take.

"Like I said your dick is fantastic, the rest of you is the problem lately."

"Luckily it's the only part you need—"

She cuts me off by slamming her mouth to mine, pausing the roll of her gorgeous hips to take possession of my mouth. Her kiss is rough and punishing, and she still tastes like the whiskey she drank. I run my hand up her lower back, stroking a path down her spine as her tongue works over mine. If I had a working fucking knee, I'd pick her up and pin her against the wall, fuck her hard to bring this whole scene to an end. I can't take much more. But as it is I'm prisoner to her torturous pace and the taste of her on my mouth.

But then, like she knows I hit my limit, she releases me and returns to fucking me, her pace picking up along with her breathing.

"Touch me," she whispers as she arches her back, and rolls her hips forward for a better angle.

And tonight, I follow this woman's orders. Whatever she

says, I do. Whatever she asks for, she gets. Because I want her last memory of me to be one she can't forget, one that makes her remember how well I gave her everything she ever wanted.

"Yes, fuck. Right there," the words come out between gasps.

"Grab my ass with your other hand. Yes. Like that." Hearing her orders come out in such a firm tone has me edging so fucking close I can barely take much more.

"Your hands are a close second by the way," she smiles and bites her lip.

I just stare. I don't trust myself to speak.

"A little more," she murmurs, her brow set as she concentrates.

Little whimpers come out of her between breaths, and it's going to break me.

"Come for me, please Liv," I whisper.

And a moment later her nails are biting into my shoulder and neck, searing pain and pleasure into me at the same time as she lets out a soft cry, and I come as she tightens around me. She rides out her aftershocks, and then takes a breath, her eyes finally opening.

She glances at me and then grabs my whiskey glass and downs the last swallow I had left. She smiles as she puts it back and presses her lips to the shell of my ear.

"No other woman will ever make you come like me, and I can't wait until that haunts you."

She pulls back, meeting my eyes and grins before she lets me go, standing and grabbing her clothes. She's throwing her T-shirt on and then her pants while I take the condom, tie it off, and throw it in the trash next to the couch. She dodges into my bathroom for a minute and when she returns, I've put myself back in some kind of order, or at least pulled my pants up. Order might be overstating it because the woman has blown me to pieces. She bends down to grab her panties off the floor and tosses them in my lap, smirking down at me.

"You can keep those. Use them to help you come when you think about me later." Another devious fucking grin and I'm lost for words. Which is fine because my mouth is too dry to form them. Because whoever this new fucking Liv is, I'm not ready for her. I don't know how you prepare for this version of her, but any preparation at all would have been better than what I had.

"Night, Liam," she calls over her shoulder as she walks out of my room and shuts the door behind her.

I sit in stunned silence for several minutes, wondering how and what the fuck just happened to me. I close my eyes and see the little smirk on her face again, and my heart twists.

She doesn't have to wait long to get what she wants, because she already haunts me at every turn.

THIRTY-FIVE

Olivia

TONIGHT, Wren is thankfully off work and the three of us are huddled in the living room with an assortment of wine bottles and glasses scattered across the coffee table, along with some cheese, bread and other odds and ends we'd pulled out of the fridge and pretended it's a fancy picnic dinner rather than what it really is— the day before our grocery run.

"I think you skipped over new-Liv era and went direct from wallflower to bad-bitch era," Wren smirks, clearly approving of the incident that I'd just recounted to them.

"I bet he is crumbling as we speak, into a million tiny pieces. Like I'd start penciling in a potential groveling session from him as soon as tomorrow," Kenz grins and takes another sip directly from the bottle.

"He's probably still sitting in front of the TV trying to remember how to use the game controller," Wren bursts out into laughter.

I shake my head, "Yeah well here's hoping." I give a mock toast and throw back the rest of my glass.

"Do you want him back? Would you even take him back after everything?" Kenz looks at me questioningly.

"I love him," I shrug, as if that's all that really needs to be said.

"You can love someone and still know they're not good for you," Wren offers.

"He is good for me though. I wish he was less bossy, less of a grumpy asshole sometimes, but in general he is really good to me. And you guys, his body, the sex... fuck. I mean I taunted him about it, but the truth is I don't think *I'll* find that again either."

"You will when you're madly in lust and love again at the same time. Ask me how I know," Kenz raises her brows at me.

"Please. You don't need love in the equation to have good sex," Wren rolls her eyes.

"I didn't say you did. I'm just saying when you do, when he's obsessed with you the way Liam was with her? The way I am with Waylon? It's better."

"If you say so."

"You sure you won't let me set you up with someone?" I ask Wren. "I have some ideas."

"I am so sure. With the bar and school and trying to prepare for the transition out of school and into a career. I have no time for dating, or all the stupid games that come along with it. Maybe you should use some of those ideas on yourself? Give you something to focus on besides Liam?"

"I haven't turned the PT guy down yet," I grin at Kenz.

"Oh god. I don't know if I can support that move. On one hand, I'd love to see him pay a little for his sins. On the other, I don't know how much more that boy can take," Kenz looks at her wine bottle thoughtfully.

"I'm not really going to, but Wren's right. I probably should get back on the dating app or something, or else I'm just going to keep going back to Mr. Grumpy hoping he'll change his mind."

"Don't give up on him just yet? He's been through a lot. I can only imagine if Waylon went through all that..."

"Do you know something I don't?"

"I'm not supposed to say."

"Spill it," Wren frowns at Kenz.

"Waylon just said that he thinks Liam really misses you. Just the discussions they've had. He thinks it's more than just the knee and football stuff that has him down. But he told me not to say anything. He doesn't want us getting involved. He's worried about what it's going to mean for us all staying friends."

"We'll all still be friends. I'll just have to learn to ignore the jerk politely."

"And find someone sensible to date in the meantime," Wren raises her brow at me.

"I'll try," I say softly as I set my glass down, because the problem is that everyone pales in comparison to him. Even with his rough edges, even with the weeks of being a raging asshole while he tries to heal, underneath it, he's still my Liam.

THIRTY-SIX

Liam

WHEN I COME DOWN for a late dinner, I find the living room of the house filled with familiar faces—Waylon and Mac, Easton, Ben, Wren and Liv. They're setting up our coffee table with food and I see Ben flicking through the movie selection on the TV. Liv is at his side, they're discussing the options they have, and she's animatedly trying to talk him into some hot-guy action flick while he tries to get her to see reason with something sci-fi. Apparently, movie night has moved to my house, but I'm not invited, interesting.

I set my plate down a little loudly and it gets the attention of several of them, eyes flicking over the backs of couches and a small wave from Mac. Liv gets up and heads toward me though, and she's dressed like a knockout. Black pants that hug her curves, a low-cut form fitting shirt, nothing close to the jeans and sweaters she normally wears on movie nights. I wonder briefly if she's done it to get my attention. If she's hoping for a repeat of the incident that's had me in a chokehold since. Except I wasn't invited to movie night. She didn't mention she was coming over at all. Which can only mean it's for someone else.

"Hey." She smiles at me, sidling up the other side of the counter and watching me put a sandwich together on a plate. "How's PT going?"

The last week I've felt strong enough on my knee to jog a bit and my doctor and PT guy have both said I can have full range of motion again, including driving. I'd texted Liv and told her I didn't need her to take me anywhere anymore and thanked her. A small part of me hated it though, that I no longer had a reason to see her regularly.

"Going well. Still have to keep going for a while to get back the strength I had before, but it's better."

"That's good," she smiles brightly at me, and hands me the chips that are behind her.

"I see movie night has moved to my place."

"We were running out of room at our place, and the land-lord is having the fireplaces cleaned for us. So Ben volunteered your guys' place tonight."

"Ah, I see. You're awfully dressed up for movie night," I glance at her.

"Oh, yeah," she looks down at her clothes as if she's forgotten she's dressed up. "I'm going out for drinks after this."

"Sounds good," I mumble, as I roll the chip bag back up. Who the hell is she going out for drinks with this late. A guy, it has to be a fucking guy. Which means she's dating again.

"Yeah. I'm kind of nervous though. It's a third date," she plays with the bracelet on her wrist, and my mind temporarily blanks. I'd figured she'd been casually dating a guy here or there. But somewhere in all this she'd gone on two with the same guy. Apparently she was right, she could help me and live her whole life outside of that. Good for her.

Bad for whatever the fuck was happening in my chest right now, though. Some combination of tightening and fire and lack of oxygen that was making it hard for me to find additional words. I toss the chips on the counter behind her.

"I'm sure it'll be good. You practiced a lot for it. I washed the clothes you left here the other week. You want to come up to my room to get them?" I sound irritated even though I don't mean to.

She looks startled by my rough tone, but she nods and follows me up the stairs.

I SET my food down on the nightstand and reach into the dresser, handing her the change of clothes.

"Thanks," she says softly.

"This way you don't have to do the walk of shame," I wink at her. I mean for it to be playful but the way her cheeks tinge, I don't think she takes it that way.

"I don't think he thinks that way... He's kind of a cute nerdy type. He's sweet. Not like all you athletes who expect all that on a short timeline," she says, staring down at the clothes in her hand.

"Us athletes, huh?" I raise a brow at her.

"You know what I mean," she flashes me a look.

"I don't think I do."

She shakes her head, and glances over her shoulder. "Can I use your bathroom? I need to finish my makeup but the downstairs one hasn't been available yet."

"Go for it," I flip the television on.

"You're not going to watch the movie downstairs?"

"I wasn't invited."

"You're always invited. They just didn't know if you'd come, especially since I was going to be there for a bit, and you don't want to be around me."

I drop my sandwich and look up at her as she runs blush over her cheeks, faking a smile as she applies it. I miss her face. I miss her smile. I want to be around her; I just shouldn't be.

"And you are pretty cranky with them lately," she adds, as she brushes another round of powder over her nose.

My eyes drift down over her form and my dick aches almost as much as my heart does to have her again. Before I can stop myself I'm on my feet and leaning in the doorway behind her.

"Because they chose you over me."

She lets out a little indignant laugh, "They didn't choose me over you. Don't be ridiculous."

"I asked them for something. You asked them for something contrary. They did what you wanted."

"They did what they thought was best."

She stares down at two perfumes she has in her hands, trying to pick.

"The vanilla one," I say and her eyes drift to mine in question. "It's sexy."

She looks at me like she's thinking about sex. Like she remembers what I feel like.

"This is what's best? You standing here in my room, getting ready for your third date?" I pin her with a look. Hoping she gives me any sign at all that she still wants me.

She blinks a few times, like she'd been lost in thought.

"I'll get out of your way," she tears her eyes away from me and puts the things she'd scattered on the counter back in her purse, and then turns to pass by me.

I hold my arm out to stop her, "Don't go."

I have no plan. I haven't thought this through. I'm acting on sheer fucking impulse, and I deeply regret asking her to come get her clothes. Having her in this room again where all I can imagine is the two of us.

"Don't go?" She looks up at me, repeating the words that don't make sense.

"Don't go tonight. Stay here. In my bed."

"Why?"

"You know why."

"Because you love me and you want to be with me, or because you won't let us be together, but you don't want anyone else to have me either?" She glares at me.

"You know I love you," I say quietly, brushing my knuckles over her cheek

She takes a breath, and her eyes soften for a moment before they shift again.

"But...?" Her eyes steel, holding mine.

But all the reasons. All the reasons she knows stand between us.

"Right. See, that silence right there? That's not good enough. Not for me. And not for you either, honestly. You deserve better. To have a girl who you can love without feeling guilty. Without always obsessing over the past."

I didn't deserve better. There wasn't fucking better. I didn't deserve her, but I could try to earn it.

"Liv..."

"I need to get going," she stretches up on her tiptoes to kiss my cheek, but I turn my head and capture her mouth with mine. I grab her around the waist and pin her up against the door. Her hands go to my shoulders for half a second like she's going to push me away but instead she wraps them around my neck, her mouth going soft for me. A few moments later she pulls back, frowning and pressing her lips together in a line like she's disappointed in herself.

She pulls away from me, and I let her go because I don't know how to fix it.

"Goodnight, Liam," she calls out without turning around.

I don't answer her. I can't. Anything I would say would sound desperate and would do no good anyway. I don't have the right words for her. I don't know how to fix it—yet. But now I know I'm going to.

THIRTY-SEVEN

Liam

I SIT in the athlete cafeteria with the rest of the guys after practice. I feel like a fraud coming here, but I'm still registered as an athlete even though my injury will last through the rest of my last season here. I still attend practices because the young backup QB we have is only a sophomore and is desperately trying to learn all the plays to keep us alive for the playoffs. We lost our second must-win game, but by a stroke of luck they did too and so we still have a snowball's chance in hell.

"I think we just need to face the fact it ain't happening this year," Easton pushes food around his plate.

The practice had been absolute shit, and none of the drills in the world seemed to be helping our new quarterback learn the routes.

"I'm working with him, but he just can't read the field as well yet. He's still learning."

"Bullshit. You could read the field your sophomore year," Waylon gripes.

"I had more play time than he's had. Coach was still trying to pick a starter, and Jones and I were getting near equal time. He's barely been in a handful of minutes, and usually when we were just trying not to run up the score."

"He's right. We need to go easy on him. I see him come in early, stay late. He's doing the best he can," Ben tries for diplomacy with the guys.

"Still fucking sucks that we're going to miss the championship."

"You don't know that," I say.

"Even if we make it, you think he can go toe to toe with whoever we get matched against? Be honest, Montgomery. Fuck. We'd probably be better with you out there on crutches than with him," Easton grouches.

"Yeah, well I've shown coach my progress and he says no fucking way."

"Because if you fucking injure it again, it *will* be career over for you." Ben shoots me a look that says I'm a moron.

"It probably is anyway."

"You don't know that," Waylon gives me a look, echoing my own words to me.

"We'll see," I shrug.

"What does appear to be over for good is any chance you had with Liv," Waylon changes the subject to one I'm even less interested in.

"How do you figure?"

"Mac says she's into that guy she's dating now. And he's no fucking Mason. She's out of his league and he knows it, which means he is all in on her. Pulling out the stops with flowers and shit."

"She said she was dating several guys, thanks to Ben's brilliant plan of getting her on a dating app, so I doubt it's serious," I shoot Ben a look before I stab the chicken on my plate.

"Keep telling yourself that," Ben makes a face but doesn't look up from his food. "She's gonna be standing at the altar and you're still gonna tell yourself it'll be fine."

"Okay! Fuck!" I drop my fork. "I want her back. I want to fucking fix it. But I don't fucking know how. I can't fucking sleep at night trying to think of how to fix it, but it's a mess. I don't know how you unfuck a situation like ours."

"You could start by apologizing," Ben offers.

"And then you talk to the girls," Waylon adds.

"What?"

"The girls? Mac and Wren? They'd help you if they thought you were sincere and ready to get your shit together. Mac especially has been rooting for you two to get together for... what? Forever? At least since the day I met her..." Waylon looks at me like I'm more than a little dense.

"I don't think either of them are my biggest fans right now. They speak to me even less than she does."

"Because you fucked up, dude." Easton shakes his head.

"You have to prove you get that you fucked up. And then you have to ask for their help. And then you fucking fix it," Ben explains to me like I'm a moron.

"If you did go to them, they would help," Waylon looks at me like he's waiting for me to take the advice.

"I don't even have a plan."

"Then let's come up with one," Ben looks at me thoughtfully.

"You're going to help me?" I ask skeptically.

"Fuck yes. We're all going to help if it means we can put a rest to this bullshit once and for all, yes." Easton glares at me.

"Well... thanks," I say uncomfortably, only feeling slightly guilty that I was going to use our friends against her the same way she had me. I smile a little, thinking of her.

"Oh, he's fucking smiling again. Someone fucking document this," Waylon laughs.

"Shut the fuck up," I gripe, but then I crack and grin anyway.

THIRTY-EIGHT

Olivia

I'D GIVEN up on the app when even the guy I'd been on three dates with just didn't work for me. He was wonderful on paper. We had good conversations. But there was zero spark, and I didn't see any reason to keep dragging things on when there didn't seem to be any real potential. He probably has half a dozen other options, and I didn't want to waste his time.

Now Kenz had set me up with someone in one of her classes, and I didn't know if I was more or less nervous. Or more or less interested, for that matter. If I was honest, I still missed *him*. Even though I shouldn't. Even though it wasn't good for me. But it's hard to make your heart listen to your brain sometimes.

I'm trying my hardest to hype myself up for this date as I get ready though. Reminding myself that Kenz has told me he's good looking, and in all the text conversations we've had so far I've really liked him. James was funny, sweet, we had a lot of the same interests, and he was taking me to see an exhibit of Roman art for a first date which was honestly impressive. As much as I'd enjoyed my foray into dating athletes, their idea of dates was usually drinking beer and partying just before hooking up. The guys from the app always just wanted to grab a drink at a bar, which I didn't mind since I could skip out after one if I didn't like them. It had its time and place, but being treated like he wanted to learn more about me and my interests? I could go for more of that in my life.

I finish curling my hair and unplug the iron, going to my room to put on my lip gloss and pick out a perfume when I stop short. A figure is sitting on my bed and I press my hand to my sternum as I try to catch my breath, the lack of oxygen the only thing that keeps me from screaming. I have to blink because the bright light of the bathroom has made it harder to see in the dim light of my bedroom, but the figure looks distinctively Liam-esque.

"Jesus Christ, Liam. What the hell are you doing?"

"Waiting for you."

"You could have said something."

"Didn't want to say something while you had a hot iron in your hand," he shrugs.

He comes into full focus now, and I wish he hadn't. He's dressed up. A dark cerulean blue button-down shirt that accents his shoulders and his arms is rolled up at the sleeves and tucked into fitted black pants. His wavy brown hair is styled and freshly cut, but several days of growth shadows his angled jaw. He looks like a fucking GQ model, just like I predicted he would if he ever bothered to put effort into his appearance. I glance down, noting he doesn't have the metal work around his knee anymore, but the shadow of a brace is visible through his pants.

"How's the knee?" I ask, regretting it immediately

because knowing how sensitive he is about it, it's the last thing I should have brought up. But I'm trying to distract myself from the rest of his appearance and bumble into it anyway.

"Good. PT guy says it's healing nicely, and I'm making better than usual progress. I think he misses seeing you there though," he smiles at me, and it hits me in the chest like a ten-pound weight.

"I bet he does," I smirk. "Who let you up here anyway?"

"Mac. She told me you were getting ready to leave, but I wanted to come say hi."

"Hi," I say quietly, walking around to my mirror to finish getting ready.

He gets off the bed and walks up behind me, glancing at me through the mirror before his eyes travel down over my outfit.

"You look nice."

"I have a date," I answer, hoping that we don't have to revisit the last time we'd been in this position in his room. I don't know if my heart could take it tonight. Especially not with the way he looks at this particular moment in time.

"Mac mentioned."

I slide my earrings in and look over him again, a sinking feeling in my gut.

"You're awfully dressed up."

He tucks his hands in his pockets and looks to the floor, "I have a date too."

"Ah. I see," I feel my heart drop to my stomach.

It makes sense. He needed to move on and so did I. We'd have to figure out how to be around each other, because even if our friendship is on ice, we still share far too many friends to stay out of each other's orbits.

I grab my lip gloss and swipe it on to distract myself.

"Doing anything fun?" he asks, still watching me.

"He's taking me to the museum to see that traveling exhibit of Roman art."

"Sounds like something you'd like."

"A slight upgrade from bags and beer pong," I say and immediately regret it. I feel like I can almost see him wince under the weight of the dig.

"Well good. You deserve that."

"Where are you taking your date?" I trace the corners of the lip gloss with a tissue to make sure the color doesn't bleed over the lines, and to hopefully cover my reaction when he answers me. I hate this conversation. It's like walking over hot coals, and I wish he'd just go back downstairs. I have no idea why he's here anyway if he has a date.

"Wherever she wants," his lip tugs up on one side in half a grin, and I hate it.

It's like he's thinking about her, and I want to know who it is. If it's Mia or one of the jersey chasers, or if he finally got on the dating app like he was threatening. If he used pictures looking like this, I bet he was drowning in women. *Ugh.*

"Why are you here if you have a date anyway?" The question comes out sharper than intended.

"Had to drop something off to Waylon."

"I see. Well... You should probably get going. Don't want to make a bad first impression by being late, right?"

I go to reach for my vanilla scented perfume, and he reaches past me, grabbing the one that smells like mandarins instead and holding it up for me. I frown at him through the mirror.

"You said vanilla the last time."

"I might have been sabotaging. Also, this one is my favorite, and I didn't want you wearing it around another guy."

I take the roller ball from him and our fingers brush in the process and it makes my heart pick up a steady thud in my chest. I repeat what he just said in my head. It doesn't make sense, unless I guess he's saying he doesn't care anymore. Why would he, when he has her. Whoever she is.

God, I hated being a jealous bitch over him. Especially when I didn't know who the new bitch even was yet. I'm sure I'd get to meet her soon. Watch her sit on his lap and kiss him at parties. Maybe she'd be the one to make sure the guys got cake and laundry done from now on. I feel like the room is spinning as fast as my jealous mind.

I take the cap off the perfume and roll it over my wrists, and then he holds out his hand for it. I give it to him. I have no idea why. But he takes it, and brushes my hair back from my neck, swiping it over my skin. And that little touch sends a flood of electricity through my body, little sparks reminding every nerve ending I have of how much I want this man. How much I like when he touches me. Flashes of the last time we had sex come crashing through my vision, and I have to close my eyes tight to try to block them out. He reaches past me to put the little glass bottle back on my dresser, brushing his hand over my waist in the process and sending another little buzz of want through me.

"What are you doing?" I whisper, suddenly very suspicious of his presence in my space. If he told me not to go again, on a night when he had a date, I was going to be furious.

He leans over, his lips ghosting against my ear, "You know what I'm doing."

His tone is unmistakable, and I lift my eyes to meet his in the mirror. It's a mistake. I turn quickly, backing up against the dresser and bracing myself when the sudden movement nearly knocks me off balance.

"Stop." I frown at him.

"Why?"

"You know why. I have a date tonight. So do you," I'm

throwing reasons up like tiny bricks in a wall that I need between us.

His lip tugs up on one side again, in that same little self-satisfied grin. He rolls his lip between his teeth as he stares at the ground.

"I have a confession," he says after way too much silence. So much that I almost cave and reach out to touch him.

"What?" I ask, my fingers tightening around the dresser. I don't need any more stomach twisting or heart pounding information out of this man. I've had more than enough.

"You know what my middle name is, right?"

I frown, "Yeah. It's James."

His eyes lift to mine, the wicked little grin spreading. And the realization hits me.

"No," The word is barely audible.

"Before you get mad, I had good intentions. I thought it would be a way for us to talk a bit without all the baggage. But I... it felt wrong, and I couldn't stay away. So I moved the time-line up a bit."

"You tricked me."

He has the audacity to only look guilty for half a second before he smirks again.

"I learned from the best."

I take a sharp breath of air, and glare at him. He wasn't wrong. But that didn't make him right either.

"So you have two choices here. You can be mad at me, and we can spend the next hour arguing about it. Or you can admit I haunt you as much as you haunt me, and we can go to the museum and look at this art you're excited about. I booked a private tour with the curator that starts in..." He pulls his phone out and glances at it. "45 minutes. So, your choice."

I stare at him, and the little self-assured smile on his face makes me scowl. I shouldn't go. He needed to apologize.

Needed to explain a lot before I could ever truly forgive him. But I also really want to go on this tour. And what's another few hours of this limbo between us if it means I get to look at gorgeous art and him? I earned that much, didn't I?

"You're evil, but let's go. We'll argue when we get back," I say at last.

"Deal." He smiles at me.

THIRTY-NINE

Liam

I WATCH her walk around the gallery and talk to the curator while I trail behind. She's utterly fascinated with each and every piece, and they spent 20 minutes discussing the design on a glass cup. I smile as I watch her face light up again as the curator explains something about the statue they're looking at, and I feel like I might have done at least one thing right by bringing her here tonight. Even if the rest of this is a complete disaster, she'll have had a couple of hours of time she enjoyed.

Another 15 minutes pass and they exchange goodbyes as the curator moves on to another tour, and she returns to my side.

"Have fun?" I ask, studying the way her eyes are still lit with amusement.

"Yes. He's brilliant. He knew so much about every single piece and every detail. He also told me about some field schools that I could attend this summer even though I only have a couple of archaeology classes. I think I might look into it."

"Yeah?"

"Yeah. It'd mean spending a month or so abroad, but I think that could be fun and it might help with my applications to grad school."

"Did you decide to apply to grad school?"

I knew she'd been thinking about it but since we'd barely spoken in weeks, I had no idea what her final decision had been.

"Yes. I found a couple of professors willing to write me last minute letters of recommendation."

"That's good. I'm happy for you."

"I still have to finish a few things on the applications, but even if I don't get in this year. The field school could help if I could get in there."

"Well they'd be stupid not to take you."

She looks up at me then, smiling.

"Have you decided what you want to do, about everything?"

"Well, I can't do The Combine this year. Which likely means no draft. If my knee continues to heal like it is, I might have a shot next year, but it'll be reduced with the year off," I shrug. "So I've been looking into other options. I've thought about maybe coaching or something in the interim."

"Coaching, eh?" She smirks at me.

"I've been told I'm pretty good at it."

"Well that's true." She bumps her hip gently into mine. "I think your backup QB would agree. I heard he's leaning pretty heavily on you."

"Yeah. He's been struggling. He wasn't really ready, but I think he has a shot if he commits."

She nods along, and I realize that we're headed back down

our usual path of talking about all things me and football, and that was not my goal tonight. When I pause she looks up at me.

"Well I hope he figures it out. I know the team is counting on him. That's a lot of pressure."

"It is."

A minute of silence passes, and she turns to me.

"So, back to the house to argue or did you want to go somewhere else?"

"I thought maybe we'd discuss it here in public, where you're less likely to murder me for fear of getting my blood on the art?"

"Ha. I reiterate that you are not funny, Montgomery."

"What would you like to do?" I ask, wanting her to have her way tonight.

"Well, I think as much fun as this has been—and thank you for this, truly—I kind of want to head home. It feels strange to be out acting like everything's normal when we left things the way we did before."

"Okay."

"And I need to know how mad I should be at Kenz for her role in this."

"She told me to tell you, when that inevitably came up, that you should remember how you all conspired against her with Waylon, and I quote 'all's fair in love and war.' So, don't be too hard on her? I did twist her arm a little. And Waylon helped."

"I'm sure you did."

WHEN WE GET BACK to her house, I park the car and turn to her.

"You're not going to come up to my room to talk?" she asks when she sees that I don't take the keys out of the ignition.

"You'd take James to your room after a first date?"

She gives me a look that tells me to be serious, but when I don't budge.

"Yes, actually. Old Liv might not have, but the new one. She might," she grins at me.

"Yeah, I can believe that," I admit, as flashbacks of our last time together flood my memory.

"Is that a problem?" She eyes me warily.

"No. I've learned that if I thought I didn't want to be on old Liv's bad side, I definitely don't want to be on new Liv's bad side," I laugh.

"All right well, new Liv gets cranky when she's cold. So let's go up to my room, okay?"

I nod and follow her up. She points to her desk chair for me to sit down and then starts to push the bench at the end of her bed over for me to prop my leg up.

"I'm good. Really."

"You were walking all night."

"I've gotta start using it more and get back to normal. You don't have to worry, Liv."

She looks at me doubtfully but pushes the bench back into place and sits down on it. She folds her hands in her lap and stares at them.

"So..." she says softly.

"So..." I answer her. I take a deep breath, summoning every ounce of courage and luck that I have that she's going to forgive me. "I fucked up pretty good, and I owe you a huge apology—for the things I said, the way I treated you. You deserve so much more than that, especially after everything."

"I fucked up too. I lied to you. Tricked you—basically, into something you didn't want to do."

"Oh, trust me. I wanted to do it. I just thought the guilt would eat me alive. I thought it would destroy our friendship."

She gives me a sad little look, and it cuts my heart to the core, "And you were right."

"Because I destroyed it. Not because it had to be that way," I sigh. "And for that I'm so sorry, Liv. I know I hurt you a lot."

"It wasn't even that you wanted to end things that hurt the worst. I could have understood that, but it was the way you pushed me away. Especially after you got hurt. Like I was no one to you."

I see the tears welling in her eyes, and I can barely stand it. I hate to see her cry ever, but knowing I caused it is a special kind of torture.

"I thought it was the only way to get you to move on. I didn't want you stuck helping me again. You'd been trying to come out of your shell and try new things, and I knew if I let you, you'd just drop everything else to take care of me and my knee. You've already given up things and spent way more time and energy on me than I ever deserved. I didn't want it to happen again, especially not after what I had just put you through by cutting things off."

"Yeah well, good thing I don't listen, and forced you to let me help you anyway." A tear still rolls down her cheek, but a little smile appears on her lips.

"Honestly, yeah. It was a really dark time, and if it wasn't for you forcing me to go to appointments and arguing with me and pushing me..." I shake my head at what I might have become in the wake of how depressed I was.

"And fucking you?" She laughs.

I choke on the memory, a little cough sputtering out of my mouth with an awkward laugh. I wasn't expecting her to bring that up.

"Yeah that... you... were fucking something else. Not to be an asshole but I did not think that version of you existed, and I was *not* expecting that."

She laughs, a little pink rising to her cheeks. "I had a good coach, and I was also pretty fed up with your bullshit at the time."

"I noticed, but fuck it was hot. Like probably the hottest sex I've ever had in my life and considering every time we've been together it feels like that, it's saying something."

"Well hopefully it at least got rid of your ideas about me being boxed into the good-girl stereotype," she gives me a playful little smirk.

"Oh, I think you're still the good girl all the time. Sometimes you're just a different kind of good."

"Stop being charming, Montgomery. I'm still trying to be mad at you." She grins at me.

I smile at her and then glance at the floor. My heart is thudding in my chest, because now I have to do the thing—say the thing that she might reject. That might rip my heart out. But it was her choice, because I'd already made mine.

"You're the love of my life Liv. I thought I could have that in half measures with us just being friends. I thought it would be enough, but it's not. I want all of you. I've wanted all of you for a long fucking time, and I just wasn't honest about it. With you or with myself. But I'm here now. I'm sorry I made a mess of everything. I'm sorry I was the stubborn one. I'm sorry I didn't listen to you sooner, that I didn't give you what you deserved when you asked for it. But I love you, and if you give me another shot I will spend every minute making it up to you."

"You want to be together? As a couple?" She looks up at me, surprise coloring her features.

"Yes."

"I was not expecting that. I thought this was just going to be the 'let's be friends again' talk."

"No. If you tell me that's all there is, fuck... I'll try. I'd try anything for you, Liv. But I want all of you."

"What about the past? Tristan? All of the guilt you say you have over that?"

"I've been working through it with the therapist they have me talking to after the injury. I still have work to do. But I realize a lot of it's survivor's guilt. That I have everything, and he has none of it anymore. And I always felt like he was the better of the two of us. And you were the best of the three of us. I realize now though that I can't let that change who we are to each other."

"Yeah. You can't. I loved Tristan. I miss him, and sometimes I feel guilty he's not here too. But... Tristan and I, we were young. He was still a boy. We hadn't gone through anything harder than arguing over what restaurant to go to for dinner or what color tie he was wearing to prom. I have no idea what would have happened when he came back, when we got to college. If we'd have made it work," she shrugs.

I nod. "I get that, but if I'm honest. It's something I still think about. If I'm just second best to what he was to you."

Her brow furrows. "Liam... what we have? Nothing comes close to that. And that's not just because he's gone. I felt it already that summer, when we almost kissed. And since then, we've been through so much. Good times. Bad times. Honestly, you've been the center of my world for a while. Then... when I thought I'd lost you? It felt like my world was ending. I missed Tristan when he was gone. It broke my heart. But losing you broke my world, you know?"

"I know. Fuck, trust me, I know. And I'm sorry. I promise I thought I was doing the right thing. I thought I was doing what was best for you."

"You have to stop that. Your bossiness is charming some-times. But you have to trust me to make my own decisions."

"You're right."

Her eyes flick up to mine.

"Can you say that again?"

"You're right?" I puzzle at her.

"Fuck that's hot." She smiles

I shake my head and smile back at her.

"You can still boss me around in bed though. For some reason I don't mind it there as much."

"Does that mean you're going to give me a chance?"

"Of course I'm going to give you a chance. I'm madly in love with you, Montgomery, you know that. Besides we're already engaged."

FORTY

Olivia

"WHAT?" His brow furrows, and I smile.

"You don't remember? Hurtful, honestly," I tease him.

"When did this engagement happen?"

"After your surgery. You told me that we needed to elope and something about pink elephants wanting you to play poker again," I burst out into laughter, still remembering how drugged he'd been in the aftermath of the surgery. "I really wish I'd filmed it, now that I think about it."

"I think I'm glad you didn't." He grimaces. "And you said yes?"

"I mean, I really felt like if I didn't play along you and the elephants might have had an outburst the nurse wouldn't have wanted to deal with, so yes I tried to placate you."

"Christ."

"Yeah, it was good times," I grin. "It wasn't that bad really.

It felt like I got to see a glimpse of what you might be like if you were happy again."

"I'm happy now," he stands and closes the distance between us.

"Me too," I admit, because the pit I've had in my stomach and the sinking sensation in my chest that I haven't been able to shake for weeks finally feels like it's healing again.

His hand cradles my cheek, stroking his thumb over my jawline as he leans in to brush his lips over mine. It's soft, sweet like we're kissing for the first time. I've missed him so much.

"Sunshine, I'm so fucking in love with you. I really am sorry I didn't just accept it and tell you a long time ago."

"You're telling me now. Better than never," I study his face, the way his brow furrows.

"Yes, but I wasted time we could have had together."

"We had it together," I counter.

"Not like it could have been though."

"I definitely wish we'd had sex sooner," I smirk.

"Are you trying to seduce me again?"

"Maybe. Is it working?"

"Always."

"Perfect, will you undo these buttons for me then," I stand and tap the small buttons that close the top portion of my sweater at the nape of my neck and he sets to work on them, gently undoing them one by one and pressing a kiss to my spine after each one comes loose.

I pull the sweater up over my head and toss it onto the bed, and then unbutton my pants and slide them off to the floor.

"Christ. James *was* gonna get laid tonight..." his eyes rake over the matching set of lingerie I have on.

I can't help but laugh. "Not necessarily. I just like it. Makes me feel confident even when I'm not."

"Yeah, this is one of my favorites from the photos," he

mutters, and then his eyes widen just slightly like he realizes what he's just admitted to.

"Oh really?" I tease him.

I swear I see the slightest hint of blush hit his cheeks as I start unbuttoning his shirt.

"I think you're allowed to admit you look at your girlfriend's boudoir photos."

"Girlfriend... right," he grins.

I undo the last button of his shirt and he pulls his arms from it, tossing it to the floor. I undo his belt, and his pants and he gets rid of them too. I bend to look at his knee, the scar is pink and healing well.

"Your knee looks good," I comment, raising my eyes to his.

"Yup. My knee. Great."

"What?" I stand, because he looks like he forgot to breathe.

"The way you look bending over like that. Fucking hell."

I palm him through the boxer briefs he has on, and he takes a sharp inhale and his eyes close. I stroke him a few times over the cotton, kissing my way across his chest and up his neck.

"Do you want me on top or do you want me to bend over the bed?"

"What?" he asks his voice choked.

"Positions that are safe for you knee."

"Did you research this?"

"Maybe."

"But if you didn't know I was James..."

"We could have had another round of hate-sex," I shrug.

"Fuck me. I don't ever want to actually have it again, but I'm very happy to role-play it anytime you want."

His hands search my body, one wrapped around my waist and the other trailing its way down the back of my neck and over my shoulders as I nip at his neck.

"So... how do you want me?"

"Say that again."

"How do you want me?" I repeat, still kissing him tentatively but confused.

"Fuck, that's hot."

I laugh against his shoulder, and he pulls me close, kissing the top of my head.

"There's just one problem."

"What?"

"I don't have a condom," he runs his fingers up and down my back.

"Why?"

"I didn't want to jinx anything."

"You're lucky I bought some. There's some in the dresser."

His fingers pause and there's a stutter to his breathing.

"They're *your* brand." I add, and he grabs my jaw gently, tilting my face up to his.

"I'm always going to be a little jealous over you, you know. I can't help it."

"When it's a little, it's hot. Just the bossy kind. Not the break faces and stomp around kind, okay?"

He kisses me, sliding his hand down over my back and grabbing my ass and pulling me tight against him until I feel him hard against my stomach.

"To answer your question, I want you any and every fucking way. But the preview I just got... I want you over the bed. Take the panties off, kneel on the bench and put your palms down on the bed for me."

I do as he asks while he grabs a condom out of the drawer and loses the rest of his clothes. When he comes behind me his hands slide up my thighs, over my ass, and ghost their way over my back.

"Fuck..." he curses.

And I look up and realize that the mirror on the dresser

frames us almost perfectly, and the sight is so perfectly fucking hot I can barely stand how much I want him. His fingers slide between my legs, testing me and teasing my clit. A soft moan comes out before I can stop it, and he pulls his fingers away.

"I need inside you right now, but I promise later you'll get my tongue and anything else you want, okay?"

"Yes," I nod. And with that he slides inside me, his hands holding my hips as he fucks me, and I watch him through the mirror. He's gorgeous, and the way he concentrates, focuses on making it good for me is so hot that he's barely started fucking me before I'm edging toward release, my fingers digging into the quilt and my hips rolling back against him.

"I can't...," I stutter out the words. "I'm sorry. It's just so deep and all the right spots."

"Fuck, don't be sorry. You're so fucking good. So fucking perfect," he mutters as I tighten around him, moaning into the quilt because I can't take watching any longer. It's only a minute longer before he's coming, breathing hard and telling me I'm perfect over and over.

He disappears into the bathroom, and I turn over, to watch his return, wondering how I got lucky enough to find a man like him who loves me. He lays down on the bed next to me, leaning on one arm so he can dot kisses over my chest and clavicle.

"Thank you. For forgiving me. For being patient with me. Fighting for us." His voice is rough, emotional in a way I've not heard in a long time.

"I will always. There is no one else but you, Liam."

EPILOGUE

Liam

I'M NERVOUSLY WAITING by the baggage carousel for Liv. We've gone almost two months apart at this point. Even though she didn't get into grad school this round, she did get into field school in Europe. She spent the better part of the summer there, and while we've video chatted almost every single day she's been there, I still miss her like fucking crazy.

I also have big news, the kind that could change our lives for good and I have no idea how she's going to take it. Or rather, I know Liv. I know she will support any and everything I do. But I want to know what she wants in all of this, and whether or not she thinks it's a good idea. Her opinion is the one I need to really decide.

I glance around the room one more time, peering over the sea of people that are greeting each other and I finally spot her. She looks tired and worn out from her journey, but her face lights up the second she sees me. I grin wide as hell, and she starts jogging toward me. When she reaches me she drops her bag and throws herself at me, and the moment I feel her in my arms again is the same moment the world feels right again for me. Like I can breathe again and part of my heart isn't living out of my body half way around the world.

"Hey Sunshine," I kiss her cheek as she wraps her arms tight around my neck.

"Oh my god! I've missed you so much. I can't believe I can actually touch you again," she spouts as she pulls me tighter.

I pick her up and spin her around once before I put her down again. She leans up to kiss me, her lips brushing over mine until I drag her close again and kiss her the way I've been wishing I could for weeks.

When she finally pulls back, she looks dazed and happy. "I missed that."

"Me too," I admit. "I missed a lot of things."

"Me too." She grins.

"Let's get your bags and get out of here then, yeah? I made a reservation for dinner."

"Do I have time for a shower because I'm pretty sure I smell like all 16 hours of flight time." She frowns.

"Yeah, we have a little buffer. And I wouldn't mind a shower."

Her eyes flash up to mine and she grins again as we hurry to grab her bags off the belt.

WE GET BACK to our studio apartment, the temporary place we've rented for the summer while we figure out what we're doing and where we're going next. I've just been working with the training camp at Highland, biding my time until she got back from field school. Now all those decisions need to be made, and I'd be lying if I didn't say I was nervous. Nervous because even though every single day I'm thankful she picked me, I still have trouble believing it's real and that she'll keep picking me for the rest of our lives.

"You want to come in with me then?" She smiles as she starts to peel off layers of travel clothes, and scatter them across the floor.

"Always," I grin, watching as each layer drops. "But it's probably not a good idea if we're going to make our reservation."

"Liam, I spent weeks in a tent with midges eating me alive and dirt in places I never thought I'd have dirt. Sleeping on a hard cot in the middle of nowhere. The only thing that kept me going some nights was the fact that I was going to come home to a hot shower and seeing my insanely sexy boyfriend naked. So, to hell with reservations if it means I finally get that. We can order pizza."

"Well, when you put it like that..." I start pulling off my shirt and jeans.

"We can make it quick, and hopefully still make the restaurant." She gives me a little smirk and given how long I've waited to be inside her again she might not be wrong about the quickness of it all.

She grabs my hand and drags me into the bathroom, flipping the water on and while we wait for it to heat she traces circles over my chest and abs.

"I missed you."

"Even with all those hot European guys?"

"Even with. I knew the one at home was much hotter, has a perfect dick, and he knows exactly how I like everything." She smiles.

"Because he taught you right," I press a whisper light kiss to her lips and slide my fingers between her legs. She's warm and wet for me already and I almost forgot how fucking gratifying it was that she wanted me this much. That I could have this effect on her.

"Just fuck me here like this. I can't wait," she mumbles against my lips, and wraps a leg around my hip.

And I'm not about to tell my girl no. Whatever she wants, she gets. So I pull her up, pinning her against the wall, lining myself up with her before I pause to look at her. How fucking gorgeous she is.

"I love you Liam," she half-says half-whimpers as she rocks her hips and slides against me.

"Fuck, that never gets old. I love you so fucking much, Sunshine," I swallow her next little moan as I slide inside her.

The sex is fast and impatient, and we both come too quickly. But I don't fucking care because I have my girl coming apart in my arms again, and it's all I need.

After a fast shower and a quick change of clothes, we're walking into the restaurant just in time for the reservation. They seat us and Liv smiles as she looks around the place.

"This place is fancy. Is it new?"

"Yeah, they opened while you were gone. I wanted to wait for you to go though." I smile at her.

"Aww I feel special." She smiles back at me over her menu.

The server takes our orders and heads off to put them in, and now I have to give her big news. Find out what she thinks of a future that's so different from the one we had been planning.

"So, I want to hear all about your trip, but I have some news first. It's pretty big and I just... want to get it off my chest so I don't have to be nervous about all night."

"Okay..." Her brow raises a little and she gives me an expectant look.

"Chicago fired their assistant offensive coach this week, and if you remember, Easton's dad is the head coach there."

"Right, I remember that now that you say it."

"Easton asked if I thought I would be interested, and I said he was crazy. No way they hire someone as young as me, but he told me to throw my hat in the ring. So I did."

My eyes lift to hers and I expect concern to be there but she's already grinning.

"And Coach Westfield recognized talent when he saw it and you have the job?"

"Something like that. It was a whirlwind trip out there. I didn't tell you because I didn't want you to be worried or distracted when you were on your way home, and I didn't think it was going to amount to anything. But then I got the call last night. They're sending over the benefits package tonight, and they want an answer by the end of the week. I told them I had to talk to you first and then I'd tell them."

"Yes. You say yes, right?"

"It would mean that my playing career is over. That I'm committing to coaching."

"I mean... You are a fantastic coach."

"And it would mean a permanent move to Chicago. We haven't had a chance to discuss where you want to go or anything, or how field school helped with your decision?" I look at her, but her smile never fades.

"There are lots of good schools in and around Chicago, Liam. I mean, assuming you'd want me to go with you."

"I'm not fucking going without you. I got lucky enough you wanted me and I'm not gonna lose that for a coaching job. If you don't want to go to Chicago, I can keep training. See how things go with the draft this time around. There'll be other coaching jobs."

"There will be other coaching jobs, but they might not be with a coach like Westfield who knows your worth."

"True," I agree as the server arrives with our drinks and appetizer.

We sit in silence for a minute while he puts things down on the table and my stomach flips in anticipation. When the server leaves she takes a sip of her drink and then looks at me expectantly, waiting for me to finish my thoughts.

I take a breath.

"I want to take the job. But I want you to come with me."

"Good. Because I want to go with you, Montgomery."

"Are you sure?"

"I'm positive. I liked field school, a lot, but it also gave me more to think about. Chicago will give me new opportunities to explore while I do it. It's perfect."

I smile, because I am so fucking relieved she wants to come. That after everything she still wants to be by my side.

"And it won't bother you that I'm not going to play anymore?"

"Liam, I liked the quarterback version of you. I loved the coach version. And I will take any version that makes you happy." She laughs softly and takes another sip of her drink.

"What about the husband version?" I ask before I can stop myself, because it's what I really want to know.

She sputters on the sip of her drink she just took, grabbing her napkin and then looking at me again.

"What?" Her brow furrows and I'm worried.

I forge ahead though because it's all I can do. What I have to do.

"I didn't want to get the ring or do the proposal yet. That felt like I was pressuring you when you were just getting back from field school. But you being gone—the time apart—just reminded me of how much I want and need you in my life. You're my best friend. You're the love of my life. I feel lucky every day I wake up and know that you still want me. That you're still mine. And I want that for good. But Liv... It's okay if you need time to think it through. Like I said, I don't want you feeling pressure. I want you to be sure it's what you want too. And you fuckin' know I don't want to stand between you and what you want for your life. I just want you to know it's how I feel."

"Yes. Yes. Always yes." She's smiling so fucking brightly.

"Yes... Really?" I feel a little tightness in my throat as I repeat it. Something that feels a little like it could be tears if that was a thing I did.

"Yes. *You* are what I want for my life, Liam. You make everything better. I can't imagine it all without you."

"Well, okay then," I say, far more emotional than I expected to be.

She reaches across and squeezes my hand, the same way she has all these years whenever I start to feel unsteady or overwhelmed.

"I love you, Liam. And I am so happy for you. You deserve this. Someone who recognizes your talent. I can't wait to see what you can do there. And I can't wait to be at every game with you."

"I don't deserve you, but I'm so fucking glad you love me, Liv." I smile at her, coughing a little to try to cover up the way my voice cracks. "Now that we've got all that out of the fucking way. Tell me about field school."

She smiles at me and starts to tell me all about her summer, and I know I'm the luckiest fucking guy on earth.

ALSO BY MAGGIE RAWDON

Play Fake

Personal Foul (Coming Soon!)

ABOUT THE AUTHOR

Maggie loves books, travel and wandering through museums. She lives in the Midwest where you can find her writing on her laptop with her two pups at her side, in between binge watching epic historical and fantasy dramas and cheering for her favorite football teams on the weekends. She loves writing characters who banter instead of flirt.

Join the newsletter here for sneak peeks: https://geni.us/MRBNews

Join the reader's group on FB here: https://www.facebook.com/groups/rawdonsromanticrebels

Get the free prequel, Pregame here: https://maggierawdon.com/pregame

instagram.com/maggierawdonbooks

tiktok.com/@maggierawdon

facebook.com/maggierawdon

ACKNOWLEDGMENTS

To you, the reader, thank you so much for taking a chance on this book and following along on Liv & Liam's journey. And thank you especially for taking a chance on me! Your support means the world.

To my editor and beta readers, thank you so much for all your feedback, critiques, guidance and help.

Kat, thank you for your constant help, support, and patience with me as I struggled to make this book a reality. Meredith, thank you for helping me see Liv & Liam through a new lens. This book wouldn't exist without both of you!

To the Sparrows, thank you for all the support you've given and continue to give through this journey! I could not have done this without you.

Made in United States
Orlando, FL
07 February 2023